"Lauren Beukes is one of the most talented writers working today. Moving from witty to sad to horrifying, she makes it all seem effortless. We're lucky to finally have her short work in one place."
—Richard Kadrey, author of the Sandman Slim series and *The Everything Box*

"Lauren Beukes is a remarkable talent, that rare writer who can go in any direction she desires and always delivers. In *Slipping*, you have the chance to see her at her most versatile and powerful. A wonderful collection from one of the strongest voices in the game."
—Michael Koryta, author of *So Cold the River* and *Those Who Wish Me Dead*

"The dazzling short pieces collected in *Slipping*, which range from reportage to tender bits of personal reflection to weird sci-fi horror, together serve to confirm the impression Beukes already created in her novels: this is a writer who can do anything."
—Ben H. Winters, author of *Underground Airlines* and the Last Policeman series

"*Slipping* is a rare surprise, and one that demonstrates Beukes's wide-ranging talent. Whether she's writing about corporate-branded future punks and celebrants, or the downtrodden casual menaces of daily life, from a compilation of tweets to a handful of remarkable non-fiction essays, her stories prove, repeatedly, that she is a masterful writer and that she has a voice that absolutely must be heard. Hold on tight to this one—you do not want it to slip away."
—Michael Patrick Hicks, author of *Emergence*

"Bold, brazen, and brilliant—now *this* is a collection to die for. Beukes fearlessly skewers personal relationships, social injustice and

pop culture (among other things), and every story is a masterclass in flair, wit and fresh ideas."
—Sarah Lotz, author of *The Three* and *Day Four*

"A ferocious collection from our brightest, sharpest talent."
—Adam Christopher, author of *Made to Kill*

"Lauren Beukes is one of the most creative, thought-provoking writers working today, and *Slipping* puts us right in the bloody depths of her brain and gives us an intimate tour. This book writhes with ideas and undeniable energy."
—Steph Cha, author of *Dead Soon Enough*

"*Slipping* is a dizzying array of stories, a 'greatest hits' from a prolific and imaginative writer. There's a mash of scenarios and genres from alternative histories to Manga, cyberpunk to feminist fairy tale. It's kick-ass speculative fiction with brains and heart. 10/10 stars."
—*Starburst*

"While each story in this collection is unique, they all have that one piece in common that make me so passionate about [Beukes's] previous novels—there's a sense of some underlying real-world threat in even the most intensely science fiction story lines. Much like Margaret Atwood's *The Handmaid's Tale*, the reader is left with feelings of unease, that though what you've just read is fiction, it still hits too close to home to not make you nervous."
—*Pages and Pints*

Praise for *The Shining Girls*

"Lauren Beukes's strong contender for the role of this summer's universal beach read. Ms. Beukes is a South African whose earlier

works have been closer to hard-core science fiction, but *The Shining Girls* is pure thriller."
—*New York Times*

"I'm all over it."
—Gillian Flynn, author of *Gone Girl*

"Utterly original, beautifully written."
—Tana French, author of *In the Woods*

"Talented Cape Town writer Lauren Beukes has managed to turn such borrowing and theft into a triumph in her new novel, *The Shining Girls*."
—NPR

"Smart prose."
—Stephen King, author of *The Stand*

"[Beukes] is so profusely talented—capable of wit, darkness, and emotion on a single page—that a blockbuster seems inevitable."
—*USA Today*

"The premise is pure Stephen King, but Beukes gives it an intricate, lyrical treatment all her own."
—*Time*

"Unreservedly recommended."
—Joe Hill, author of *Heart-Shaped Box*

"One of the summer's hottest books."
—*Wired*

"Very smart . . . completely kick-ass. Beukes's handling of the

joints between the realistic and the fantastic is masterful."
—William Gibson, author of *Neuromancer*

"Brilliant. A book about the duel of two fabulously realized characters. A triumph."
—*Independent*

"From something horrific and inexplicable, she makes delicate and redemptive magic."
—*Chicago Tribune*

"Disturbing, smart and beautifully written."
—Erin Morgenstern, author of *The Night Circus*

"Science fiction and psychological thriller collide spectacularly in this heart-thumping tale of a time-traveling serial killer."
—*Entertainment Weekly*

"Imagine Poe and Steinbeck in a knife fight where Poe wins and writes Jack the Ripper's version of *The Grapes of Wrath*. *The Shining Girls* is even scarier than that."
—Richard Kadrey, author of *Sandman Slim*

Praise for *Broken Monsters*

"Beukes's captivating *Broken Monsters* defies the standard tropes of the serial killer genre to become a thoroughly modern, supernatural thriller . . ."
—*Los Angeles Times*

"This wickedly unpleasant thriller has a rare and intriguing capacity to make the reader think."
—*The Telegraph*

Praise for *Zoo City*

"Beukes's energetic noir phantasmagoria, the winner of this year's Arthur C. Clarke Award, crackles with original ideas."
—Jeff VanderMeer, *New York Times Book Review*

"Fabulous wordplay, imaginative settings and scenarios, and such a dark and cynical heart that I was totally riveted by it."
—Cory Doctorow, author of *Little Brother*

★ "Beukes (*Moxyland*) delivers a thrill ride that gleefully merges narrative styles and tropes, almost single-handedly pulling the 'urban fantasy' subgenre back towards its groundbreaking roots."
—*Publishers Weekly*, starred review

"If our words are bullets, Lauren Beukes is a marksman in a world of drunken machine-gunners, firing her ideas and images into us with a sly and deadly accuracy, wasting nothing, never missing."
—Bill Willingham, creator of *Fables*

"Lauren Beukes brings to *Zoo City* the observant, cynical eye for the intersection of media, business, and pop culture that animated her debut, *Moxyland*."
—*Ideomancer*

Other books by Lauren Beukes

Novels
Moxyland (2008)
Zoo City (2010)
The Shining Girls (2013)
Broken Monsters (2014)

Non-fiction
Maverick: Extraordinary Women from South Africa's Past (2005)
Maverick: Extraordinary Women from South Africa's Past 2nd edition
with Nechama Brodie (2015)

Graphic fiction
Strange Adventures #1, "All The Pretty Ponies"
with Inaki Miranda (2011)
Fairest: The Hidden Kingdom with Inaki Miranda (2012, 2013)
The Witching Hour, "Birdie" with Gerhard Human (2013)
Wonder Woman, "The Trouble with Cats"
with Mike Maihack (2015)
Strange Sports Stories #1, "Chum" with Dale Halvorsen and
Christopher Mitten (2015)
Survivors' Club with Dale Halvorsen and Ryan Kelly (2015, 2016)

LAUREN BEUKES
Slipping: Stories, Essays & Other Writing

LAUREN BEUKES

SLIPPING

Stories,
Essays
&
Other Writing

TACHYON
SAN FRANCISCO

Tachyon Publications LLC
1459 18th Street #139
San Francisco, CA 94107
(415) 285-5615
tachyon@tachyonpublications.com

www.tachyonpublications.com
smart science fiction & fantasy

Series Editor: Jacob Weisman
Project Editor: Jill Roberts

ISBN 13: 978-1-61696-240-1

Printed in the United States of America by Worzalla

First edition: 2016
9 8 7 6 5 4 3 2 1

CONTENTS

Fiction

1. Muse

2. Slipping

29. Confirm / Ignore

32. Branded

40. Smileys

49. Princess

57. My Insect Skin

64. Parking

74. Pop Tarts

86. The Green

106. Litmash

108. Easy Touch

126. Algebra

136. Unathi Battles the Black Hairballs

157. Dear Mariana

166. Riding with the Dream Patrol

173. Unaccounted

183. Tankwa-Karoo

191. Exhibitionist

202. Dial Tone

205. Ghost Girl

Nonfiction

227. Adventures in Journalism

236. All the Pretty Corpses

241. Judging Unity

248. Inner City

258. On Beauty:
A Letter to My Five-Year-Old Daughter

262. Glossary

MUSE

The gloves arrived in the mail in a box lined with tissue paper.
There was no return address.
They were elbow-length. Lace-up. Finest suede.
Muse-skin, the attached note said.
These will get you unblocked, the note said.
It was only when she put them on and sat down to write
That she realized there were fishhooks in the fingertips
That drew blood with every keystroke.

SLIPPING

1. High Life

The heat presses against the cab, trying to find a way in past the sealed windows and the rattling air-conditioning. Narrow apartment blocks swoop past on either side of the dual carriageway, occasionally broken up by a warehouse megastore. It could be Cape Town, Pearl thinks. It could be anywhere. Twenty-three hours travel so far. She had never been on a plane before.

"So what's the best thing about Karachi?" Tomislav, her promoter, asks the cab driver, trying to break the oppressive silence—the three of them dazed by the journey, the girl, the promoter and the surgeon, who has not looked up from his phone since they got in the car because he is trying to set up a meeting.

The driver thinks about it, tugging at the little hairs of his mustache. "One thing is that this is a really good road.

Sharah e Faisal. There's hardly ever a traffic jam and if it rains, the road never drowns."

"Excellent." Tomislav leans back, defeated. He gives Pearl an encouraging smile, but she is not encouraged. She has watched the World Cup and the Olympics on TV; she knows how it is supposed to be. She stares out the window, refusing to blink in case the tears come.

The road narrows into the city and the traffic thickens, hooting trucks and rickshaws covered in reflecting stickers like disco balls, twinkling in the sun. They pass through the old city, with its grand crumbling buildings from long ago, and into the warren of Saddar's slums with concrete lean-tos muscling in on each other. *Kachi abadi*, the driver tells them, and Pearl sounds it out under her breath. At least the shacks are not tin, and that's one difference.

Tomislav points out the loops of graffiti in another alphabet and taps her plastic knee. "Gang signs. Just like the Cape Flats."

"Oh they're gangsters all right," the driver says. "Same people run the country."

"You have gangsters in your government?" Pearl is shocked.

The cab driver clucks and meets her eyes in the rear-view mirror. "You one of the racers?"

"What clued you in?" Dr. Arturo says, without looking up. It's the first thing he's said all day. His thumbs, blunt instruments, tap over the screen of his phone. Pearl rubs her legs self-consciously, where the tendons are visible under the joint of her knee, running into the neurocircuitry. *It's a showcase*, Dr. Arturo told her when she asked him why it couldn't look like skin. Some days she thinks it's beautiful. But mostly, she hates seeing the inside-out of herself.

"Why do you think you're in Pakistan?" the driver laughs. "You think anyone else would let this happen in *their* country?" He rubs his thumb and fingers together and flings them to the wind.

2. Packed with Goodness

Pre-race. A huge +Games banner hangs above the entrance of the Karachi Parsi Institute, or KPI. It's an old colonial building that has been extended to accommodate them, the track built over the old cricket ground and into the slums. The original school has been turned into the athletes' village, classrooms converted to individual medical cells to cater to their unique needs. Pearl's, for example, has hermetic bio-units and sterile surfaces. The window has been fused shut to prevent polluted air from leaking in.

In the room next door, they installed extra generators for Charlotte Grange after she plugged in her exo-suit and tripped the power for the whole building. Pearl can hear her grunting through the walls. She doesn't know what Siska Rachman has. Do the technically braindead still need to eat?

She sits on the end of her bed, paging through the official program while Tomislav paces the room, hunched over his phone, his hand resting on his nose. *"Ajda!* Come on!" he says, in that Slavic way that makes the first part of the sentence top-heavy. Like Tomislav himself, still carrying his weightlifter bulk all squeezed up into his chest and neck. He doesn't compete anymore, but the steroids keep him in shape. The neon lights and the white sheen off the walls make his eyes look bluer, his skin paler. "Peach" she was taught in school, as if "peach" and "brown" were magically less divisive than "black" and "white," and words could fix everything. But Tomislav's skin is not the warm orange of a summer fruit, it's like the milky tea she drinks at home.

Tomislav has thick black hair up his arms. She asked him about it when they first met at the Beloved One's house on the hill. Fourteen, too young and too angry to mind her elders, even though her mother gasped at her rudeness and smacked her head.

Tomislav had laughed. *Testosterone, kitten.* He tapped the slight fuzz above her top lip. *You've got it too, that's what makes you so strong.*

He's since made her laser all her unsightly hair. Sport is all about image. Even this one.

He sees her looking at him and speaks louder. "You want to get a meeting, Arturo, we gotta have something to show." He jabs at the phone dramatically to end the call. "That guy! What does he think I'm doing all day? You all right, kitten?" He takes her by the shoulders, gives them a little rub. "You feeling good?"

"Fine." More than fine, with the voices of the crowd a low vibration through the concrete, and the starting line tugging at her insides, just through that door, across the quad, down the ramp. She has seen people climbing up onto the roofs around the track with blankets.

"That's my girl." He snatches the program out of her hands. "Why are you even looking at this? You know every move these girls have."

He means Siska Rachman. That's all anyone wants to talk about, the journos, the corporates. Pearl is sick of it, the interviews for channels she's never heard of. No one told her how much of this would be *talking* about racing.

"Ready when you are," Dr. Arturo says into her head, speaking through the audio implant in her cochlear. Back online as if he's never been gone, checking the diagnostics. "Watch your adrenaline, Pearl. You need to be calm for the install." He used to narrate the chemical processes, the shifting balances of hormones, the nano-enhancing oxygen uptake, the shift of robotic joints, the dopamine blast, but it felt too much like being in school; words being crammed into her head and all worthless anyway. You don't have to name something to understand it. She knows how it feels when she hits her stride and the world opens up beneath her feet.

"He's ready," she repeats to Tomislav.

"All right, let's get this show pumping."

Pearl obediently hitches up her singlet with the Russian energy drink logo—one of Tomislav's sponsors, although that's only spare change. She has met the men who have paid for her to be here, in the glass house on the hill, wearing gaudy golf shirts and shoes and shiny watches. She never saw them swing a club, and she doesn't know their names, but they all wanted to shake her hand and take a photograph with her.

She feels along the rigid seam that runs in a J-hook down the side of her stomach, parallel with her hysterectomy scar, and tears open the velcroskin.

"Let me," Tomislav says, kneeling between her legs. She holds her flesh open while he reaches one hand up inside her abdomen. It doesn't hurt, not anymore. The velcro releases a local anesthetic when it opens, but she can feel an uncomfortable tugging inside, like cramps.

Tomislav twists off the valves on either side, unplugs her stomach and eases it out of her. He sets it in a sterile biobox and connects it to a blood flow. By the time he turns back, she is already spooling up the accordion twist of artificial intestine, like a magician pulling ribbons from his palm. It smells of lab-mod bacteria, with the faintest whiff of feces. She hands it to Tomislav and he wrinkles his nose.

"Just goes to show," he says, folding up the crinkled plastic tubing and packing it away. "You can take the meat out of the human, but they're still full of shit!"

Pearl smiles dutifully, even though he has been making the same joke for the last three weeks—ever since they installed the new system.

"Nearly there." He holds up the hotbed factory and she nods and looks away because it makes her queasy to watch. It's a sleek bioplug, slim as a Communion wafer and packed with goodness, Dr. Arturo says, like fortified breakfast cereal. Hormones and nanotech instead of vitamins and iron.

Tomislav pushes his hand inside her again, feeling blindly for the connector node in what's left of her real intestinal tract, an inch and a half of the body's most absorbent tissue for better chemical uptake.

"Whoops! Got your kidney! Joking. It's in."

"Good to go," Dr. Arturo confirms.

"Then let's go," Pearl says, standing up on her blades.

---

3. Forces Greater Than You

You would have to be some kind of idiot. She told her mother it was a bet among the kids, but it wasn't. It was her, only her, trying to race the train.

The train won.

4. Why You Have Me

The insect drone flits in front of Pearl's face, the lens zooming in on her lips to catch the words she's murmuring and transmit them onscreen. *"Ndincede nkosi undiphe amandla."*

She bends down to grab the curved tips of her legs, to stretch, yes, but also to hide her mouth. It's supposed to be private, she thinks. But that's an idea that belonged to another girl: the girl before Tomislav's deals and Dr. Arturo's voice in her head running through diagnostics, before the Beloved One, before the train, before all this.

"It's because you're so taciturn, kitten," Tomislav tries to comfort her. "You give people crumbs and they're hungry for more. If you just talked more." He is fidgeting with his tie while Brian Corwood, the presenter, moves down the starter's carpet with his microphone, talking to Oluchi Eze, who is showing off her tail for the cameras.

Pearl doesn't know how to talk more. She's run out of words, and the ones Dr. Arturo wants her to say make her feel like she's chewing raw potatoes. She has to sound out the syllables.

She swipes her tongue over her teeth to get rid of the feeling that someone has rigged a circuit behind her incisors. It's the new drugs in the hotbed, Tomislav says. She has to get used to it, like the drones, which dart up to her unexpectedly. They're freakish—cameras hardwired into locusts, with enough brain stem left to respond to commands. Insects are cheap energy.

Somewhere in a control room, Dr. Arturo notes her twitching back from the drones and speaks soothing words in her head. "What do you think, Pearl? More sophisticated than some athletes we know." She glances over at Charlotte Grange, who is also waiting to be interviewed. The big blonde girl quakes and jitters, clenching her jaw, her exo-suit groaning in anticipation. The neural dampeners barely hold her back.

The crowd roars their impatience, tens of thousands of people behind a curve of reinforced safety glass in the stands high above the action. The rooftops are also packed and there are children swarming on the scaffolding of an old building overlooking the track.

The people in suits, the ones Dr. Arturo and Tomislav want to meet, watch from air-conditioned hotel rooms five kilometers away. Medical and pharmaceutical companies looking for new innovations in a place where anything goes: drugs, prosthetics, robotics, nano. That's what people come for. They tune in by the millions on the proprietary channel. The drama. Like watching Formula 1 for the car crashes.

"All these people, kitten," Tomislav says, "they don't care if you win. They're just waiting for you to explode. But you know why you're here."

"To run."

"That's my girl."

"Slow breaths," Dr. Arturo warns. "You're overstimulated."

The insect drone responds to some invisible hand in a control room and swirls around her, getting every angle. Brian Corwood makes his way over to her, microphone extended like a handshake and winged cameras buzzing behind his shoulder. She holds herself very straight. She knows her mama and the Beloved One are watching back home. She wants to do Gugulethu proud.

"Ndincede nkosi." She mouths the words and sees them come up on the big screens in closed captions below her face. They'll be working to translate them already. Not hard to figure out that she's speaking Xhosa.

"Pearl Nit-seeko," the presenter says. "Cape Town's miracle girl. Crippled when she was fourteen years old and here she is, two years later, at the +Games. Dream come true!"

Pearl has told the story so many times that she can't remember which parts are made-up or glossed over. She told a journalist once that she saw her father killed on TV during the illegal mine strikes in Polokwane and how she covered her ears so she didn't have to hear the popcorn pa-pa-pa-pa-pa of the gunshots as people fell in the dust. But now she has to stick to it. Tragedy makes for a better story than the reality of a useless middle-aged drunk who left her mother to live with a shebeen owner's daughter in Nyanga so that he didn't have to pay off the bar tab. When Pearl first started getting famous, her father made a stink in the local gossip rags until Tomislav paid him to go away. You can buy your own truth.

"Can you tell us about your tech, Pearl?" Brian Corwood says, as if this is a show about movie stars and glittery dresses.

She responds on autopilot. The removable organs, the bath of nano in her blood that improves oxygen uptake. Neural connectivity that blows open the receptors to the hormones and drugs dispatched by the hotbed factory. Tomislav has coached her in the newsworthy technical specs, the details that make investors' ears prick up.

"I can't show you," she apologizes, coyly raising her shirt to let the cameras zoom in on the seam of scar tissue. "It's not a sterile environment."

"So it's hollow in there?" Corwood pretends to knock on her stomach.

"Reinforced surgical-quality graphene mesh." She lightly drums her fingers over her skin, as often rehearsed. It looks spontaneous and shows off her six-pack.

She hears Dr. Arturo's voice in her head. "Put the shirt down now," he instructs. She covers herself up. The star doesn't want to let the viewers see too much. Like with sex. Or so she's been told. She will never have children.

"Is that your secret weapon?" Corwood says, teasing, because no one ever reveals the exact specs, not until they have a buyer.

"No," she says. "But I do have one."

"What is it, then?" Corwood says, gamely.

"God," she says and stares defiantly at the insect cameras zooming in for a close-up.

---

5. Things You Can't Hide

Her stumps are wrapped in fresh bandages, but the wounds still smell, like something caught in the drain. Her mother wants to douse the bandages in perfume.

"I don't want to! Leave me alone!" Pearl swats the teardrop bottle from her mother's hands and it clatters onto the floor. Her mother tries to grab her. The girl falls off the bed with a shriek. She crawls away on her elbows, sobbing. Her Uncle Tshepelo hauls her up by her armpits, like she is a sack of sorghum flour, and sets her down at the kitchen table.

"Enough, Pearl," he says, her handsome youngest uncle. When she was a little girl, she told her mother she was going to marry him.

"I hate you," she screams and tries to kick at him with her stumps, but he ducks away and goes over to the kettle while her mother stands in the doorway, face in hands.

Pearl has not been back to school since it happened. She turns to face the wall when her friends come to visit, refusing to talk with them. During the day, she watches soap operas and infomercials and lies in her mother's bed and stares at the sky and listens to the noise of the day: the cycles of traffic and school kids and dogs barking and the call to prayer vibrating through the mosque's decrepit speakers and the traffic again and men drunk and fighting at the shebeen. Maybe one of them is her father. He has not been to see her since the accident.

Tshepelo makes sweet milky tea for her and her mother, and sits and talks: nonsense, really, about his day in the factory, cooking up batches of patés, which he says is like fancy flavored butter for rich people, and how she should see the stupid blue plastic cap he has to wear to cover his hair in case of contami-nation. He talks and talks until she calms down.

Finally she agrees to go to church—a special service in Khayelitsha Site B. She puts on her woolen dress, grey as the Cape Town winter sky, and green stockings, which dangle horribly at the joint where her legs should be.

The rain polka-dots her clothes and soaks into her mother's hat, making it flop as she quicksteps after Tshepelo, who carries Pearl in his arms like an injured dog. She hates the way people avert their eyes.

The church is no more than a tent in a parking lot, although the people sing like they are in a fancy cathedral in England, like on TV. Pearl sits stiffly at the end of the pew between her uncle and her mother, glaring at the little kids who dart around to stare. "Vaya," she hisses at them. "What are you looking at? Go."

Halfway through the service, two of the ministers bring out the brand-new wheelchair like it is a prize on a game show, adorned with a big purple ribbon. They carry it down the stairs on their shoulders and set it down in front of her. She looks down and mumbles something. Nkosi.

They tuck their fingers into her armpits, these strangers' hands on her, and lift her into the chair. The moment they set her down, she feels trapped. She moans and shakes her head.

"She's so grateful," her mother says and presses her down with one hand on her shoulder. Hallelujah, everyone says. Hallelujah. The choir breaks into song and Pearl wishes that God had let her die.

———————

6. Heat

Pearl's brain is micro-seconds behind her body. The bang of the starting gun registers as a sound after she is already running.

She is aware of the other runners as warm, straining shapes in the periphery. Tomislav has made her study the way they run. Charlotte Grange, grunting and loping, using the exo-suit arms to dig into the ground, like an ape; Anna Murad with her robotics wet-wired into her nerves; Oluchi Eze with her sculpted tail and delicate bones, like a dinosaur bird. And in lane five, furthest away from her, Siska Rachman, her face perfectly calm and empty, her eyes locked on the finish line, two kilometers away. A dead girl remote-controlled by a quadriplegic in a hospital bed. That is the problem with the famous Siska Rachman. She wins a lot, but there is network lag-time.

You have to inhabit your body. You need to be in it. Not only because the rules say so, because otherwise you can't feel it. The strike of your foot against the ground, the rush of air on your skin, the sweat running down your sides. No amount of biofeedback will make the difference.

"Pace yourself," Dr. Arturo says in her head. "I'll give you a glucose boost when you hit eight hundred meters."

Pearl tunes in to the rhythmic huff of her breath, and stretches her legs longer with each stride, aware of everything: the texture of the track, the expanse of the sky, the smell of sweat and dust and oil. It blooms in her chest—a fierce warmth, a golden glow, and she feels the rush of His love and she knows that God is with her.

She crosses third, neck-and-neck with Siska Rachman and milliseconds behind Charlotte Grange, who throws herself across the finish line with a wet ripping sound. The exo-suit goes down in a tumble of girl and metal, forcing Rachman to sidestep.

"A brute," Dr. Arturo whispers in her ear. "Not like you, Pearl."

7. Beloved

The car comes to fetch them, Pearl and her mother and her uncle. A shiny black BMW with hubcaps that turn the light into spears. People came out of their houses to see.

She is wearing her black dress, but it's scorching out, and the sweat runs down the back of her neck and makes her itch under her collar.

"Don't scratch," her mother said, holding her hands.

The car cuts between the tin shacks and the government housing and all the staring eyes, nosing out onto the highway, into the winelands, past the university and the rich people's cookie-cutter townhouses, past the golf course where little carts dart between the sprinklers, and the hills with vineyards and flags to draw the tourists, and down a side road and through a big black gate which swings open onto a driveway lined with spiky cycads.

They climb out, stunned by the heat and other things besides—the size of the house, the wood and glass floating on top of the hill. Her uncle fights to open the wheelchair Khayelitsha Site B bought her, until the driver comes round and says, "Let me help you with that, sir." He shoves down hard on the seat and it clicks into place.

He escorts them into a cool entrance hall with wooden floors and metal sculptures of cheetahs guarding the staircase. A woman dressed in a red and white dress with a wrap around her head smiles and ushers them into the lounge where three men are waiting: a grandfather with two white men flanking him like the stone cats by the staircase. One skinny, one hairy.

"The Beloved One," her mother says, averting her eyes. Her uncle bows his head and raises his hands in deference.

Their fear makes Pearl angry.

The grandfather waves at them to come, come. The trousers of his dark-blue suit have pleats folded as sharp as paper, and his shoes are black like coal.

"So this is Pearl Nitseko," the Beloved One says, testing the weight of her name. "I've heard about you."

The stringy white man stares at her. The lawyer, she will find out later, who makes her and her mother sign papers and more papers and papers. The one with heavy shoulders fidgets with his cuffs, pulling them down over his hairy wrists, but he is watching her most intently of all.

"What?" she demands. "What have you heard?" Her mother gasps and smacks her head.

The Beloved One smiles. "That you have fire in you."

8. Fearful Tautologies

Tomislav hustles Pearl past the religious protesters outside the stadium. Faiths and sects have united in moral outrage, chanting, "Un-natural! Un-godly! Un-holy!" They chant the words in English rather than Urdu for the benefit of the drones.

"Come on!" Tomislav shoulders past, steering her towards a shuttle car that will take them to dinner. "Don't these cranks have bigger things to worry about? Their thug government? Their starving children?" Pearl leaps into the shuttle and he launches himself in after her. "Extremism I can handle." He slams the door. "But tautology? That's unforgivable."

Pearl zips up her tracksuit.

The crowd surges towards the shuttle, bashing its windows with the flats of their hands. "Monster!" a woman shouts in English. "God hates you."

"What's tautology?"

"Unnecessary repetition."

"Isn't that what fear always is?"

"I forget that you're fast *and* clever. Yeah. Screw them," Tomislav says. The shuttle starts rolling and he claps his hands. "You did good out there."

"Did you get a meeting?"

"We got a meeting, kitten. I know you think your big competition is Siska, but it's Charlotte. She just keeps going and going."

"She hurt herself."

"Ripped a tendon, the news says, but she's still going to race tomorrow."

Dr. Arturo, always listening, chimes in. "They have back-up meat in the lab, they can grow a tendon. But it's not a good long-term strategy. This is a war, not a battle."

"I thought we weren't allowed to fight," Pearl says.

"You talking to the doc? Tell him to save his chatter for the investors."

"Tomislav says—" she starts.

"I heard him," Dr. Arturo says.

Pearl looks back at the protestors. One of the handwritten banners stays with her. "I am fearfully and wonderfully made," it reads.

9. She Is Risen

Pearl watches the buses arrive from her bed upstairs in the headquarters of the Church of the Beloved Pentecostal. A guest room adapted for the purpose, with a nurse sitting outside and machines that hiss and bleep. The drugs make her woozy. She has impressions, but not memories. The whoop of the ambulance siren and the feeling of being important. Visitors. Men in golf shorts and an army man with fat cheeks. Gold watches and uniform stars, to match the gold star on the tower she can see from her window and the fat, tapered columns like bullets at the entrance.

"Are you ready?" Dr. Arturo says. He has come from Venezuela especially for her. He has gentle hands and kind eyes, she thinks, even though he is the one who cut everything out of her. Excess baggage, he says. It hurts where it was taken out, her female organs and her stomach and her guts.

He tells her they have been looking for someone like her for a long time, he and Tomislav. They had given up on finding her. And now! Now look where they are. She is very lucky. She knows this because everyone keeps telling her.

Dr. Arturo takes her to the elevator where Tomislav is waiting. The surgeon is very modest. He doesn't like to be seen on camera. "Don't worry, I'll be with you," he says and taps her face near her ear.

"It's all about you, kitten," Tomislav says, wheeling her out into a huge, echoing hallway under a painted sky with angels and the Beloved One, in floating purple robes, smiling down on the people flowing through the doors, the women dressed in red and white and the men in blue blazers and white shirts. This time, she doesn't mind them looking at her.

They make way for the wheelchair, through the double doors, past the ushers, into a huge room with a ceiling crinkled and glossy as a sea shell and silver balconies and red carpets. She feels like a film star, the red blanket over her knees her party dress.

From somewhere deep in the church, women raise their voices in ululation and the hair on her neck pricks up as if she is a cat. Tomislav turns the wheelchair around and parks it beside a huge gold throne with carved leaves and flowers and a halo of spikes. He pats her shoulder and leaves her there, facing the crowd, thousands of them in the auditorium, all staring at her. "Smile, Pearl," Dr. Arturo says, his voice soft inside her head, and she tries, she really does.

A group of women walk out onto the stage, swaying with wooden bowls on their hips, their hands dipping into the bowls like swans pecking, throwing rose petals before them. The crowd picks up the ululating, and it reverberates through the church. Halalala.

The Beloved One steps onto the stage, and Pearl has to cover her ears at the noise that greets him. Women are weeping in the aisles. Men too, crying in happiness to see him.

The Beloved One holds out his hands to still them. "Quiet, please, brothers and sisters of the Pentecostal," he says. "Peace be with you."

"And also with you," the crowd roars back. He places his hands on the back of the wheelchair.

"Today, we come together to witness a miracle. My daughter, will you stand up and walk?"

And Pearl does.

10. Call to Prayer

The restaurant is fancy, a buffet of Pakistani food, korma and tikka and kabobs and silver trays of sticky sweet pastries. The athletes have to pose for photographs and do more interviews with Brian Corwood and others. The journalist with purple streaks in her hair and a metal ring in her lip asks her, "Aren't you afraid you're gonna die out there?" before Tomislav intervenes.

"Come on! What kind of question is that?" he says.

But the athletes can't really eat, and there is a bus that takes them home early so they'll be fresh the next day, while the promoters peel away, one by one, in fancy black cars that take them away to other parts of the city, looking tense. "Don't you worry, kitten." Tomislav smiles, all teeth, and pats her hand.

Back in her room, Pearl finds a prayer mat that might be aligned toward Mecca. She phones down to reception to ask. She prostrates herself on the square of carpet, east, west, to see if it is any different, if her God will be annoyed.

She goes online to check the news and the betting pools. Her odds have improved. There is a lot of speculation about Grange's injury, and whether Rachman will be disqualified. There are photographs of Oluchi Eze posing naked for a men's magazine, her tail wrapped over her parts.

Pearl clicks away and watches herself in the replay, her strikes, her posture, the joy in her face. She expects Dr. Arturo to comment, but the cochlear implant only hisses with faint static.

"Mama? Did you see the race?" The video connection to Gugulethu stalls and jitters. Her mother has the camera on the phone pointed too high so she can only see her eyes and the top of her head.

"They screened it at the community center," her mother says. "Everyone was very excited."

"You should have heard them shouting for you, Pearl," her uncle says, leaning over her mother's shoulder, tugging the camera down so they are in the frame.

Her mother frowns. "I don't know if you should wear that top, it's not really your color."

"It's my sponsor, Mama."

"We're praying for you to do well. Everyone is praying for you."

11. Desert

She has a dream that she and Tomislav and Jesus are standing on the balcony of the main building of the Karachi Parsi Institute looking over the slums. The fine golden sand rises up like water between the concrete shacks, pouring in the windows, swallowing up the roofs, driven by the wind.

"Did you notice that there is only one set of footsteps, Pearl?" Jesus asks. *The sand rises, swallowing the houses, rushing to fill the gaps, nature taking over.* "Do you know why that is?"

"Is it because you took her fucking legs, Lord?" *Tomislav says.*

Pearl can't see any footsteps in the desert. The sand shifts too fast.

12. Rare Flowers

Wide awake. Half-past midnight. She lies in bed and stares at the ceiling. Dr. Arturo was supposed to boost her dopamine and melatonin, but he's busy. The meeting went well, then. The message from Tomislav on her phone confirms it. *Good news!!!! Tell you in the morning. Sleep tight kitten, you need it.*

She turns the thought around in her head and tries to figure out how she feels. Happy. This will mean that she can buy her mother a house and pay for her cousins to go to private school and set up the Pearl Nitseko Sports Academy for Girls in Gugulethu. She won't ever have to race again. Unless she wants to.

The idea of the money sits on her chest.

She swings her stumps over the side of the bed and straps on her blades. She needs to go out, get some air.

She clips down the corridors of the old building. There is a party on the cricketing field outside, with beer tents and the buzz of people who do not have to run tomorrow. She veers away, back towards the worn-out colonial building of the KPI, hoping to get onto the race track. Run it out.

The track is fenced off and locked, but the security guard is dazed by his phone, caught up in another world of sliding colorful blocks. She clings to the shadows of the archway, moving past him and deeper into the building, following wherever the doors lead her.

She comes out into a hall around a pit of sunken tiles. An old swimming pool. Siska Rachman is sitting on the edge, waving her feet in the ghost of water, her hair a dark nest around a perfectly blank face. Pearl lowers herself down beside her. She can't resist. She flicks Rachman's forehead. "*Heita.* Anyone in there?"

The face blinks and suddenly the eyes are alive and furious. She catches Pearl's wrist. "Of course, I am," she snaps.

"Sorry, I didn't think—"

Siska has already lost interest. She drops her grip and brushes her hair away from her face. "So, you can't sleep either? Wonder why."

"Too nervous," Pearl says. She tries for teasing, like Tomislav would. "I have tough competition."

"Maybe not," Siska scowls. "They're going to fucking disqualify me."

Pearl nods. She doesn't want to apologize again. She feels shy around Siska, the older girl with her bushy eyebrows and sharp nose. The six years between them feels like an uncrossable gap.

"Do they think Charlotte is *present?*" Siska bursts out.

"Charlotte is a big dumb animal. How is *she* more human than me?"

"You're two people," Pearl tries to explain.

"*Before*. You were half a person before. Does that count against you?"

"No."

"Do you know what this used to be?" Siska pats the blue tiles.

"A swimming pool?"

"They couldn't maintain the upkeep. These things are expensive to run." Siska glances at Pearl. In the light through the glass atrium, every lash stands out in stark relief against the gleam of her eyes. "They drained all the water out, but there was this kid who was . . . damaged, in the brain, and the only thing he could do was grow orchids. So that's what he did. He turned it into a garden and sold them out of here for years, until he got old. Now it's gone."

"How do you know this?"

"The guard told me. We smoked cigarettes together. He wanted me to give him a blowjob."

"Oh." Pearl recoils.

"Hey, are you wearing lenses?"

She knows what she means. The broadcast contacts. "No. I wouldn't."

"They're going to use you and use you up, Pearl Nit-seeko. Then you'll be begging to give some lard-ass guard a blowjob, just for spare change."

"It's Ni-tse-koh."

"Doesn't matter. You say tomato, I say ni-tse-koh." But Siska gets it right this time. "You think it's all about you.

Your second chance and all you got to do is run your heart out. But it's a talent show, and they don't care about the running. You got a deal yet?"

"My promoter and my doctor had a meeting."

"That's something. They say who?"

"I'm not sure."

"Pharmaceutical or medical?"

"They haven't told me yet."

"Or military. Military's good. I hear the British are out this year. That's what you want. I mean, who knows what they're going to do with it, but what do you care, little guinea pig, long as you get your payout."

"Are you *drunk*?"

"*My body* is drunk. I'm just mean. What do you care? I'm out, sister. And you're in, with a chance. Wouldn't that be something if you won? Little girl from Africa."

"It's not a country."

"Boo-hoo, sorry for you."

"God brought me here."

"Oh, that guy? He's nothing but trouble. And He doesn't exist."

"You shouldn't say that."

"How do you know?"

"I can feel Him."

"Can you still feel your legs?"

"Sometimes," Pearl admits.

Siska leans forward and kisses her. "Did you feel anything?"

"No," she says, wiping her mouth. But that's not true. She felt her breath, burning with alcohol, and the softness of her lips and her flicking tongue, surprisingly warm for a dead girl.

"Yeah," Siska breathes out. "Me neither. You got a cigarette?"

13. Empty Spaces

Lane five is empty and the stadium is buzzing with the news.

"Didn't think they'd actually ban her," Tomislav says. She can tell he's hungover. He stinks of sweat and alcohol and there's a crease in his forehead just above his nose that he keeps rubbing at. "Do you want to hear about the meeting? It was big. Bigger than we'd hoped for. If this comes off, Kitten . . ."

"I want to concentrate on the race." She is close to tears, but she doesn't know why.

"Okay. You should try to win. Really."

The gun goes off. They tear down the track. Every step feels harder today. She didn't get enough sleep.

She sees it happen out of the corner of her eye. Oluchi's tail swipes Charlotte, maybe on purpose.

"Shit," Grange says and stumbles in her exo-suit. Everything comes crashing down on Pearl, hot metal and skin, a tangle of limbs and fire in her side.

"Get up," Dr. Arturo yells into her head. She's never heard him upset before.

"Ow," she manages. Next to her, Charlotte is climbing to

her feet, a loose flap of muscle hanging from her leg where they tried to attach it this morning. The big girl touches it and hisses in pain, but her eyes are already focused on the finish line, on Oluchi skipping ahead, her tail swinging, Anna Murad straining behind her.

"Get up," Dr. Arturo says. "You have to get up. I'm activating adrenaline. Pain blockers."

Pearl sits up. It's hard to breathe. Her singlet is wet. A grey nub of bone pokes out through the skin under her breast. Charlotte is limping away in her exo-suit, her leg dragging, gears whining.

"This is what they want to see," Dr. Arturo urges. "You *need* to prove to them that it's not hydraulics carrying you through."

"It's not," she gasps. The sound is wet. Breathing through a snorkel in the bath when there is water trapped in the u-bend. The drones buzz around her. She can see her face big on the screen. Her mama is watching at home, the whole congregation.

"Then prove it. What are you here for?"

She starts walking, then jogging, clutching the bit of rib to stop the jolting. Every step rips through her. And Pearl can feel things *slipping* inside. Her structural integrity has been compromised, she thinks. The abdominal mesh has ripped and where her stomach used to be is a black hole that is tugging everything down. Her heart is slipping.

Ndincede nkosi, she thinks. Please, Jesus, help me.

Ndincede nkosi undiphe amandla. Please, God, give me strength.

Yiba nam kolu gqatso. Be with me in this race.

She can feel it. The golden glow that starts in her chest, or, if she is truthful with herself, lower down. In the pit of her stomach.

She sucks in her abdominals and presses her hand to her sternum to stop her heart from sliding down into her guts—where her guts used to be, where the hotbed factory sits.

God is with me, she thinks. What matters is you feel it.

Pearl Nitseko runs.

CONFIRM/ IGNORE

Yellow is my favorite color. That's what I'd like you to believe. Other things you should believe if we are to remain friends: that my gender is female. That my birthday is 19 August 1988, with its pleasing arrangement of numbers. That I am interested in women and men but currently single, although you may find that hard to believe.

My religious views are "eyes on eternity," which is vague enough to appeal to theists and atheists alike. My political views are "pragmatic optimist egoist," which says that I am smart and sunny and witty and irreverent, but also that I am beautiful and cool and I know it. But you already determined that from my profile picture. "About me" says I am just a girl. There's humility in that. But not truth.

My favorite artists are Mikhael Subotzky and David Goldblatt. My favorite musicians are Spoek Mathambo and Lady Gaga, in all her incarnations. My favorite film is *Jennifer's*

Body. My favorite author is Haruki Murakami. I don't watch TV. Who cares that these things are incompatible? People are complicated. I've said so myself. Or did you say it first?

I post arty photographs, washed out or heavily filtered by tungsten film, taken on my Nikon F2S or my Lomo Diana or my Polaroid camera. I post status updates bitching about how hard it is to get hold of Polaroid film. Also: philoso-phemes poached from pop culture. Michel Houellebecq. Alexander McQueen. Mae West. Anaïs Nin.

One day I get Bette Davis and Bettie Page confused. This is not my fault. It's yours. And how are we supposed to know anyway? We weren't even born yet, we snipe in different conversation threads in parallel universes. On your page, this conversation goes nowhere. On mine, it leads to a riff on the best Bettys of all time. This should tell you something.

You have your friends. I have mine. *And also yours.* It's easy. This city is small. It is not unlikely that we'd have friends in common. And all I need is one. One pragmatic optimist egoist opens all doors. You might not trust me, but you trust your friends. It's a vicious unicycle, as I said once, clowning around.

These are not my words. But be honest, they're not yours either. Nothing belongs to anyone anymore. Culture wants to be free. This is not my original thought. But who of us can claim to be truly original? Aren't we all remixes of every influence we've ever come across? Love something, let it go. If it comes back, it's a meme. There's a double me in meme.

It hurts when you accuse me of being fake. But it's not a surprise. Your jealousy is a poison flower. If anything, I expected it to bloom sooner. You get off on playing detective, sniffing out the trail of other people's photos I've "stolen," other people's status updates I've "plagiarized." Why, you ask, if I'm so popular, has no one ever met me IRL?

I unfriend you, trying to control the damage, but you raise your voice on other pages, rousing the rabble, until I have no recourse but to kill Amber Richards. A whole life erased with one click. One of you jokes that you should create a memorial page.

"Amber" would probably love that, I say on another page in another voice.

Did you think I wasn't prepared for this? Already I am among the chorus condemning the ghost of an alter ego.

This time I will be more careful.

BRANDED

We were at Stones, playing pool, drinking, goofing around, maybe hoping to score a little sugar, when Kendra arrived, all moffied up and gloaming like an Aito/329. "Ahoy, Special-K, where you been, Girl, so juiced to kill?" Tendeka asked while he racked up the balls, all click-clack in their white plastic triangle. This pool bar was old-school. But Girl just smiled, reached into her back pocket for her phone, hung skate-rat style off a silver chain connected to her belt, and infra'd five rand to the table to get tata ma chance on the next game.

But I was watching her, and as she slipped her phone back into her pocket, I saw that telltale glow beneath her sleeve. Plus long sleeves in summer didn't cut it. So it didn't surprise me none when K waxed the table. Ten-Ten was surprised, though. He slipped his groove. But Boy kept it in, didn't say anything, just infra'd another five to the table and racked 'em again. Anyone else but Ten woulda racked 'em hard, woulda slammed those balls on the table. But Ten . . . Ten went the other way. You could see how careful he was. Precise, like an assembly line.

Boyfriend wasn't used to losing, especially not to Special-K. I mean, the Girl held her own against most of us, but Ten could wax us all six-love, baby. Boyfriend carried his own cue, in a special case. Kif shit. Lycratanium, separate pieces that clicked into each other, assembled slick and cold, like he was a soldier in a movie snapping a sniper rifle together. But Kendra, grinning now, said, "No, my bra, I'm out." Set her cue down on the empty table next to us.

"Oh ja, like Ten's gonna let this hook slide," Rob snorted into his drink. Jasmine looked a little worried, but that's Jazz for you.

"Best of three," Tendeka said, and smiled loose and easy. Like it didn't matter. Chalked his cue.

Girl hesitated, then shrugged. Picked up the cue. Tendeka flicked the triangle off the table, flip-rolling it between his fingers. "Your break."

Kendra chalked up, spun the white ball out to catch it at the line. Edged it sideways so's it would take the pyramid out off-center. Leaned over the table. Slid the tip of the cue over her knuckles once, taking aim, pulled back and cut loose, smooth as sugar. Crack! Balls twisting out across the table. Sunk four solids straight-up. Black in the middle and not a single stripe down.

Rob whistled. "Damn. You been practicing, K?"

Kendra didn't even look up. Took out another two solids and lined up a third in the corner pocket. Girl's lips twitched, but she didn't smile, didn't look at Ten, who was still saying nothing. He chalked his cue again, like he hadn't done it already, and stepped up. The freeze was so tight I couldn't take it. I knew what was coming. I was off by the bar, but nears enough to check the action. Ten lined 'em up and took out two stripes at the same time, rocketing 'em into different pockets. Bounced the white off the pillow and took another, edged out the solid K had all ready to go. Another stripe down, and Boy lined up a fifth blocking the corner pocket. "You're up."

Girl just stood there, looking like she was seizing up.

"K. I said: you're up."

She snapped her head towards Tendeka. Tuned back in. Took her cue, leaned over, standing on tiptoes, and nicked the white ball light as candy-floss, so it floated, spinning, into the middle of the table. Smiled at Ten, and that ball just kept on spinning. Stepped back, set her cue down and started walking over to the bar, to me, while that white ball was still spinning. Damn.

"Hey! What the fuck?"

"Ah c'mon, Ten. You know I gotcha down."

"What! Game ain't even started. And what's with this, man? Party tricks don't mean shit."

"It's over, Ten."

"You on drugs, Girl? You tweaked?"

"Fuck off, Tendeka."

Ten shoved his cue at Rob, and rounded on Kendra. "You're mashed, Girlfriend!" He grabbed her shoulder, spun her round, "C'mon, show me!"

"Kit Kat, baby. Give it a break," Kendra says.

"Lemme take a look at you. C'mon."

"Fuck off, Tendeka! Serious!"

People were rubbernecking. Cams too, though in a place like Stones they probably weren't working too well. Owner paid a premium for faulty equipment.

Jazz was arguing with Ten, defending Kendra now. Not that she needed it. We all knew the Girl wasn't a waster. Even Ten.

Now me, I was a waster. I was *skeef.* Jacked that shit straight into my tongue, popping candy capsules right into my piercing. Lethe or supersmack or kitty. Some prefer it old-style, pills and needles, but me, the works work best straight in through that slippery warm pink muscle, into the bloodstream and salivary glands. That mouth of yours is the perfect disseminator. But, tell you true? Everything I take is cheap shit. Black-market. Ill legit. Not like sweet Kendra's high. Oh no, Girl had gone the straightenarrow. All the way, baby. All the way.

"C'mon Ten, back off, man." Rob was getting nervous. Bartender too, twitching to call his defuser. But Kendra-sweet had had enough, spun on Ten, finally stuck out her tongue at him like a laaitie.

Jazz sighed. "There. Happy now?" But Ten wasn't. For yeah, sure as sugar, Special-K's tongue was virgin. Never been pierced by a stud, let alone an applijack. Never had that sweet rush, microneedles releasing slick-quick into the fleshy pink. Never had her tongue go numb so's you can't speak for minutes. Doesn't matter though. Talking'd be least of your worries, supposing you had any.

But then Ten knew that all along. Cos you can't play the way Girlfriend did on the rof. Tongue's not the only thing that goes numb. And Boyfriend knows it. And everything's click-clicking into place.

"You crazy little shit. What have you done?" Ten was grabbing at her tough-like, and she was swatting back at him, pulling away as he tried to get hold of her sleeve. Jazz was yelling again, "Ease off, Tendeka!" Shouldn't have wasted her airtime. Special-K could look after herself now. After those first frantic swats, only to be expected when she's so fresh, something leveled. You could see it kick in. Sleek. So one instant she's flailing about, and the next she lunges, catches him under his chin with the heel of her palm. Boy's head snaps back, and at the same time she shoves him hard he falls backwards, knocks over a table on his way. Glasses smash and the bartender's pissed. Everyone frozen, except Rob who laughed once, abrupt.

K gave Ten a look. Cocky as a street kid. But wary too. Not of him, although he was already getting up. Her battery was running low, you could see it when she first set down her cue. And Boy was pissed indeed. But that look, boys and girls, that look was wary of herself.

Ten was on his feet now, screaming. The plot was lost. He'd cut himself on the broken glass. Bleeding like paint splats on the wooden floor. Lunged at Kendra, who backed away, hands up, but still with that look. And Boy was intent on serious damage, yelling, not hearing his cell bleep first warning, then second.

Then his defuser kicked in. Higher voltage than necessary, but the bartender was peeved. Ten jerked epileptic. Some wasters I know set off their own phones' defusers, low settings for those dark and hectic beats. Even rhythm can be induced, boys and girls. But it's not easy. Have to hack SAPScom to SMS the trigger signal to your phone. Harder now the cops have privatized, upgraded the firewalls. It's that or you can tweak the hardware so the shocks come random. But that can crisp you KFC.

Me, I defused my defuser. 'Lectric and lethe don't mix. Had a cherry in Sea Point who pulled the plug one time. Simunye. Cost ten kilos of sugar, so's it don't come cheap, and if the tec don't know what they're doing, ha, you're crisped. Or worse, disconnected. Off the networks. Solitary confinement-like. Not worth the risk, boys and girls, unless you know for certain the tec is razor.

So, there's Ten, jerking to imaginary beats. Bartender hit endcall finally and Boy collapsed, panting, his phone still crackling. Jazz knelt next to him. VIMbots scuttled over to clean up the blood and glass and spilled liquor. Other patrons were turning away now. Game over. Please infra another coin. Kendra stood watching one more second, then also turned away, walked over to the bar where I was sitting.

"Cause any more kak like that, and I'll crisp you too," the bartender said as she sat down on the bar stool next to me.

"Oh please. Like how many dial-ins you got left for the night?" Kendra snapped, but she was looking almost as strung out as Ten.

"Yeah, well, don't make me waste 'em all on you."

"Just get me a Ghost, okay?"

Behind her, Jazz and Rob were holding Tendeka up. He made as if to move for the bar, but Jazz pulled him back. Not least cos of the look the bartender shot them. Boy was too fried to stir shit anyway, but said, loud enough for all to hear, "Sell-out."

"Get the fuck out, kid." Dismissive. The bartender knew there was no fight left in him.

"Corporate whore!"

"C'mon, Ten. Let's go." Jazz started escorting him out.

Kendra ignored him. Girl had her Ghost now, downed it in one. Asked for another.

Already you could see it kicking in.

"Can I see?" I asked, mock sly-shy.

Kendra shot me a look I couldn't figure, and then slid up her sleeve slowly, revealing the glow tattooed on her wrist.

The bartender clicked his tongue as he set her drink down. "Sponsor baby, huh?"

The logo was emblazoned not on her skin, but under it, shining through, with the slogan "Just be it."

No rinkadink light show this: she'd signed up for nanotech that changed the bio-structure of her cells, made 'em phosphorescent in all the right places. Nothing you couldn't get done at the local light-tat salon, but corporate sponsorship came with all the extras. Even on lethe, I wasn't oblivious to the ad campaigns on the underway. But Kendra was the first I knew to get Branded.

Girl was flying now. Ordered a third Ghost. Brain reacting like she was on some fine-ass bliss, drowning her in endorphins and serotonin, the drink binding with aminos and the tiny bio-machines humming in her veins. Voluntary addiction with benefits. Make her faster, stronger, more coordinated. Ninja-slick reflexes. Course, if she'd sold her soul to Big Red Cola instead, she'd be sharper, wittier. Big Red nano-lubes the transmitters. Neurons firing faster, smarter, more productive. All depends on the brand, on your lifestyle of choice, and it's all free if you qualify. Waster like me would never get with the program, but sweet Kendra, straight-up candidate of choice. Apply now, boys and girls, while stocks last. You'll never be able to afford this high on your own change.

Special-K turned to me, on her fourth now, blissed out on the carbonated artificial sugars and the tech seething in her hot little sponsor-baby bod. "And one for my friend," she said to the bartender. And who was I to say no?

SMILEYS

Thozama is not a sheep. Not like these heads in their bloody packets at her feet, pink tongues lolling from their mouths, lips curled back revealing sharp and yellowed herbivore incisors, like a smile, like a sneer, like men when you can't tell what they are thinking. Like this man, Soldier, who has swung into the scalloped plastic seat facing her on the train and leaned over to introduce himself.

There are plenty of open seats. The trains going to town are gagging with people, literally choking them out onto the platform with every heave of the doors, but there are not so many heading *back* to Langa at eight fifteen in the morning.

She would go earlier if she could; it takes all day to prepare the smileys, but the butcher in Salt River only opens for trade at seven, which means that on a Monday, she must leave at five, because now that her house has arrived, she lives in Delft.

Get a house, lose a neighborhood. She knows people who have sold up their neat little brick houses from the government and moved right back to Langa or Nyanga or Khayelitsha, back to a shack, because it's better to be among people you know, better to be twenty minutes to town instead of an hour, better to get water for free, even if from a shared public tap, than to have to pay bills, all the bills that come with houses.

So she lives in Delft, but her customers are in Langa, where they have been for these past eight years. Sometimes she will sleep at a friend's for the week and only go back to her house on the weekends. She has a trolley at the station waiting for her to load it up with heads and trundle them to her stall in the hub of Chinatown.

The name is misleading. There are no Chinese people here, like there are no Spanish in Barcelona overlooking the highway or Serbs in Kosovo, where the shacks lean stubbornly against the sharp slope running down to the small tributary of the Black or the Liesbeek or some other dead river bloated with garbage. These are names picked from the news, from the Olympics, from the genocide.

Older settlements are named for the struggle, like talismans of protection. But where is that communist when the paraffin fires tear through Joe Slovo every summer, turning the clutter of shacks into a maze of heat and smoke, flames riding the wind like boys on the train, leaping between rooftops, eating up the shacks. Where is Joe then? Thozama can tell you: dead in the ground, with all the other promises.

She has a good spot in Chinatown, on a corner between her friend, Nosingile, who sells mealies, a good complementary business, and a stall, rigged with shadecloth and plastic chairs, that sells phone calls and airtime. Sometimes the boys complain about the flies that cloud around like *miggies*. They say it drives customers away to the competing phone container down the way, but Thozama says no, it's the opposite. The heavy smell of the boiling mutton soaks into the air, lures people by their noses so they come floating in on the breeze. They should pay her commission.

The train rattles and sways through Maitland industria, warehouses and factories slipping away past the window that only opens halfway, that is greasy and scratched and jaundiced. There is a fat blue fly maintaining a holding pattern of misshaped rectangles over the bags of sheeps' heads. The flies always manage to find the blood. She waves it away.

"You sell smileys, Mama?" Soldier says, as if it is not obvious. She is not overly concerned. He is too old to be trouble. Forty-five, she reckons by the sag of his face, the creases like gutters on either side of his mouth, and it is only the start of the day—she has no money yet to hide in her bra—or tuck into her panties, because the tsotsis on the trains are getting more brazen. Besides, a bag of heads is too much work to be worth stealing.

It takes all day to prepare. It is a procedure. You need patience and a fridge to store them in and a place to cook them where the neighbors will not complain about the smoke or the smell.

First you must wash them and squeeze out the excess blood. You must stuff the nostrils with newspaper to stop the flies, always the flies, getting in. Then cut off the hair with the edge of a sharp knife. She could be a barber given the precision with which she does this, shaving men's scalps instead of mutton, but there are already two hair salons near her corner in Chinatown, dueling businesses run by two girls who used to be friends, who have set up right next to each other, out of spite as much as anything else.

Once the hair is removed, you burn the heads in the fire, a quick *tsss-tsss*, and then scrape them again, this time with a metal rod that has been lying in the coals. Then they must be washed and scraped once more, with steel wool to get rid of any last stubborn straggles of hair, because customers will judge the quality of your meat by how clean the heads are. Then you take your axe, cut the head in half—she splits a skull with one blow—and set it to boiling with the others, in a metal drum on the fire. And then wait for the lunchtime traffic.

Smileys are a delicacy. Or used to be. Now, any man, single men mostly, with no wives to cook for them, can buy for only twenty rand for a half; men like this Soldier, for instance.

"You're playing with me," she says in answer, nudging a bag full of heads with the toe of her shoe.

"I'm sorry, I can see. I was making conversation. Maybe finding a new place to eat?" Is he flirting with her? Why, when she is almost twenty years his senior?

"My heads are very clean, excellent quality. Like Woolworths. You should tell your friends."

"Business is good then, Mama?" Soldier asks, and suddenly she is wary.

"So-so. Better at the end of the month, when people have money. But with the holidays coming, everyone is going back to the Ciskei, Transkei, then it's very slow. Too slow." She tsks and shakes her head, playing old lady down-on-her-luck.

"But, hey, these skollies, you must watch out for them," Soldier says, like the thought has just occurred to him, when she can tell it has been sitting, waiting on his tongue, like that fat blue fly. "They'll rob a woman like you, a businesswoman. They'll watch you, coming to the station with heads, coming home with money. They'll be waiting for you."

"I'm all right. My cousin's boy comes with me." This is a lie. Her cousin's son sometimes helps her at the stall, for ten rand for the day, for a pack of cigarettes, but it is too far to travel all the way to Delft, especially on the weekends when young men have other priorities.

"You know, Mama," Soldier says, "these politics and what-what. They've messed us up. I'm not talking now with everything, but the old days, you know?"

She does know. The young people don't see it. It's all nonsense, they say, apartheid is over and done, leave it behind. But the past infests everything, like worms. They've cut down the old trees, the new government, but the roots of the past are still there, can still tangle round your feet, trip you up. They go deep.

"You know why they call me Soldier?'

"You fought in the struggle. Were you with MK?"

"APLA. The Azanian People's Liberation Army. But when I came back from the fighting, when we were free, I applied to the police for work. But they said I didn't have matric and what-what, so now what was I supposed to do. This is what I'm talking about, Mama, this is why I came to sit with you."

The way he says it worries her.

"Because you see, people like me, we come back with all this training and what good are we in our community? We're dangerous people, Mama. We were lions fighting that apartheid struggle, lions defending our communities, but what happens when you bring the lions into the kraal, among the sheep?"

"They eat them."

"They eat them, Mama. These men, APLA, MK, the Transkei Defense Force, those Ciskei military wings, now they have nothing to do, they turn to armed robbery or hijacking. It's easy for them, and that's why we would rather use these men to initiate protection and defense. So we started the Anti-Crime Association."

She has heard of ACA, of course. The man stripped naked and beaten in the streets, on the word of another man and a R150 "transport fee," of the man found hanging behind the taxi rank, his eyes blindfolded. Vigilantes.

"So what do you want with me?"

"We are working hard. We are all volunteers. We work for free. Maybe sometimes the people in the community bring us some food."

"That is what you want? Food?"

"No, no, like I was saying, a businesswoman like you, sometimes it is dangerous. We could accompany you. I could accompany you, get you home safe with your day's earnings. The police are useless, you know. There are places they can't go or don't want to go. ACA doesn't have to follow all the rules the police do. We're more effective than the police. ACA doesn't have any boundaries. ACA is everywhere. ACA is like the Scorpions, but better."

"I thought you were lions, not insects?" She always had a problem with her tongue getting away from her. With smileys, the tongue is the part that is most savored.

"You joke, Mama, but this is very serious, very serious. Even Nelson Mandela said we must all engage in the fight against crime. But fighting crime costs money."

"This is my station," she says, getting up, trying to cut the conversation, burn it away like unwanted hair.

"I'll walk with you."

"No, no, it's fine. My cousin's boy . . ."

"You can't be carrying those heads. They must be heavy. Let me help you."

"Are you *volunteering*?" she snaps, but he is already holding her bags, following her out of the train onto the platform. She searches the crowd for someone she knows. But there is no one she recognizes, no one to help her.

"My trolley is behind here," Thozama says, leading him round the back of the station, past the Diamond shebeen and the SASKO stage, where they are doing a roadshow with megaphones, as if the company had not been fixing bread prices all this time. "Those are the real criminals," she says, nodding at the production where they are giving out prizes to make people forget.

"It's terrible, terrible," Soldier agrees.

"So how much will it cost me?"

He pretends to misunderstand her. "It's volunteer stuff. But we need uniforms, so the skollies can see when we are around, and they know not to commit crime and what-what. So we have a presence. And we need computers and phones. It's all unpaid."

"How much will it cost me?"

"We don't work for reward, Mama, but you know, businesses need protection. Women like you, they are vulnerable, working on their own. And sometimes those businesses make a contribution. A donation. You don't want to be robbed. You don't want to lose all your hard earnings and you know what skollies are like now, no respect. You don't want to go through that."

Thozama thinks about the things she *has* been through. Her husband working in Germiston as a petrol attendant, both of them bringing in money, building their home, a family from two different cities over a thousand kilometers apart, when he died in the fighting between the Zulus and the ANC in 1993. She thinks about her twenty-six-year-old daughter who drinks up her government grant, drinks to drown the anger and the shame of her diagnosis, and forgets to give her baby, Thozama's grandson, his anti-retroviral medicine.

She thinks about her best wishes: to live with her kids (all grown up, the customs done, her son has already been to the bush), for her business to grow and her kids to take over, so she can relax, stop riding the train to the butcher, stop shaving the heads, boiling the heads, selling the heads.

And she thinks about this man, this Soldier, this lion, and she stoops, as if she has dropped something, as if she is an old woman who needs to take a break. And she picks up a broken half-brick from the ground.

"What is it, Mama?" he says. "Don't worry, it's not much money. We all have to make a living."

And she hits him on the side of the head.

It is a clean blow. Her arm is strong from her work. It is much easier, in fact, than chopping a sheep's skull in half. Although the sound it makes is almost the same.

He drops to the ground, collapsing from the knees like one of those cheap Chinese toy figurines with the button at the bottom, the bags slipping from his hand, dropping with him.

A smiley rolls out, comes up grinning at him, the tongue thick and pink between its teeth. But he can't see it, because his eyes are closed. Blood smears the side of his head. It will draw flies. It will leave a scar.

There is a chance he might find her. There is a chance he might retaliate.

But he has made one big mistake.

"I am not a sheep," she says to the man sprawled on the ground behind the station.

She picks up her bag, restores the prodigal brother to his place among the smiling-sneering heads, and walks away into the crowds at the market towards Chinatown.

Princess

It should come as no surprise that the princess found her pea, not beneath the teetering pile of mattresses, quilted and cotton-rich, with pocket coils and high-density foam, but nestled among the wiry coils between her legs.

You might wonder how she'd missed it in the first place. How could she have overlooked the marvel that would turn her blood to treacle and pin her like a butterfly on the fulcrum of her desire? The princess wondered at this herself.

But the unfortunate truth is that, like many princesses—and princes besides—she had always been too preoccupied with her princess-y duties, which included making the cover of *Heat* and *People* and *Us Weekly*, dabbling in music or fashion or reality TV, looking hot at all times, dancing on tables and, most importantly, Being Seen.

Delighted with her discovery, feeling like an explorer who has unexpectedly stumbled upon a lost temple in humid tangles of jungle, the princess rose from her tower of mattresses, calling impatiently for her infinitely patient handmaid.

Now, this handmaid was a loyal servant and true. An economic refugee from Ecuador, she had seen many things and weathered many tempests with the princess, including that video scandal—all the more sordid for its tediousness—where the princess lolled limp and bored while the prince, who turned out to be a pornographer, grunted and heaved away. But that was before the princess found her pea. And the handmaid was willing to bet her immigrant work visa that everything was about to change.

She set about helping the princess prepare, which was not technically in her job description. But in this matter—being that of the flesh and the delights thereof—the handmaid was far more experienced and had much wise knowledge to impart.

But before you cry foul over class exploitation, consider that the handmaid had a secret—a secret that had allowed her to stick by the princess throughout her wastrel shenanigans and wasted affairs. For the handmaid deeply loved the princess in a manner not entirely appropriate or approved, despite what you may have seen on those Spring Break reality TV specials.

So, at the princess's insistence, the handmaid plucked and shaved and waxed the plump, velvety casing, all the better to show off the sultry treasure within. Then she teased back the folds and burnished the princess's pea to a glistening jewel. And the princess shivered and shuddered and gasped and finally cried, which the handmaid thought was a tad melodramatic, but then she hadn't been let down all her life by fumble-fingered and feckless princes.

She dabbed the princess's tears (and other damp bits) with an indulgent three-ply tissue. Then she brushed out her hair, pinning it up in a style that only seemed effortless, and rifled her wardrobe for an outfit to match. After much deliberation, the handmaid picked out a pale starry sheath of a dress by a designer whose name you would recognize.

It was the kind of dress that clung in all the right places, the kind that might easily ride up as a princess swung open the door of a limousine, or attach itself with static attraction to a silver pole that a princess might be slithering against in a nightclub, or simply be hoisted up at the right moment of intoxication at the right prompting from a man with a camera.

And it's not that this didn't make the handmaid sad. But she had long ago given up judging the princess, who was quite the worst combination of headstrong and insecure. For in this matter, too, the handmaid was also wise and experienced, having been motivated by that selfsame troublesome formula to abandon wool-gathering on the alpaca farm where her family worked, and to sneak across dusty borders in cramped and stinking trucks, to have many adventures both wild and frightful.

Then the princess kissed the handmaid goodbye and clattered across the entrance hall of her luxury apartment toward the limo that awaited her, just like every other night, weekday or weekend, on a princess's rather busy social calendar.

But this was not like every other night. This was different. Because the princess was different.

The doorman noticed it as he held open the door with a sharp snap of his heels. And the limo driver noticed as the princess slipped onto the back seat among her so-called friends. And even those bespangled and twittering girls noticed, despite their notable lack of observational skills, which were generally limited to spotting a fake designer label or a cheap haircut at fifty paces.

The princess was more sparkly than usual, more sparky, more radiant. The scent of confidence came off her like she'd been doused in a bottle of the stuff. And, more than that, she was smugly sated.

Her friends interrogated the princess with barbed banalities like "What's up with you?" But the princess, still simmering in the heat and thrall of afterglow, could not be roused by their bile. Behind their perfectly whitened smiles, her friends rumbled and muttered with venomous envy.

At the nightclub, all swished past the velvet rope and the huddled plebs clamoring after them for acknowledgement or autographs. Her friends dismissed them, but the princess found herself for once moved by their plaintive and probably unhealthy adoration—and did something she never did: she stopped to chat.

Horrified, her friends seized her arm and hustled her inside the building before she could exchange more than a sentence with the ecstatic couple at the front of the queue, leaving the large but hapless bouncer to deal with the fandom hysteria spreading fast as the pox or a viral video.

Inside the club, it was hot and pulsating with people, like the flush and the rush through a heart's central chambers. Before they made it to the VIP bar, the princess found herself ensnared by the music, the deep house-beat insistent and sweet as the throb between her legs. She started to dance, not for show, as she usually did, atop a table above the masses, but for pleasure, in the thick, sweaty press of the crowd. Her friends on the sidelines rustled and murmured with gleeful scorn, disguised as concern.

Seeing his opening, a predatory prince prowled over to grind and gyrate in what passed for foreplay. But his mistake was in assuming that she was well fucked, rather than fucked well, and she shrugged him off to dance on her own, lost in the flow of the rhythms resonating inside her and out.

Gradually, the whole room began to take note of the difference in the princess. The crowd parted and swirled and started to orbit her, like electrons—or sharks. The envious friends and the prowling prince found their way to the center, circuiting closer and closer. Then one touched her hair and another her elbow, one plucked at her strap and another at her skirt, hands reaching and grasping as if she were a religious relic, a crying statue, a totem, a vodoun doll.

The princess tried to bat them away, laughing, as if it were a game—but these courtiers played rough. They kept pawing and groping her, the circle getting tighter and closer, until she had no route to escape.

It was a day for new feelings, it seemed, for now the princess experienced another emotion she'd never had before. It was not dissimilar to the feelings induced by the handmaid's deft fingers, the fluttering in her chest and the thrill down her vertebrae. But whereas before these were soporific and dreamy, this sensation left her cold and bright as the hard, glittering eyes of her one-time friends.

"What is it with you?" and "Who do you think you are?" they heckled and sneered, snagging manicured nails on that silver shimmer of dress, their movements savage and jerky in the hiccuping strobe.

They ripped and they tore, shredding and stripping the flimsy fabric as easily as you might a reputation. In vain, the bewildered princess struggled and wept. Her cohorts didn't stop until her dress lay in strips at her feet—and her secret lay bared to all.

The predatory prince was not the only one to recoil in shock, crying that he'd never seen the like when the truth was, he'd never thought to look. The rest of the assembly gasped in wonder and fright as the princess tried to shelter that lustrous pearl, that giddying pea that she had fully intended to show off that night—but, not like this, not to these hyenas in designer clothing, who jostled and jeered, buoyed by outrage and superstition and fear.

The princess moaned and curled over herself, trying to shield her nakedness, trying to deflect the blows that came not from fists but from pretty mouths lined with lip-gloss or ringed by designer stubble. She collapsed to the ground, writhing from hurt and humiliation. And then, a voice blasted the crowd.

The source of the command to "Back off, bloodsuckers!", was so unlikely that, at first, it caused tittering ripples. Standing defiantly in the doorway was a girl with dark hair, wearing supermarket jeans and, worst of all, practical shoes. It was the handmaid. And when it was clear that the contemptuous mob had no intention of obeying, she drew herself up and waded right in.

The empty-eyed courtiers tried to resist, to fight back, but they were no match for a girl who had wrestled alpacas and the bureaucracies of borders—not to mention the princess's vanity. They were so one-dimensional, their personalities so paper-thin, that they proved no trouble at all. One push, one shove, one shoulder and they wafted up and away like helium balloons. They floated to the ceiling, where they bumped against the rafters and tangled in the light fittings.

The handmaid hefted the princess to her feet, wrapped her up in her anorak and escorted her out from that awful place, between the drifts of celebrity, bobbing in the cross-currents of the air-conditioners.

But outside the front door, worse was waiting. There were snapping shutters and flashes and the terrible scrutiny of zoom lenses. Unfortunately, the baying paparazzi were made of sturdier stuff and used to the worst kinds of abuse. They didn't give, they didn't crumble in the face of the handmaid's wrath. Their shutters whirred and clicked, snapping relentless shot after shot after shot.

The handmaid faltered, blinded by flashbulbs. She felt her confidence draining from her, as if those ancient legends about photographs stealing a piece of your soul might be true. She batted at the air, as if she could swat away the popping flashes, but it was too much. She was exhausted. She was done. With a moan and a whimper, the handmaid fell to her knees on the curb, scuffing her jeans.

And that's when the princess stepped forward, out from under the handmaid's protective arm. She took center stage, where she'd always been most comfortable, although never this exposed. When she had the paparazzi's full attention, meeting those cold lenses with uncharacteristic calm, the princess shrugged her shoulders and let the anorak drop.

The cameras all automatically dipped as if weighted, down past the slope of her diminutive breasts and her taut gym-toned belly to the undercurve of her body and her pink velvet box and the still glistening treasure nested within.

For a full minute, the hungry cameras feasted. And then something happened. A paparazzo lowered his camera, then looked away, ashamed. Then another, and a third and a fourth. The fifth nudged the sixth, who ripped the seventh's camera from his hands, and a clatter of memory chips fell to the pavement, to be scrunched beneath stamping boots.

The princess stood naked before them, still and collected and candidly open, so that none of them could stand up to her, or stand to look, as she showed off their shame, her pride, her voluptuous pea.

And so it was that the princess found not only her pea and her pleasure, but also her heart.

The princess and the handmaid fled the bright and terrible city. They bought a farm in the mountains of Ecuador and launched a trendy fashion label of hypoallergenic alpaca wool products in couture cuts.

The handmaid still struggled with the princess from time to time; people aren't readily cured of a lifetime of bad habits, not even by fairy-tale miracles. She found the alpacas to be generally sweeter of temperament, although when riled, they would spit a sour green slobber of saliva and stomach acid and half-dissolved grass. And at least, in her experience, the princess had never done that.

MY INSECT SKIN

It starts with Kafka.

—But you should love me anyway, I tell Joe.—If I turned into a giant cockroach, I'd still be me.

—Ja, except you'd be crunchy and gross and you wouldn't have these, he says, lifting my breasts. I squirm away, slapping at his hand.

—Oh, so now you just love me for my body. I see. And here I thought it was who I am that did it for you.

—Lien. Your body is part of who you are. You can't just divorce your mind. Although if you do, I get custody of the pussy.

—Do I have to pay you alimony?

—I'm sorry. I just would not be attracted to you if you had six legs and insect skin.

—Carapace, I correct.

—Exactly. Trust me, not attractive.

—But what if I was horribly disfigured in a terrible accident? What if I got burned and my skin melted like plastic?

—That wouldn't be the same as you being a giant cockroach.

—But what if I was? What if I fell through a window and cut my face to shreds?

He sighs and rolls over to look out the window framing Signal Hill.

—Okay, okay. What if I was a man? Would you still love me?

—You are not a man, his voice says from under the pillow he's pulled over his face.

—What if I was. Before. Before you met me? I straddle him, leaning on my elbows on his chest. What if I had a sex change in Thailand and my old name is Michael. Would you still love me?

Joe lifts the pillow and looks up at me.

—Are you trying to tell me something, Lien?

—Um. Maybe.

—You're just wrong. You know that? He shakes his head, then rears up to kiss me on my forehead.—You need to stop reading that book. And stop watching so much daytime TV. And shave your toes.

—What's wrong with my toes? I'm indignant. Mortified.

—Nothing. Except if you shaved them, maybe I wouldn't almost believe you when you say you used to be a guy. He waits a beat.—Michael.

I whack him with a pillow and he wrestles it away from me and we make love again, breathless, laughing.

Only the next day, Thursday, I wake up feeling slippery. Not like a giant cockroach exactly, but something is out of sync with my body, more even than recent changes. I ease out of bed, careful not to wake Joe, pull on my tracksuit and my sneakers and click the door shut behind me. Outside, the sky is pale like water. A minibus taxi roars past, the guy in the back singing out Keptown-Keptown! I drop my leg from stork position and push my toe against a wall to stretch my calves. The wind battering against the flagpoles of the hotel across the road has chipped the sea into dark and angry little caps.

The Afrikaans poet Ingrid Jonker killed herself here. Just walked into the sea one day. When they found her body, there were tiny sea shells in the curves of her ears. When I mention this to Joe when we are out walking, eating Flake 99s, he tells me to stop being such a melodrama queen, only he says it like this: mellow drama queen.

I start a slow warm-up jog to the promenade, speeding up as I reach the rails that fence off the Atlantic. There is a homeless guy on the beach, shuffling among the gulls and pigeons that lift and resettle behind him, a screeching, fluttering wake. My legs are starting to burn and an arrowhead grazes my lung every time I breathe. It feels good though, like I'm on cruise control.

—Would you still love me if I cheated?

—Cheated at PlayStation or cheated on me with someone else?

—Either.

—No.

—Even with a girl?

—Am I there?

—No!

—Then no.

I did kiss a girl, once, before I met Joe. Coked off our faces at one of those season clubs in summer, she'd pushed me up against a wall in a dark corner, pressed her lips to mine and tried to put her hand up my skirt. I didn't really resist, but I didn't go home with her either. She decided I was too straight for her. I guess I was. Am. Breeder.

The arrowhead has shifted from my ribs. I know I can run out a stitch, only now the pain has moved to my belly and it's heavy and gnawing, like cramps. It can't be cramps. I know, although Joe doesn't. I haven't told him yet. It's uncomfortable though, so even though I still have a ways to go, and I need to stay fit, especially now, I slow down to a walk, just for a little bit.

There's finally someone else out here: a man walking a huge dog, a Weimaraner. It's not on a leash and it bounds up to me and shoves its nose into my crotch as I raise my hands defensively.

—Nushka! Nushka! Down! I'm so sorry. The man wrestles the dog away and slaps at its nose. I'm really sorry. He's just excitable around pretty girls.

—No, it's okay. It's fine. There is a shiny snail-trail of dog slobber on my tracksuit. I suddenly feel sick.

—Hey, I've seen you jogging around here a lot. Do you live nearby?

I barely hear him. Gravity spins out for an instant, so that it feels like the world takes a leap in strobe.

—What? Yes. No. My boyfriend does.

—Oh. Yeah? Well. I live nearby. Maybe we could get a cup of coffee?

—What?

—I mean, after you're done jogging. Sometime.

Is he hitting on me?

—Are you hitting on me?

The world strobes again. I think he has the decency to look a little embarrassed, but right now I don't care. I feel wrong. Like my insides have been strung around a fork that someone is twisting.

—Well, you know, Nushka likes you, and you seem pretty cool. Maybe I could get your number and . . .

—I left it at home, I snap, and brush past him to the hospital-blue box of the public toilets.

—Well, jeez. I'm sorry for asking. I was just being friendly. What's your fucking problem? Bitch.

I push against the door of the ladies' bathroom, only it doesn't budge. I push again and then stumble around the side to the men's bathroom, shove the door open, reel as a fist clenches on my guts and nearly fall to the concrete that is spattered with damp grey sand.

—Okay, how about if I killed someone?

—Did they deserve it?

—Kind of. But it was pre-meditated murder rather than self-defense.

—Hmmm. I dunno. Do the cops know you did it?

—Does it matter?

—It does if I have to pay for the lawyer.

I'm crumpled in the stall, my shorts around my ankles, doubled over my knees, holding the door shut with one hand because the lock doesn't work. I can't breathe. I can't think. God god oh fuck god fuck!

And now the slipperiness has moved to between my legs. The pain moves like breath, builds with bright intensity, tearing through me, then easing, fluttering, then steadily building again. My fingers are pressed white into my belly, trying to hold it in, oh god please. Time stutters and drags. I will someone to come and find me, to make it stop.

Only, when I hear the door open and footsteps on the concrete, it's accompanied by the click of claws.

—Hey! Are you still in here? Are you okay?

I can hear the dog panting, big doggy gasps, and meanwhile he's waiting. Listening. A shadow over the slice of light beneath the door. I bite down on the back of my hand and lock my arm against the door. Go away go away go away please just please please.

—He-ll-o? Are you in there? He rolls his knuckles over the door.

I'm trying not to breathe, not to let out the tight sounds catching in my throat.

He stands there for a long time. But then the shadow moves, there's a scrunch of sand under boots, soft clothing sounds, the squeal of a zipper. Oh god. And the dog panting.

Something is tearing loose. Outside, there's a splash of piss. Then the urinal flushes. Footsteps, the creak of his jeans and the dog *tjanks* once.

—I'm just looking out for you, you know. I can hear the

dog, Nushka, I can hear Nushka breathing, I can hear his fingers in the dog's fur, his hand ruffling its head. I can hear the drone of the morning traffic. There is blood in the toilet bowl.

Or maybe it's the waves. I can't tell.

Dark clots of it.

And he's still standing there, blocking the sliver of light under the door. I think about Joe and the police station not even two hundred yards from here and the traffic and the homeless guy and the other joggers. And he's still here. And our breathing, me and him and the dog playing counterpoint. And we're not even a foot apart. Jesus please. And I wonder if his hand is on the door, if it's touching mine through the wood. And it's like we've always been listening to each other breathe on the other side of three centimeters of wood, white paint flaking, graffiti and dirty fingerprints. And my body can't fucking hold it. Oh god, Joe. Would you still? Would you? I lean my head against the door. And the sound escapes.

—Hey.

My hand is pressed tight against my mouth, my fingers digging into the shape of my jaw, but I'm sobbing, the sound raw against my teeth, against my fingers.

—Hey!

Would you wouldyouwouldyouwouldyouwouldyouwould you, and I'm screaming now. So I can't hear the dog panting, so I can't hear him breathing, so I can't hear the fetus slipping from my body. I'm screaming so I can't hear myself scream.

PARKING

His name is Nikolas van Rooyen. He is an officer with the metropolitan police. A traffic marshal. It doesn't escape him that most of his colleagues are women. They say it is a tough job, that people are rude. They are defensive. They try their luck. But he is twenty-two and grateful for the work.

He works on Long Street, which is good, because it is always busy. There is always a bustle and a hustle here. He likes being outside. He likes the noisiness of the street, although he also likes it when it is quiet, early in the morning, before the city is swollen with cars and people. He likes it when the streets are empty, when the spaces are still white lines waiting to be filled. It is hard to find parking in town.

His job is to ensure that people put money in the meter or rather that they swipe their prepaid cards. His job is to recharge cards that have run out of credit, to sell brand-new cards to people who don't have one at all, or to sell them minutes off his own card. Parking costs R3.40 for half an hour. His salary comes out of the meters.

He has been watching her for three weeks now. She comes here often, to Long Street. Not always, not every day, but often. Usually in the afternoons, every second or third day. At first he thought she might work here, but she is only here for a couple of hours at the most, and what kind of job would let her to do that?

She drives a red Toyota Tazz. The license plate is CA 087-169. He has it memorized so that he can look out for her. She is often in his area, on his beat. He thinks he is in love with her, although he doesn't know her name. Only her car.

She tries to park in Pepper or one of the other cross-streets between Long and Loop, where there aren't any meters. But everyone else knows this too, and these spaces are rarely free. Sometimes she gets lucky, though. It depends on the time of day. Sometimes he has seen her circle the block several times, going all the way down Long and turning up at the restaurant on the corner, until a parking space opens up on one of the cross streets, or she surrenders and takes the first available space with a meter.

When she is here, she goes to Mr. Pickwick's Coffeeshop and Eatery. She knows the waiters well. They hug her when she goes in. It is better when she sits outside, where he can see her. She smokes, Stuyvesant Blue (he has checked at the café, matched the color of the box), and drinks coffee and meets many different people. When one of the men who walks the streets here flashes her a pair of sunglasses, she shakes her head and looks angry, and this makes him feel like he knows her, because he wouldn't take them either—although the man has Oakleys and Ray-Bans.

Her car is a 1300, bottom of the range, but new enough, maybe three or four years old, so he can tell that she has money. She has looped a necklace of flowers, like the ones they hang around your neck at the airport in Hawaii (he has seen it once on TV), around her headrests. The flowers are faded in the sun, but still colorful. He sometimes thinks when he is passing her car that he can smell them, although he knows they are made of silk, like the ones in his mother's house in Beaufort West.

There is a scratch on her front bumper, a nasty one that wraps around the edge, as if she has grazed a pole or perhaps another car. She is a careless driver. She pulls out from between the lines of her parking space without indicating, and her parallel parking is terrible. He wishes sometimes that he were a car guard in an orange vest rather than a warden, that he could guide her in with whistles and gestures and tap the trunk smartly, not so as to give her a fright, but to tell her to stop. Like Emmanuel, who is from the DRC, who only comes at 4 p.m., when the rest of them are going off shift.

Part of his job is to chase away the informal car guards and the street people and the barefoot children who sleep in doorways. His job is to keep the city safe, especially for the visitors, to chase away the rubbish. It is a respectable job, and they say that this is how they sorted out the crime situation in New York. That by stopping the small crimes, you can stop the big ones. But this is the work he tries to avoid, when he can. Emmanuel says he is soft, that he would not last in the Congo, if he can't even handle children.

There is another scratch on her rear bumper. Though he's not quite sure what could have caused it. The bumper is the same dark cherry red as the rest of her car. He thinks she could be *his* cherry, and is instantly ashamed at how childish the thought seems. It is something his father would say.

The paint on the bumper is cracked and ugly like a scar. It is flaking off in patches, like burned skin peeling off. Once, when he was certain no one was looking, he pried off a flake of paint with his fingernails and palmed the thin curl. It was too small to put in his pocket, so he put it on his tongue instead. It tasted like nothing. He was expecting it to be cold, metallic, or at least to taste of dust and dirt and the city streets, but it was like a piece of plastic, like he had ripped a packet of chips with his teeth and got a snag of it left in his mouth. He couldn't think what else to do, so he swallowed it.

At first, he didn't think much of it when he didn't see her for a few days, because it was the weekend and it was his Saturday off. They rotated shifts every weekend, one on, one off. She wasn't there on Friday, so that made three days, including Sundays when no one works, but then she didn't come to town on Monday or Tuesday or Wednesday. He wondered if she had left. If she was ever coming back.

She never notices him. His uniform is like camouflage, as if he is part of the street, smudging into the background like the pigeons. On Thursday, he nearly misses her, because she parks on Loop and walks down. It is only by chance, because he is crossing the road to help a woman who has run out of minutes on her card, that he sees her disappearing into one of the fashion shops. He recognizes her hair, with its streaks of color and its scruffy cut, like it is her own special camouflage.

When she emerges from the shop with its headless mannequins and ugly clothes, he nearly walks over to her, nearly opens his mouth, but then she is already stepping into the street. He imagines that there is a car bearing down on her, speeding, like the cars do here, despite the pedestrians, that he could grab her out of the way, that she would turn and see him. But this is stupid, he knows. Just dreaming.

He likes to think that her life doesn't exist outside this street, that as soon as she clears the traffic lights where Long becomes Kloof, she simply winks out of existence. That she is only real when she is here.

Her car is always dirty, inside and out. She leaves a lot of things on the back seat: empty cool-drink cans and magazines and Happy Meal wrappers. He wishes she had more respect, but at the same time, it gives him clues into her life, like fingerprints on a detective show. For example, the cans are always Coke Light and sometimes the rims are smeared with lipstick, although he hasn't seen her wear any, at least not during the day, when he is on duty.

He doesn't think she has a boyfriend, but Rudy, who works with him, who comes by to chat and have a smoke and to talk about God, says you never know with women.

"They're bad news," Rudy says. "You can't trust them. They tell you one thing, but meantime, they're stringing along five guys! Women are not *ordentlik* any more. They sleep around. Like these bloody foreigners bringing AIDS." But he knows she doesn't. He's sure. He can tell.

Another two weeks go by and then, on a rainy Monday morning, he gets his chance. She parks on the corner of Long and Wale and dashes from her car, down the street. She has not paid the meter. But she has not seen him either. On at least two separate occasions, he has topped her up from his own card when her time was about to run out. This time, he will not. Instead, he radios for the clamping company to come.

"Oh no," she says. "Oh no, please. I was only gone for a minute. I was just dropping something off."

"Sorry, ma'am," he says, thrilled that this is easy, that his official script, played out so many times before, does not leave him stumbling for words. "You have to pay for your parking."

"I was out of money on my card!"

"I'm sorry, ma'am. You should have refilled your card. I'm just doing my job."

"Oh please, Officer, I promise I won't do it again. It was just this once. Please."

"I'm sorry. There's nothing I can do."

"Well how much is the clamping fee?"

"It's a two hundred rand spot fine."

"Two hundred rand! Oh no, please, I'm a student. I've got a student loan to pay off. I'm working as a waitress, I probably earn less than you do! Please don't do this to me. Please."

"Okay. But then you must have coffee with me." The words are out fast, before he can think to stop them, and isn't this what she does all the time?

"What?"

"Just to talk. We can talk." His heart is like a fish in his throat. He opens his hands out to her.

"You're kidding me."

"Tomorrow. Over there."

"Pickwick's?" She turns to look.

"Yes. At five. I finish at five."

"Jesus."

"Okay?"

"Ja. Okay, okay. But unclamp me first."

He pretends to unlock the clamp, but the truth is that Albert from the clamping company has not locked it at all. For twenty bucks, the price of a joke, he says, Albert is across the road talking to a street vendor who sells Chappies and Simba chips. He straightens up with the clamp in hand and notices with alarm that her face is blotchy.

"Hey, thanks, Officer. And don't worry, I won't do it again." But she is not smiling. She has already climbed into her car and started the engine. The Toyota peels away from the curb without indicating, and she is gone. He half-raises his hand, only to realize that the clamp is still in it, clumsy, like a bear trap.

On Tuesday, his day goes badly. He has to get the street kids to wake up and move on, but they are drunk with sleep and other things besides, and they are slow. A woman at the restaurant on the corner shouts at him, "Hey, leave them alone!" and the children spit and curse, but they are only children, and there is only so much he can do.

After lunch, a man in a suit who is going to the court, he can tell, yells at him too. "Just give me a fucking break, okay? I'm going to be one fucking second. I don't see why I should have to pay three bucks if I'm only going to be here for one second!" He wants to explain that it is his salary, that it is the law, that it is his job, but he doesn't feel like this today. Instead, he lets it go, lets him go, although he knows, and he is proved right, that the man will be twelve and a half minutes, not one second at all.

He should see it as a warning of things to come, but he chooses to ignore it. He has brought a button-up shirt from home. He changes in the bathroom of another coffee shop, where they let him use the toilet during the day when he is on duty.

He thinks of buying her a rose, but decides not to; he does not want to scare her or for her to think he is coming on to her. And besides, he doesn't know if she likes them, and she has strange tastes. Like her clothes.

He sits in the window of Mr. Pickwick's, at the counter, so he can be sure not to miss her. He orders a glass of water, not sure what she will want to drink when she gets here. He studies the menu to find an appropriate choice, but also so that he will not have to meet the eyes of the other customers, who might wonder what he is doing here all alone. He looks up whenever someone comes in the door. A lot of people come through here, and the waiter with the dreadlocks and the tattoo like a black bullseye on his shoulder smiles at him once, briefly, as he steps through the entrance carrying empty beer bottles from the table outside.

At six, he orders a Black Label. He makes it last. But not long enough. He orders another beer and lets exactly one minute pass, timing it on his watch, between sips, between each time he is allowed to lift the bottle to his lips and then barely wet his mouth. He peels off the label and carefully sticks it onto his glass because it is something to do.

At eight, he pays the bill and finally gets up from the counter and walks out onto the street. It is too late to take the train, so he must catch a taxi. He walks down Long all the way to Strand, before he turns down to the station. Just in case.

Four days go by before he sees her again. She is sitting outside the restaurant on the corner. She is with two people, a man and a woman, and although his first instinct is to duck away, to leave it, he turns towards her instead. He walks up to the table and stands in front of her, waiting until she notices him. It only takes a second, but it might as well be forever, and later he will wish that she hadn't.

"Oh god! This is the blackmailing freak I was telling you about." She turns back to him. "What? Like I'd go out with a, what are you, what, a bloody traffic cop?" She leans back, her arms spread across the back of her chair and says it again for the benefit of her friends, "Like I'd go out with a fucking traffic cop." She draws on her cigarette, the flare of orange at the tip is nearing her fingers, and exhales the smoke at him. She leans forward, towards him, her lips slightly open as if for a kiss, "You're lucky I don't report you for sexual harassment, you psycho."

He could clamp every wheel of her car, wallpaper every inch of glass with pink tickets. Instead he sinks down next to it. It is parked up the street, above Loop, on Dorp, where he normally would have no reason to go. He had to search up and down the streets to find it. He sits on the pavement beside it, his feet in the road, and rests his hand on the bumper. She still has not had the paint fixed. He picks off another flake and thinks to put it in his mouth again, to peel off all the paint, to sit here and eat her bumper. Instead, he just holds it in his hand, closes his fist on it and squeezes it, tensing every muscle in his arm, in his shoulders, in what feels like his whole body, until it feels like he is shaking with the effort. But it feels like nothing, like he is holding air, and when he opens his hand, uncurling his fingers, spreading them wide, there is indeed nothing there at all.

Pop Tarts

I've thought about it myself, you know. Who hasn't? But you need a catch, a hook, a way of delaying the restless trigger finger on the remote just long enough to grab the audience before the next commercial break. Because it's not just static entertainment for zombie voyeurs anymore. You have to engage with your viewers. And Jude does that better than anyone else. But you have to be consistent. You have to stay fresh. It's not easy.

But Jude's doing okay, if the queue snaking out from the Biko Bar is anything to go by. *Special Appearance.* She seems to be doing a lot of these lately. But then she has a lot of adoring fans. Much more than when she was just Koketla.

Adil and I are fashionably late, which would not normally be a problem, except that it means we don't have Jude's security guys to protect us from the plebs, and someone in the line recognizes me. It starts a Mexican wave of excitement, and suddenly, everyone is screaming for Jude and surging forward, grabbing at my jacket as if she has left her mark on me and I can somehow convey it to them, like a saint's relic. It takes two bouncers to fight them off, while the door girl quickly ushers us in.

We push through into a crush of beautiful people and Adil whistles, or at least I assume he does by the way he's pursing his lips. It's hard to hear over the music.

"How we gonna find her?" he yells.

"Easy. Just look for the densest concentration of people." And it's true, for all that these posers are pretending to be about their own shit, they are drawn into a haphazard orbit swirling around the glittering magnet that is Jude. Whether they admit it or not. That and the cameras, of course.

Craig, the camera guy, picks us up before she does, swinging the glassy eye towards us as we shove our way towards her. This always makes me uncomfortable, no matter how many times she ropes me in as supporting cast. It's knowing that they're there, watching, all the time. Live. I don't know how she deals.

"Hey Craig," I say, raising my hand, only to have Jude's manager Dirk, who is always lurking, but always just out of frame, grab me by the elbow.

"Babes, please. How many times I gotta tell you? Don't talk to the cameraman."

"Sorry," I mumble, but Craig has already turned the camera back on Jude, radiant, like all the world loves her. I suppose much of it does. Or at least those parts of it with satellite access or broadband Internet.

She changed her name three months back, just after she

started. It was Dirk's idea. He persuaded her that she was going to lose out on the *very lucrative* overseas market with a name like Koketla. Americans wouldn't be able to wrap their tongues around it. "Think of your *audience*, babes!" And "Hey, Jude!" does make a catchy name for a TV-show, I have to admit.

"Did the mic pick that up?" Dirk mouths at the PA standing near the sound guy, still on about my talking-to-the-camera-guy-faux-pas-deluxe. But she shakes her head and shrugs. No big deal. Dirk still huffs at me: "How many times you been guesting now?" as if he intends to drop me like last season's Italian shoes. As if he could.

"Well, I am the best friend," I hiss back.

"For now, babes. For now."

I think she should have used her name, owned it, made it a running joke that no one outside of South Africa could pronounce it. Heck, most of the whiteys *inside* South Africa couldn't manage it, but hey, whatever works for you, right? Anything to appease the ratings gods.

It's a very competitive market now that everyone and their domestic worker has public access broadcast rights and a private channel to call their own. Not to mention big-time sponsor deals. Even that grunty plumber Faisal who was voted celebrity most likely to choke on his own boringness is now the official spokesman for Drano.

Koketla—sorry, *Jude*—could have gone the sex tape route, like that chick Magda: devouring men like they were going out of fashion. She worked her way through most of Cape Town's eligible straight population—and that was just in the first season. Of course, some of Magda's once-off studlings asked to have their faces or um, other body parts, blanked out, but I was surprised at how many men were totally happy to appear live on camera, naked, in front of half the world. No *skaam* whatsoever. Or maybe we're all publicity whores when it comes down to it.

Dirk has been much smarter with Jude. No cheap-and-nasty booty shows or lip-smacking tell-all *YOU* magazine exposés for Mrs. Mugudamani's little girl. Although there's been an *FHM* shoot and at least one *Marie Claire* cover. And sure, there have been lovers—she's South Africa's official Most Desirable after all—but it's all tastefully shot, soft focus, low light. Dirk has stylists and everything. So much for reality TV.

In front of us, Jude winds up her sparkling conversation with that old vulture of a gossip columnist, who must nevertheless be courted, be allowed to bask in her glow. And the PA, who has been waiting for this moment, makes urgent hand motions to us. I know my cue after three months of this. The crowd parts like the Red Sea, Jude turns her full radiance on us, frothy signature Smirnoff cocktail in hand, and purrs in real delight: "*Hola*, guys!"

And this is part of Jude's hook. Her authenticity despite all the artifice surrounding her. She is so genuinely warm and *nice* that you cannot help liking her. Even the *Mail & Guardian* arts critic is head over heels with her, despite himself, he says. And being so wonderful and cool and smart and gorgeous, Jude attracts other wonderful, cool, smart, gorgeous people who are interesting to watch.

Her friends are all artists and DJs and rappers and poets—the creative elite. And occasionally, some reasonably attractive academics as wildcards, folk who can throw in a twist of gender theory or Marshall McLuhan-isms, to even the most arb conversations, about rock versus kwaito, say. That's where I come in.

Of course, you get the occasional product placement, like the Smirnoff cocktails or Adil, for example, who is apparently a shit-hot up-and-coming filmmaker who needs the exposure. And for a *very reasonable* fee, Dirk will place him center stage.

If you ask me, Dirk should be the one with the show, with his pedicures and hair plugs and deliberately awful shirts in floral print or bold stripes, not forgetting his manipulative Sun Tzu stratagems. (That would be the ancient Chinese general guy who killed the king's favorite wife to make a point about army discipline—I might say in an aside, during my highbrow guest slot.)

Oh, Dirk comes off as sweetie-darling charming, but trust me, he's the coldest, savviest, most flamboyantly evil bastard of a marketing pimp you ever could meet. Although when I pointed this out to Jude once, in a rare off-camera moment, she just smiled in that devilishly cute way she's cultivated, tipping her jaw slightly down and raising an eyebrow, half-sly, half-sweet, like it was obvious. "Ja-*a*. Lucky for me!"

Right now, Jude kisses me warmly on the cheek and links her arm with Adil's. Hmm. Is he to be a love interest, then? And I wonder, cynically, if that costs extra. While Koketla was genuinely that nice, that friendly, that generous, I'm realizing more and more that Jude only seems that way. And some bitter part of me hopes that she'll mess up.

"Shall we check out the VIP room?" Jude beams, taking my hand in hers. "I heard a little rumor that Lucas Radebe is here!" As her adoring sidekicks for the evening, we traipse obediently after her, Dirk's security guards parting the crowd, off-camera of course, to let her through.

It turns out that the famous soccer player is not in the building. Is not even in the country right now, and with the party starting to fizzle, we are ushered off stage left as fast as possible, because Jude absolutely *cannot* be associated with a dud night out, not if her sponsors are to be kept happy.

I notice that Adil has been left behind somewhere along the way, which makes me feel a bit ashamed of my earlier suspicions, but then Dirk sidles up to me, while Jude is flirting with a star-struck fan, asking her to sign his arm: "And then I'm gonna go straight to a tattoo shop and get it inked over," he says, a little too enthusiastically, which has the security guys edging closer.

"So, we're leaving now," Dirk says.

"Ja. I know. I'm catching a ride."

Dirk smiles, all teeth. "Well, I thought that it might be past your bedtime."

"No," I say, "I'm good," steadily meeting his look. A knot of irritation creases above one eyebrow, but then he grins again and slaps me on the back. "Okay, babes, have it your way. But don't say I didn't warn you. It's going to be one *helluva* night!"

There is still a line snaking outside the bar as Jude's little entourage—cameras and minders and manager and me—spills out onto the street. Her signature limo, covered in graffiti by her brand-name boyfriends, is waiting at the curb, vapor billowing from the exhaust in the cold. "Brrr!" Jude says, with a giggle, rubbing her arms—she is seriously underdressed for the Jozi winter—and clambers into the limo.

Dirk slips in the front with the driver, which is weird, I think. He normally follows in a car with security and the rest of the crew. But I don't think anything of it until I climb in after Craig the camera guy, not even managing to close the door before the limo pulls away, tires screaming.

"Hey!" I yell, realizing only now that I am fairly drunk. But then I see that there is someone else in the back of the limo with us, drinking a bottle of extra-dry Savanna (because he also has sponsorship deals) and wearing a black ski mask.

He points two fingers at us, his thumb cocked like a gun, and jerks his hand up. "Bang!" he whispers in that signature husky Chris Isaak voice. "You've been jacked." His cameraman, wedged into the far corner to try and take in the whole scene, zooms in on our startled faces.

I am too shocked to say anything, but Jude, who is more outspoken than Koketla ever was, lets rip. "Excuse me, what the fuck do you think you're doing?"

"Hey now! Hey! Do you know who you're talking to?" he says, patting the dull black weight of a Glock 9mm resting in his lap, still talking soft and low, cowboy-style. But of course she knows who she's talking to. Half the world does.

Joshua-X. Joburg's number one white-boy hijacker, whose daring criminal exploits go out 24-7 on 136 channels around the world, not including subscriber Internet. He's even started his own station, Tsotsi-TV, with a spin-off that has him mentoring aspiring juvenile offenders. Of course, a lot of it's faked these days, but then so is Jude's show.

"You asshole! You can't hijack my ratings!" Jude is effervescent with anger. I've never seen her more beautiful.

"Just did, baby." He looks directly into her camera, mugging, and says another one of his trademark lines, "So, let's say we go for a little ride." Weirdly, this reassures me, reminds me that it's just a show and that Dirk is sitting up front. Jude realizes this at the same time and lunges forward, leaning over Joshua-X to beat on the glass separating us from the driver.

"Dirk! Dirk! Goddammit!" She is almost sobbing with rage. Squashed next to Craig, I hear Dirk's voice crackling in his headphones: "Okay, let's cut to commercial break." Craig lowers the camera and makes a slicing motion across his throat to Joshua-X's camera guy, who looks disgusted, but nevertheless switches his camera to standby. Joshua-X looks amused and raises his cider to me, tilting his head past Jude's armpit as she continues to beat on the glass. The limo pulls over.

"Okay," Craig says into his headset microphone and the dividing window glides down.

"Dirk! What the fuck!"

"Easy, babes. I thought we discussed this."

"You didn't discuss *him*!"

"But I said we needed a little *drama*. A way to spice things up a bit."

"We've been over this! Why can't you trust me? The show works! Everyone loves it! Everyone loves me!"

"Babes," Dirk says, "I didn't want to tell you. But MTV Europe is threatening to *drop* us."

"What?" Jude rocks back into her seat.

"Serious."

"I don't understand."

"Audiences are fickle, babes. Why do you think we been doing so many parties, so many openings? But this will *make* you, trust me. I spoke to Nike and they like it a lot. They're *very* interested."

"You've already discussed this? With sponsors?"

"Yeah, listen, it's perfect. The country's hottest criminal hijacks the most adored superstar. The ratings will go through the roof, I'm talking *inter*-stellar."

"Oh," Jude says. "Oh. God. Well. Couldn't you have told me, Dirk? Instead of springing this . . . this—whatever this is?"

"Aw c'mon, babes, we know your *acting* needs a little work. It had to be a surprise." Joshua-X snickers at this, and Jude scowls at him.

"So, whaddaya say?" Dirk grins and throws a little fake one-two punch. "We on, champ?"

"Okay, okay," she wafts her hand in resignation. "Whatever you say, Dirk,"

"Love ya, babes. Now, Craig, we're still on a five-minute time delay, right?" This is something all the live TV producers cottoned onto after that whole thing with Janet Jackson's boob. It's already come in handy for Jude—there was that time when a street kid threw a bunch of carrot tops at her during her Durban tour. Just blipped out of the broadcast, no worries.

Dirk checks his watch. "Right, we've got enough time, let's take it from the top, from when you climbed into the limo."

But I can't keep quiet anymore. "Don't you think this is a little disingenuous? What happened to reality, Jude? People *trust* you."

"Okay, that's it," Dirk snaps. "I've had it. You! Out!"

"Oh no, Dirk, please . . ." Jude whines. "She's my best friend. I need her here for moral support."

"For the love of . . . fine. But she's not in the scene."

"Hey, mind if I take a smoke break?" Joshua-X asks, bored by the proceedings.

"Just make it snappy," Dirk says, turning back to Jude. "Now, babes, let's talk about how we're gonna handle this . . ."

I stand on the pavement with Joshua-X, shivering in the cold night air, while Dirk goes over an ad-lib script with Jude. Joshua-X looks me up and down and purses his lips. I smile back, uneasily. "So. How's it going?" I ask.

"Yeah, all right, you know. Got all these wannabes, though. Would you believe I got cats cruising around looking for me, actually trying to get hijacked?"

"That's pretty messed up."

"Yeah, they use cell phones to track my whereabouts, there's like this whole SMS network or something."

"Hectic."

"And then I got guys muscling in on my act and I don't just mean other cats with cameras, you know what I'm saying, I mean real criminals out there, real tsotsis, you know, pretending to be me, using my schtick to rob people. Now *that's* messed up! Like, not cool at all."

Dirk emerges from the limo, a reassuring arm around Jude's shoulders. "Good to go? Everyone?" We take our positions, Joshua-X climbing back into the limo, draping himself back into the seat with a fresh beer and the Glock in his lap. His camera guy susses it out through the viewfinder and gives him a thumbs-up.

"Okay, now just like she was leaving the club," Dirk says. He pulls me aside. "But not you. You can ride up-front with me." Jude smoothes down her dress and shakes out her braids, drawing herself up and turning on her kilowatt smile, like she's totally oblivious to what's waiting for her in the limo.

I climb in next to Dirk, but just as the cameras are about to start rolling, he slides down the glass divider. "And babes? One more thing. You gotta take a bullet. Just in the leg. Don't worry, it'll be great. It'll make CNN."

"What?" Jude says, dazed, but then Craig shoves her forward and she trips into the limo.

"What!" I shout, but Dirk rolls up the divider as the limo screeches away, the momentum throwing me back. He leans over and clicks on the intercom so we can hear what's happening in the back without transmitting anything on our side. I twist round, shaking with adrenaline, frantically trying to find the button that will lower the divider, with some idea of clubbing Joshua-X on the back of the head.

"Hey there, lady, you've been jacked."

"Please! Omigod! Please! No!"

Dirk smacks the back of my hand. "Now, now, don't interfere." He pops the cigarette lighter, and smirks. "Or I'll have to burn you."

"So, let's say we go for a little ride."

"No! Wait! Please!"

"Just kidding," Dirk says, lighting up a cigarette instead.

"Don't! Joshua, I mean it. Don't you dare!"

"You ever thought about it?" Dirk says, offering me the pack with one hand. "You've got the look. And the mouth. Although you gotta stop using so many long words. You could do it, though. Have your own show, I mean."

"Noooooo!"

Inside, the gun goes off with a bang and a flash that lights up the interior and Koketla's horrified face, her eyes scrunched-up, her body desperately twisting away. And I'm in shock and this is how I will later justify my thought at the time—that this is not one of her better-looking moments.

"So, kid." Dirk leans over to turn down the volume on the screaming from the back, taking a long drag on his cigarette. "What do you say?"

THE GREEN

The Pinocchios are starting to rot. Really, this shouldn't be a surprise to anyone. They're just doing what corpses do best. Even artificially preserved and florally animated ones. Even the ones you know.

They shuffle around the corridors of our homelab in their hermetically sealed hazmat suits, using whatever's left of their fine motor functioning. Mainly they get in the way. We've learned to walk around them when they get stuck. You can get used to anything. But I avoid looking at their faces behind the glass. I don't want to recognize Rousseau.

They're supposed to be confined to one of the specimen storage units. But a month ago, a Pinocchio pulled down a cabinet of freeze-dried specimens. So now Inatec management lets them wander around. They seem happier free-range. If you can say that about a corpse jerked around by alien slime-mould like a zombie puppet.

They've become part of the scenery. Less than ghosts. They're as banal a part of life on this dog-forsaken planet as the nutritionally fortified lab-grown oats they serve up in the cafeteria three times a day.

We're supposed to keep out of their way. "No harvester should touch, obstruct or otherwise interfere with the OPPs," the notice from Inatec management read, finished off with a smiley face and posted on the bulletin board in the cafeteria. On paper, because we're not allowed personal communications technology in homelab. Too much of a security risk.

Organically Preserved Personnel. It's an experimental technique to use the indigenous flora to maintain soldiers' bodies in wartime to get them back to their loved ones intact. The irony is that we're so busy doing experiments on the corpses of our deceased crew that we don't send them back at all. And if we did, it would have to be in a flask. Because after they rot—average "life-span" is twenty-nine days—they liquefy. And the slime-mould has to be reintegrated into the colony they've been growing in lab three.

It's not really slime-mould, of course. Nothing on this damn planet is anything you'd recognize, which is exactly why Inatec has us working the jungle in armored suits along with four thousand other corporates planet-side, all scrambling to find new alien flora with commercial applications so they can patent the shit out of all of it.

"Slime-mould" is the closest equivalent the labtechs have come up with. Self-organizing cellular amoebites that ooze around on their own until one of them finds a very recently dead thing to grow on. Then it lays down signals, chemical or hormonal or some other system we don't understand yet, and all the other amoebites congeal together to form a colony that sets down deep roots like a wart into whatever's left of the nervous system of the animal . . . and then take it over.

We've had several military contractors express major interest in seeing the results. Inatec has promised us all big bonuses if we manage to land a military deal—and not just the labtechs either. After all, it's us lowly harvesters who go out there in our GMP suits to *find* the stuff.

Inatec's got mining rights to six territories in four quadrants on this world. Two subtropical, one arid/mountainous, and three tropical, which is where the big bucks are. Officially, we're working RCZ-8 Tropical 14: 27° 32' S / 49° 38' W. We call it The Green.

We were green ourselves when we arrived on-planet. The worst kind of naïve know-nothing city hicks. It was all anyone could talk about as we crammed around the windows— how fucking amazing it all looked as the dropship descended over our quadrant. We weren't used to nature. We didn't know how hungry it was.

The sky was rippled in oranges and golds from the pollen in the air, turning the spike slate pinnacles of the mountains a powder pink. The jungle was a million shades of green. Greens like you couldn't imagine. Greens to make you mad. Or kill you dead.

Homelab squats in the middle of all that green like a fat concrete spider with too many legs radiating outwards. Uglier even than the Caxton Projects apartment blocks back home. Most of us are from what you'd call underprivileged backgrounds. The Caxton stats when I left were 89% adult unemployment, 73% adult illiteracy, 65% chance of dying before the age of forty due to communicable disease or an act of violence. Who wouldn't want a ticket out of there? Even if it was one-way.

Besides, our work is a privilege. We're getting to work at the forefront of xenoflora biotech. At least that's what it says on the "Welcome to Inatec" pack all employees are handed when they've dotted the i's and crossed the t's on the contract. Or maybe just made an X where you're supposed to sign. You don't need to be literate to pick flowers. Even in a GMP.

Of course, by forefront, they mean front lines. And by harvesting they mean strip-mining. Except everything we strip away grows back, faster than we can keep up. Whole new species we've never seen before spring up overnight. Whole new ways to die.

You got to suffer for progress, baby, Rousseau would have said (if he was still alive). And boy, do we suffer out there.

The first thing they do when you land is strip you, shave you, put you through the ultraviolet sterilizer, and then surgically remove your finger- and toenails. It's a biologically sensitive operation. You can't be bringing in contaminants from other worlds. And there was that microscopic snail parasite incident that killed off two full crews before the labtechs figured it out. That's why we don't have those ultra-sensitive contact pads on our gloves anymore, even though it makes harvesting harder. Because the snail would burrow right through them and get under the cuticle, working its way through your body to lay its eggs in your lungs. When the larvae hatch, they eat their way out, which doesn't kill you, it just gives you a nasty case of terminal snail-induced emphysema. It took the infected weeks to die, hacking up bloody chunks of their lungs writhing with larvae.

Diamond miners used to stick gems up their arses to get them past security. With flora, you can get enough genetic material to sell to a rival with a fingernail scraping. "Do we have any proof there was ever a snail infestation?" Ro would ask over breakfast. "Apart from the company newsletter?" he'd add, before practical, feisty, *educated* Lurie could get a word in and contradict him. He was big into his conspiracy theories and our medtech, Shapshak, only encouraged him. They'd huddle deep into the night, getting all serious over gin made from nutri-oats that Hoffmann used to distill in secret in his room. It seemed to make Shapshak more gloomy than ever, but Ro bounced back from it invigorated and extra-jokey.

Ro was the only one who could get away with calling me Coco, and only because we were sleeping together. Dumb-fuck name, I know. Coco Yengko. Mom wanted me to be a model. Or a ballerina. Or a movie star. All those careers that get you out of the ghettosprawl. Shouldn't have had an ugly kid, then, Ma. Shouldn't have been poor. Shouldn't have let the Inatec recruiter into our apartment. And hey, while we're at it, Ro shouldn't have died.

Fucking Green.

Green is the wrong word for it. You'd only make that mistake from the outside. When you're in the thick of it, it's black. The tangle of the canopy blocks out the sunlight. It's the murky gloom after twilight, before real dark sets in. Visibility is five meters, fifteen with headlights, although the light attracts moths, which get into the vents. Pollen spores swirl around you, big as your head. Sulfur candy floss. And everything is moist and sticky and *fecund*. Like the whole jungle is rutting around us.

The humidity smacks you, even through the suit, thick as +8 gravity, so that you're slick as a greased ratpig with sweat the moment you step out. It pools in your jockstrap, chafes when you walk, until it forms blisters big as testicles. (A new experience for the girls on the crew.) Although walking's not what we do. More like wading against a sucking tide of heat and flora.

The rotting mulch suffocates our big, clanking mechanical footsteps. Some of the harvesters play music on their private channels. Ro used to play opera, loud, letting it spill into The Green, until it started attracting insects the size of my head. I put a stop to it after that. I prefer to listen to the servo motors grinding in protest. I have this fantasy that I'll be able to hear it when my suit gets compromised. The *shhht* of air that lets through a flood of spores like fibrous threads that burrow into metal and flesh. The faint suck of algae congealing on the plastic surfaces, seeping into the seams of the electronics, corroding the boards so the nanoconnections can't fire. The hum of plankton slipping between the joints of my GMP between the spine and pelvic plates, to bite and sting.

The base model GMPs aren't built for these conditions. The heat is a problem. The servo motors get clogged. The armor corrodes. The nanotronics can't sustain. Every joint is a weak point. The damn flora develops immunity to every vegicide we try. Assuming they're actually *using* vegicides, Ro would point out. Why risk the harvest when harvesters are replaceable?

Management has determined that the optimum number for a harvesting team is five. I'm the team leader. Look, Ma, leadership material. Our medtech is Shapshak, who sometimes slips me amphetamines, which he gets under the counter from the labtechs along with other pharmaceuticals he doesn't share. (It's not like management don't know. They're happy if we're productive and sometimes you need a little extra something to get through out there.) Lurie is our ambot; a high school education and eight weeks of training in amateur botany specimen collection puts her a full pay scale above the rest of us plebs, plus she gets the most sophisticated suit—a TCD with neuro-feedback tentacle fingers built into the hands for snagging delicate samples that aren't susceptible to snail invasion. Rousseau and Waverley were our clearers— manual labor, their GMPs suitably equipped with bayonet progsaws that'll cut through rock, thermo-machetes for underbrush, and extra armor plating for bludgeoning your way through the jungle with brute force when everything else failed.

In retrospect, we could have done with less brute force. Could have done with me spotting the damn stingstrings before we blundered into the middle of a migration. Could have done with being less wired on the under-the-counter stuff. One minute Waverley and Ro are plowing through dense foliage ahead, the next, there are a thousand mucusy tendrils unfurling from the canopy above us.

This wouldn't have been a problem usually. Sure, the venom might corrode your paintwork, leave some ugly pockmarks that'll get the maintenance guys all worked up, but they're not hectic enough to compromise a GMP.

Unless, say, someone panics and trips and topples forward, accidentally ripping a hole in Rousseau's suit with the razor edge of a machete, half-severing his arm. Waverley swore blind it wasn't his fault. He tripped. But GMPs have balance/pace adjustors built-in. You have to be pretty damn incompetent to fall over in one. If Ro wasn't a roaming brain-dead corpse-puppet right now, he might be suspicious, might think it was a conspiracy to recruit more guinea pigs for the OPP program. We know better. We know Waverley's just a fucking moron.

There was a lot of screaming. Mainly from Ro, until Shapshak shot him up with morphine, but also Lurie threatening to kill Waverley for being so damn stupid. It took us ninety minutes to get back to homelab, me and Shapshak dragging Ro on the portable stretcher from his field kit, which is only really useful for transporting people—not armored suits—but it was too dangerous to take him out. Waverley broke through the undergrowth ahead of us—the only place where we would trust him, leaving traces of Ro's blood painted across broken branches.

When we got to homelab, Lurie still had to file the specimens and we all had to go through decontam, no matter how much I swore at security over the intercom: *Just let us back in right fucking now.*

We had to sit in the cafeteria, the only communal space, listening to Rousseau die, pretending not to. It should have been easy. The loud drone of the air conditioner and the filters and the sterilizer systems all fighting The Green is the first thing you acclimatize to here. But Ro's voice somehow broke through, a shrill shriek between clenched teeth. We hadn't known anyone who'd ever died from the stingstrings. The labtechs must have been thrilled.

Shapshak spooned oats into his face, drifting away from it all on some drug he wasn't sharing. Lurie couldn't touch her food. She put on her old-school security-approved headphones, bopped her head fiercely to the music. Made like she wasn't crying. I restrained myself from hitting Waverley, who kept whining, "It wasn't my fault, okay?" I took deep breaths against the urge to bash his big bald head on the steel table until his brains oozed out. If Ro was here and not lying twisting around on a gurney while the meds prepared the killing dose of morphephedrine, he would have cracked the tension with a joke. About crappy last meals maybe.

The other crews were making bets on what would kill him. Marking up the odds on the back of a cigarette packet. Black humor and wise-cracking is just how you deal. We'd have been doing the same if it wasn't one of ours. Yellow Choke 3:1. Threadworms 12:7. The Tars 15:4. New & Horrible: 1:2.

Ro's voice changed in pitch, from scream-your-throat-raw to a low groaning—the kind that comes from your intestines plasticinating. The spores must have got in to the rip in his gut through the tear in his armor.

OhgodohgodohgodeuggghgodOHpleasefuckgodOH

Across from us, Hoffmann from F-Crew leapt to his feet, whooping in delight and making gimme gestures. "Tars! I fucking knew it! Oh yeah! Hand over the cashmoney, baby!"

Ro's screaming tapered off. Which meant either he was

dead or just sub-auditory under the concert of laboring machinery. Waverley tried to say something encouraging, "At least we know it's the fast kind of fatal," and I punched him in the face, knocking the porridge out of his mouth in a grey splatter tinged with blood—along with two teeth.

I got a warning, but no demerit, "under the circumstances," human resources said. They declined my request to have Waverley reassigned to another unit.

"It's for the best," they said. Which was the same line my mom spun me when she took me to the sterilization clinic in Caxton, mainly for the incentive kickback the government provided, but also to make sure I didn't end up like her, pregnant and homeless at fourteen, working double shifts at the seam factory—which is what she did after I was born, to keep the pair of us alive. That only makes me feel more guilty—all the sacrifices she made so I could get out of Caxton. And here I am, letting my sometime-lover die on my watch. Sorry, Ma, I think. But you don't know what it's like out here.

Within forty-eight hours, Ro's replacement arrived. Joseph Mukuku. Another ghettosprawl kid sprayed, shaved, irradiated, de-nailed and ready to go. We had three whole days to mourn while he ran through the simconditioning and then we were back out there in the thick of it, harvesting. I found a request for stingstrings in my order log. The results of Ro's venom burns were, according to the labtechs, "fascinating." The note attached to the order read: "Lash-wounds were cauterized. Unclear whether this is common to stingstrings or whether it was reacting with other flora or spores. Living specimens (ideal) required for further study. Deceased specimens okay."

We couldn't get them. That's what I reported anyway. Threatened to peel the skin off Mukuku if he said different. The kid learned quick, didn't cause any shit and we made Waverley walk five meters up front where he'd only take out flora if he tripped again. Shapshak offered me chemical assistance from his stash of pharmaceuticals, but by then I was already contemplating it and I knew drugs would only get in the way. I didn't want to get better. I wanted out.

It was the encounter with Rousseau that cemented it.

I'd managed to avoid him for twelve whole days after he died. Every time I spotted a Pinocchio shuffling down the corridor or standing spookily motionless facing a wall, I did a 180 in the other direction. Didn't make a big deal about it, just managed to spend more time in the gym or doing routine maintenance on my GMP. Anything to keep busy. It's the thinking about it that kills me. I try to leave no space for thinking.

I was doing leg-presses when he found me. It was the automatic door that tipped me off. It kept opening and closing, opening and closing, like someone didn't have enough brains to get out of the way of the sensors. I knew it was him even before I saw the limp, sagging sleeve where his left arm should have been.

"What do you want?" I said, standing up and moving over to rest my hand casually on the 10kg barbells. Ready to club him to death. Re-death. Whatever. Not expecting an answer.

Through the faceplate, I could see a caul of teeming, squirming green over his face. You could still make out his features, still tell it was Ro under there. I thought about his cells starting to break down under his new slime-mould skin, his organs collapsing, nerves firing sluggishly through sagging connections in dead tissue.

He opened his mouth, his tongue flopping uselessly inside. He worked his jaw mechanically. Individual amoebites, attracted by the motion, started sliding into the cavity, triggering others, oozing past his lips—coating his teeth, his tongue, with the seething furry growth. Inside the suit, Ro tipped his head back, his mouth open in something like a scream as more and more amoebites flooded in to colonize his mouth, soft furry spores spilling down his chin. "Misfiring neurons," human resources had assured us when they first let the Pinocchios out.

"Nothing to worry about," they said. Neither, it turns out, is the GMP progsaw I put to my forehead, positioning it right against my temple for maximum damage before I flick the on switch.

I have a dream about my mom. I am scampering over the factory floor, back when she still had the job, dodging the electric looms to collect scraps of fabric that she will sew into dishcloths and dolls and maybe a dress, to sell to the neighbors, illegally. We are not allowed to remove company property. They incinerate leftovers every evening, specifically to prevent this. *Be careful*, she whispers, her breath hot against my cheek. But I'm not careful enough. As I duck under the grinding, whirling loom, the teeth catch my ear and shear down my face. My skin tears all the way down to my belly button and unfurls, flopping about, obscenely, like wings, before the flaps stiffen and wrap around me like a cocoon. In the dream, it feels like I am falling into myself. It feels safe.

I wake up in a hospital bed, with my right arm cuffed to the rail. There is a woman sitting on the edge of the bed wearing a pinstripe skirt and matching blazer. She is blandly pretty with blonde-streaked hair, wide blue eyes, and big, friendly teeth in a big, friendly mouth. A mom in a vitamin-enriched living commercial. Not someone I've seen in homelab before. Too neatly groomed. I sit up and automatically reach up to touch my head, to the place where the progsaw had started ripping into my temple, only to find layers of bandage mummifying my skull.

"We do pay attention, Coco," the woman says, and then adds, more softly, "I'm very sorry about what happened to Malan."

"Who?" I say. My cheek is burning. I try to rub the pain away and find a row of fibrous stitches running from my temple down to my jaw.

"Malan Rousseau? Your coworker? It's quaint how you call each other by surnames. This isn't the army you know. You're not at war."

"Tell that to The Green," I mutter. I am angry to be alive.

"Yes, well. We installed new safety measures into the GMPs after the accident. Chemical agents that would clog up the blades of your weaponry with fibrous threads if it came into contact with human pheromones. It's based on threadworms. One of the technologies you've helped make possible, Coco. Saved your life."

"Didn't want to be saved." My throat feels raw like it's been sandblasted from the inside.

"Pity about your face," she says, not feeling any pity at all.

"Never going to be a model now." I try to laugh. It comes out as a brittle bark.

"Unless it's for a specialist scar porn, no, probably not. Do you want some water? It's the painkillers making you so thirsty. Even with our new safety measures, you still managed to do quite a bit of ruin to yourself. No brain damage though."

"Damn," I deadpan, but the water is cold and sweet down my throat.

"My name is Catherine, I'm from head office. They sent me here especially to see you and do you know why? It's because you've made us reevaluate some things, Coco, how we work around here." Every time she says my name, it feels like someone punching me in the chest. A reminder of Ro.

"Don't call me that. It's Yengko. Please."

"As you prefer," her mouth twists impatiently, "Ms. Yengko. You'll be pleased to know, I think, that after your *incident*, Inatec has elected to relocate the OPPs—what do you call them?"

"Zombie puppets." But I'm thinking, Living prisons cells.

She looks down to her hands folded in her lap, at her perfect manicure, and smiles a little tolerant smile. But what I'm thinking is, That bitch still has her fingernails, which also means she has no intention of sticking around. "Pinocchios, right? Isn't that what you call them? That's cute. But we've come to realize, well, you made us realize that having them in homelab puts undue stress on our employees. I guess we were so busy focusing on this huge medical breakthrough—"

"Profit, you mean."

She ignores me. "That we didn't think about how it was affecting you guys on a personal level. So, I'm sorry. *Inatec* is sorry. We've moved the OPPs to another facility. We've already paid stress compensation into everyone's accounts and we're implementing mandatory counseling sessions."

"He was trying to talk."

"No. He's dead, Coc—Ms. Yengko," she corrects herself. "It must have been very upsetting, but he can't talk. The OPP symbiote sometimes hooks into the wrong nerves. We're still learning, still figuring each other out."

"How buddy-buddy of you. Didn't realize this was a partnership."

"We're a bio-sensitive operation. It's about finding a balance with nature, no matter how foreign it is."

"So what happens now?"

"We'd like you to stay on, if you're willing. Under the circumstances, Inatec is willing to retrench you with two weeks' payout for every year you've worked, plus stress bonus, plus full pension. Which is, I'm sure you'll appreciate, very generous considering your attempt to damage Inatec property and injure personnel, which would normally be grounds for instant dismissal. Your non-disclosure still applies either way, of course."

"Wait. You're blaming me for Ro's death?"

"By injuring personnel, we mean your attempted suicide. You're a valuable asset to the company. Which is why I'd encourage you to hear my alternate proposition."

"Does it involve letting me fucking die like I wanted?"

"As I said, you're a valuable asset. How long have you been here? Two years?"

"Twenty months."

"That's a lot of experience. We've invested in you, Ms. Yengko. We want to see you achieve your potential. I want you to walk away from this . . . challenge in your life, stronger, more capable. You've got a second chance. Do you know how rare that is? It's a unique personal growth opportunity."

"Double pay."

"One and half times."

"Plus my pension payout. You wire it to my mom in the meantime."

"You don't want to hear about the alternative?"

"More of the same, isn't it?"

"It's better. We're running a pilot program. New suits. We want you to head it up. We've learned from our mistakes. We're ready to move on. It's a new day around here. What do you say?"

She thinks I don't know. She thinks I'm an idiot.

Homelab has been renovated in the time I've been out. A week and a half, according to Shapshak, who is strangely reproachful. He follows me around, as if trying to make sure I don't try to off myself again. He can't look at my face—at the puckered scar that runs from my ear to the corner of my mouth, twisting my upper lip into a permanent sneer. He's more stoned than ever—and so are most of the other crews. Whatever else Catherine's proposed "new day" involves, obviously restricting access to recreational pharmaceuticals isn't part of it. Or maybe it's the mandatory counseling sessions, which involve a lot of antidepressants that Mukuku says leave him feeling blank and hollow. I wouldn't know. I felt that way already.

The Pinocchios are, true to Catherine's word, gone. Along with some of the staff. Lurie has been shipped out, together with Hoffmann, Ujlaki and Murad, all the A-level am-bots, half the other team leaders, and 60 percent of the labtechs. Leaving a shoddy bunch of misfits, unsuitable for anything except manual labor. Or guinea pigging.

Labs one to three have been cleared to accommodate the new suits, ornate husks floating in nutrient soup in big glass tanks. Like soft-shelled crabs without the crab. The plating is striated with a thick fibrous grain that resembles muscle. The info brochure posted on the bulletin board promises "biological solutions for biological challenges." There is grumbling about what that means. But underneath all that is the buzz of excitement.

The operations brochure talks about how the suit will harden on binding, how the shell will protect us from anything a hostile environment can throw at us and process the air through the filtration system to be perfectly breathable without the risk and inconvenience of carrying compressed gas tanks around. We'll be lighter, more flexible, more efficient—and it's totally self-sufficient, provided we take up the new nutritionally fortified diet. "No more fucking oats!"

Mukuku rejoices. He's not Ro, but he's not an asshole and that's about all we can ask around here.

Lab four is still cranking. The reduced complement of labtechs are busier than ever, scurrying about like bugs. They wear hazmat suits these days. They've always been offish, always above us, but now they don't talk to us at all.

Inatec management send in a state-of-the-art camera swarm to record the new suit trials—for a morale video, Catherine explains. Exactly the kind of camera swarm they supposedly can't afford to send out into The Green to scout ahead of us to avoid some of the dangers. "You won't have to worry about that anymore," she says. I believe her.

Harvest operations are called off while they do the final preparations, leaving us with too much leisure time, too much time to think. Or maybe it's just me. But it allows me to make my decision. *Not* to blow it wide open. (As if they wouldn't just hold us down and do it to us anyway.) Because I'm thinking that a cell doesn't have to be a bad thing. It doesn't have to be a prison. It could be more like a monk's cell, a haven from the world, somewhere you can lock yourself away from everything and never have to think again.

On Tuesday, we're summoned to lab three. "You ready?" Catherine says.

"Is my pension paid out?" I snipe. There is nervous laughter.

"Why can't we use our old suits?" Waverley whines. "Why we gotta change a good thing?"

"Shut up, Waverley," Shapshak snaps, but only half-heartedly. And then because everyone is jittery—even us uneducated slum hicks can have suspicions—I volunteer.

I step forward and shrug out of my greys, letting them drop to the floor. Two of the labtechs haul a suit out of the tank and sort of hunker forward with it, folding it around me like origami. It is clammy and brittle at the same time. As they fold one piece over another, it binds together and darkens to an opaque green. The color of slime-mould.

The labtechs assist others into their suits, carefully wrapping everyone up, like a present, leaving only the hoods and a dangling connector like a scorpion tail. The tip has a pad of microneedles that will fasten on to my nervous system. Nothing unusual here. The GMPs use the same technology to monitor vital signs. Nothing unusual at all.

"Don't worry, it won't hurt. It injects anaesthetic at the same time," Catherine says. "Like a mosquito."

"Not the ones on this planet, lady," Waverley snickers, looking around for approval, as they start folding him into his suit.

Back in Caxton, I tried converting to the Neo-Adventists for a time. They promised me the pure white warmth of God's love that would transform me utterly. But I still felt the same after my baptism—still dirty, still broken, still poor.

"Can we hurry this along?" I ask, impatient.

"Of course," Catherine says. And maybe that's a glimmer of respect in her blue eyes, or maybe it's just the reflection of the neon lighting, but I feel like we understand each other in these last moments.

The labtech slips the hood over my face. She presses the bioconnector up against the hollow at the base of my skull, and clicks the switch that makes the needles leap forward.

Suddenly the armor clamps down on me like a muscle. I fight down a jolt of claustrophobia so strong it raises the taste of bile in my mouth. I have to catch myself from falling to my knees and retching.

"You okay, Yengko?" Shapshak says, his voice suddenly sharp through the glaze of drugs he's on. He must really care, I think. But I am beyond caring. Beyond anything.

I wondered what it would feel like. The soft furriness of the amoebites flooding through the bioconnector, the prickle as they flower through my skin. What's better than a dead zombie? A live one. And maybe God's touch is cool and green, not pure white at all.

"Yes," I say and close my eyes against the light, against the sight of the others being parceled up in the suits, at Waverley starting to scream, tugging at the hood as he realizes what's going on, what's in there with him. "I'm fine." And maybe for the first time, I actually am.

LITMASH

As part of a Twitter fiction festival, I asked followers to propose genre mash-ups and wrote tweet-sized stories, live.

#Sex&TheDystopianCity I
Picked up the most adorable bespoke pink tutu. Only had to gun down eight people. #win #summersales.

#Sex&TheDystopianCity II
Miranda was the first to go. All the lawyers up against the wall. Carrie was executed for looting. Samantha ran a brothel for a while. But Supreme General Commander Charlotte came out best of all. She always was the most ruthless.

#KamaSartre
Hell is sex with other people.

#MuppetPrisonDrama
They shaved Animal to reveal the map, Gonzo picked the lock. But Warden Piggy was waiting for them. "Going somewhere, Frog?"

#PotterxPalahniuk
I am Benjamin Bunny's vented spleen. His gutted innards. His roast haunch on a plate.

#MyLittlePonyNoir
Ain't no rainbows here, Dash said. Not since Pinkie Pie turned up hooves up in an alley.

#ColdWarFairyTale I
The sad truth was that magic gets mired in bureaucratic red tape, same as everything.

#ColdWarFairyTale II
He opened up the warhead and found her heart. All glass and nuclear love.

EASY TOUCH

Dearly beloved
   is a good way to start.
   So is:
Hello my friend
   Or:
Greetings to you and your family
   Or even an exotic:
Salut

In the end, it doesn't matter how you address them. You don't even need a name. They will give you everything. Roll over to show you their bellies like dogs, their tails wagging. Money talks, you see. It roars like a stadium of soccer fans, drowning out that little voice of doubt.

Laryea has never had any doubt: people are greedy and stupid; they get what's coming to them. People like Hilda

Varone, whose name is printed in big block capitals on his cardboard sign, so she can't miss seeing him in the clog of people waiting in the arrivals hall of OR Tambo International. Not that she could miss him anyway. He is a big man—more fat than muscle these days, if he is honest, but still good-looking, in a button-up shirt and chinos and a flat-top you could stand a glass on. He likes to look professional for his clients.

He knows from experience that Hilda will be feeling anxious, that all those hours and hours on a plane from Mexico City via New York will have given her too much time to think. And it's her first time without her husband, Oscar. In these kinds of circumstances, it's important to stick to routine. People like routine. It makes the world seem safe and predictable.

The glass doors from baggage claim glide open and spit out a flurry of people with suitcases and backpacks and wheelie carry-ons. He spots Hilda right away. She looks rumpled and tired, dragging her big grey suitcase with the dodgy wheel. He has chosen a spot right in front of the doors, but her eyes skid over him and his neatly lettered sign, searching the crowd as if she is expecting someone else.

He's always thought of her as chubby, but she's lost weight since he last saw her. Now, she's just a short compact package of a woman with over-plucked brows and a frizz of dark hair that doesn't like being told what to do. Much like Hilda herself.

Laryea has always found Oscar easier to deal with. For an ambulance driver, Oscar is a meek man, as if all the shout has been drained out of him by the yowl of the sirens as he navigates the sprawl of Mexico City, his arthritic hands clamped on the wheel, wishing for power steering. He should retire, but how can he, considering the circumstances?

The couple has been to Johannesburg three times since they first made contact eighteen months ago. But Oscar opted to stay home in sunny Me-hi-co this time round. It gets expensive, all these flights, all these meetings, all the administration. Supposedly, this is the last trip. A mere formality and it will all be done.

Laryea knows better.

"Ms. Varone!" he calls out to Hilda. "Over here."

"Laryea," she says, noticing him at last, but sounding less than thrilled. Jet lag is a bitch. He moves to welcome her with a kiss on both cheeks.

"You still dragging this old thing around?" he says, taking the suitcase from her. "Don't worry, soon you'll be able to afford Louis Vuitton. A matching set for you and Oscar!"

"I think we have *más importante* things to spend the money on, no?" she says, sharply.

"Of course. Forgive me, *señora*. How *is* Gael?"

"The same," she says, bleakly.

Life can change in an instant. One moment your six-year-old son is stepping out of a bodega, the next he is on his back under a car, the axle pressing down on his stomach, crushing his spine, his spleen, his pelvis, so the doctors say he will probably never walk again. A burst tire. A freak accident.

It's not that Laryrea doesn't feel sorry for Hilda and Oscar. But the world is full of tragedy.

PLEASE HELP TSUNAMI VICTIMS!

THE RED CROSS INTERNATIONAL AMSTERDAM, THE NETHERLANDS ZONE (B) HEREBY APPEALLING TO YOU FRIENDS,PUBLIC,FAMILIES AND COMPANIES, TO HELP US WITH ONLINE FUND RAISING TO ENABLE US TREAT OVER 1.5 MILLION CHILDREN AFFECTED WITH QUAKE/TSUNAMI DESASTER ACROSS ASIA.VISIT WWW.CNN.COM/ TSUNAMI TO SEE WHY YOUR HELP/ MONEY IS HIGHLY NEEDED.

HELP THE NEEDY,POOR AND SICK, NO AMOUNT IS SMALL FOR GOD LOVES A CHEERFULL GIVER.

Hilda is quiet on the drive to the restaurant. But the question lurks in the tension of her shoulders, the clench of her jaw. *When?*

"You have to be patient," Laryea soothes her. "These things take time."

"These things take time. These things take time," she parrots angrily. "This is what you always say, Laryea."

He imagines her telling off her water-cooler clients in the same tone, more fluently perhaps in her native Spanish, but no less bolshy. He imagines entire office complexes living in fear of Hilda Varone, employees willing to risk drinking Mexico City tap water rather than face her wrath.

"This is the way third-world governments work," he says,

"This is what makes it all possible. You know that. Your mother—"

"Leave my *mamá* alone." She glares out at the hawkers selling superglue at the traffic lights.

"You know what I'm saying, Hilda, if Pinochet hadn't—"

"I said to leave it. It was different in Chile. There was none of this . . . *lawyers*." She spits the word out.

"Of course not. She didn't have time to set anything up when she fled the country."

"She leaves everything. Just pack up and go."

"Imagine if she had managed to hide her money away before she left; how hard it would be to get it out of the country? This is par for the course. You shouldn't expect it to be easy. Have patience, *señora*. This is the last time, I promise."

He suspects it will have to be. They have taken her for $47,453 so far and he can't see how they will squeeze any more juice from her.

The secret is in not using round numbers. Round numbers are too much like a bribe, a ransom. All those gaping zeros like holes in a story. To short-circuit suspicion, you need the kind of numbers beloved by bureaucrats and auditors. Numbers that suggest fourteen per cent tax or built-in administration charges or adjustments for the exchange rate. Official numbers. Numbers that can keep clicking up, because there is always another cost, another agency fee, another unforeseen surcharge.

"I can't do this again," she says, staring out the window as if the sweep of trees lining Jan Smuts Avenue requires her fullest concentration. *"No puedo más."* Laryea pretends not to notice her dabbing angrily at her eyes.

"The last time. I promise. Mr. Shaik is waiting for us at the restaurant. In half an hour, less, the last of the paperwork will be signed and sealed. If you want, we don't even have to check into the hotel. You can get straight back on the plane and go home to Oscar and Gael. *Sí?*"

"Yes, okay," she sniffs. "But this Mr. Shaik is corrupt. I read the newspapers."

"Do you know a lawyer who isn't? And his corruption, *señora*, is what we are counting on."

It is a fact that names in the news have more credibility.

I know that this mail might come to you as a surprise as we have not met before, My name is Mrs. Grace Mugabe, the wife of Mr. Robert Mugabe the president of Zimbabwe. Our country is currently facing international saction all over the world and my effort to so speak peace into my husband prove abortive because he already have a wrong notion towards the western nations.

As the first lady of our country i have been able to use my position to raise some money from contracts which i deposited with a European diplomatic security company the sum of US$35M(Thirty Five Million US Dollars) knowing fully that our government will soon be brought down by international communities because of the manner at which things are degenerating in Zimbabwe.

I contacting you because I want you to go to the security company and claim the money on my behalf. I ask you to also pray for me to survive the

internal threat i am experincing from my husband
President Robert Mugabe because as i am sending
you this urgent proposal tears flow from my eyes as
i am living with a human monster.

Laryea is *not* a monster. He is a student of human behavior. He admires Oscar and Hilda's fortitude. They are not without resources. They borrowed the money he has extracted from family and friends. They could have used it to fly Gael to a private hospital in the United States. It would have paid for the specialist spinal surgery, at least. Instead, they've given it to Laryea's syndicate. Is it the syndicate's fault that the pair of them are so naïve and greedy as to believe a fairy tale about $12.5 million?

It helps that the fairy tales are set in countries too far away to be able to check up on the details. It helps that Laryea's format, his bait, is grammatical with none of the gross spelling mistakes or lazy typos endemic to the genre.

First my Father was a king in our village before
he died and left behind some Gold as the King
of our town that God bless with Gold, he was
enntitle to some quantity every end of the Month
this was the way he acquired the quantities of
Gold the family is having today. the only thing
i want from you is either you buy the Gold from
me or you help me for shipment of the gold to your
destination and sell it on my behalf and get your
own percentage.

No, Laryea's English is excellent. He has a talent for languages, a way with words. It's why he was bumped up from catcher to guyman. Now, instead of fielding emails, he does fieldwork. He deals with actual clients, in person, face-to-face. This is not why his mother worked for forty years as a post-office administrator to pay for his university education. Still, he has been able to put his political science degree to some practical use. Current affairs make for topical lures. So do Hollywood movies.

> *My name is Captain Andrew McAllister; I am an American Soldier and serving in the US Military in the 3rd Armored Cavalry Regiments, Patrols Tail Afar, in Iraq. I am desperately in need of assistance and I have summoned up courage to contact you. I am presently in Iraq and I found your contact particulars in an address journal. I am seeking your assistance to evacuate the sum of $1,570,000 (One million Five Hundred and Seventy Thousand US dollars) to the States or any safe country of your choice, as far as I can be assured that it will be safe in your care until I complete my service here. This is no stolen money and there are no dangers involved.*

Better that he had become a journalist. Like the photographer he had assisted in Ghana in 2005. Since then, he has seen his name around a lot, that photographer. He keeps an eye out for it, he sees it in the newspapers, sometimes on the cover of fancy art magazines. While he was waiting for a client in the lobby of the Sandton Sun once, Laryea picked up a flyer for the photographer's new exhibition. His photographs were selling for 20,000 rand each. Easy money. Fame. And for what? Pointing and clicking? Now *that's* a scam.

The Zoo Lake Restaurant is a tourist destination, which means, Laryea supposes, that tourists don't have to *destine* any further north. It's just enough, a taste of the real Africa, diluted, exaggerated. A glamorous movie-land of ornate masks and hanging lamps of dyed leather and food tamed for feeble Western palates.

"Did I ever tell you about the bees?" he asks as he pulls out Hilda's chair for her. It's a signature story in his repertoire. He uses patter to set clients at ease, to make them feel like they're bonding. You aren't supposed to use real stories, in case you reveal yourself in the details. But Laryea would take a bet, any amount you like, that the famous photographer doesn't remember his name, let alone know how to find him.

"The bees? No, I do not think so. Is Mr. Shaik coming *pronto*?" Hilda looks anxiously around the restaurant.

"He'll be here any minute, you just relax. Have a glass of wine. The food here is excellent. Really authentic."

"You know I have trusted you all this while, Laryea."

"I know, Hilda."

He has arranged a happy ending for her. Or the semblance of one. In return for the last outstanding $6,572, which is the absolute limit of her gullibility he reckons, she will receive 108 pages of paperwork from Mr. Shaik, filed in triplicate and stamped by the Reserve Bank as evidence of the transfer to her account in Mexico City.

She will have about a week to enjoy the idea of her wealth before she realizes that it is all fake, that the money has not been deposited, that it never will be. By that time she will be 10,000 kilometers away, and Laryea will have switched to a new cellphone number, a new email address. It could be worse. Ask the Swiss guy who was kidnapped last year. Or the German who was murdered . . .

Laryea has always thought of the syndicate like a swarm on the move. If the queen dies, you make a new queen, if a worker bee dies, you replace it with another drone. Their business is decentralized. Untouchable. The hive will always survive. And honey is one of the best ways to catch mugus, of course.

> *Hi my friend,*
> *it's nice and lovely for me to mail you and, I thank God that I find you, Am kristinacain female, 24 years of age and i am from USA . . . I will like us to be friends because friendship is like a clothes, without clothes one is naked and without friends one is lonely and to avoid loneliness we all need friends, i guess i am right?*
> *Kristina*

Romance scams always seemed too cruel to Laryea—and too much trouble. Like catching a shark: easy to hook, but a struggle to reel in. Besides, there is too much typing involved with all the instant messages and emails that stand in for passion these days.

Laryea takes a sip of wine—Warwick Trilogy 2006, because he likes to indulge his clients in these final meetings. He likes to think of it as an act of grace, although he notes with irritation that Hilda has barely touched hers. She is fiddling with her fork, tapping it nervously on the edge of the table. *Rat-tat-tat. Rat-tat-tat.* The restaurant is filling up, conversation and the clatter of cutlery relegating the Senegalese gospel album to ambient noise.

"Now, this story," he says, trying to recapture her attention. "It's more about honey collectors than bees, really. I was working with a photographer, a famous one, you might have heard of him—"

"Was this before or after you work in Burger King?"

He had forgotten he'd told her about that. Why had he told her? About exactly where a political science degree will get a young man with big dreams and no work permit; not to the *Economist*, but the Burger King at Paddington Station, lost like the storybook bear with his red Wellington boots.

"Before," he says, trying to recover. "The photographer, he did these hyena photographs. You might have seen them?"

"No." She fishes a soft pack of smokes out the bowels of her bag and taps out a cigarette. Laryea pinches it from her lips before she can light it.

"We're in the non-smoking section," he says, laying the cigarette on the table perfectly parallel to the woven placemat. Her mouth twists into a stony pout in its absence.

"Anyway, I was translating for him." This part is a lie. He was carrying the photographer's equipment, all the lights and battery packs and loops of cable. It was only when the real translator, an environmental journalist for the UN, fell ill with gastroenteritis that Laryea had stepped in to untangle the local dialect.

"It was about an hour and a half from Techiman, where

the jungle runs right up to the highway, like it's trying to swallow the road. The whole town was three houses. And also *mashambas*, you know, like mud huts? Maybe forty or fifty people living there, women pounding cassava or sitting with blankets spread out on the ground selling soft drinks, fruit, loose cigarettes, warm beer and gin. They call it gin, but it's actually liquor they make themselves in Coca-Cola bottles."

"We have towns like this in Mexico."

"Maybe not quite like this, but close enough, I'm sure. So the women sell basic stuff and pound cassava and the men collect honey."

"Mmf," Hilda says.

"No, but it's terrible, just listen. The way they do it. These are African bees. And African bees are crazy. *Loco*."

"I know what crazy is."

"They're incredibly aggressive. They'll attack at the slightest provocation. So what these guys do is smoke them out. They spend hours going through the jungle, sometimes days, trying to find the hives, and when they do, they tie cassava leaves and plastic bags around their heads and hands, because insects don't like the smell, and then they set fire to the bush around the tree."

"And then the bees fly away and they get the honey." Hilda is less than impressed.

"The point is that it's a disaster. They burn down half the forest in the process—and they ruin the honey. The smoke gets into everything"

"You can see this in the honey, *acaso*?"

"That golden glow? Poof!" He kisses off his fingertips. "Gone. It still tastes sweet, but it's dusty with soot. So, they can only sell it on the local markets. It's an economic tragedy. If they had hives, if they learnt how to cultivate the honey, they could sell it internationally. Organic, fair trade, all that stuff, they could make real money. But instead they're trapped in this subsistence life, burning down the forest, destroying the trees where the bees make their hives, so every time they have to travel deeper into the jungle."

"This is very sad. But it is like this everywhere, no? All over the world there is *tragedia*. Refugees. Economics. Earthquakes. *Genocidios*." Hilda fiddles with the cigarette, puts it down, exchanges it for the fork. *Rat-tat-tat. Rat-tat-tat.*

"I'm not comparing it," Laryea says. "Not with what happened to *our friend*." But he doesn't like the echoing of his own thoughts. How does he explain that he was moved by the poignancy of this self-defeating cycle?

The reality is that Laryea is as much a mugu, a believer in false promises, as Hilda, carried along by his worthless degree and a British Airways flight to London, only to end up washing dishes in a Lebanese restaurant in King's Cross, flipping patties at Burger King, cleaning the public toilets at an outdoor rock festival. Disappointment is the reek of shit and teenage vomit in a plastic Portaloo on an August afternoon, with guitars buzzing like sick bees in the background.

He was made an offer to move to Johannesburg. He took it. Dealing in dreams seemed easier than drugs.

Need extra INCOME! Become our [MYSTERY SHOPPER]: Earn [NO LESS THAN $500.00] Per Venture: It is Very Easy and Very Simple: No

*Application fees: Mystery shoppers are Needed
Throughout America Great Pay. Fun Work. Flexible
Schedules.No experience required. If you can shop-
you are qualified!*

*A mystery shopper is like being 007 at the mall.
Mystery shoppers must complete their assignments
and go un-detected. You do not have to use any
money from your pockets. So We will provide you
the money for all your assignments.*

The waitress comes over to the table to let them know that
their friend has arrived. "He's just on the phone. He said
he'll be with you in a minute." She indicates a tall man in
a crisp dark suit with a cellphone clamped to the side of his
head, pacing up and down in the foyer and talking loudly
in Algerian French. Another deal on the go. Another mugu
biting.

*This is a business proposition. I represent an in-
dependent investment consultancy and brokerage.
We have recently been asked to invest funds
outside Scotland and have decided to seek partners
outside Scotland to cooperate with us in investing
the available funds.*

"He doesn't look like his *foto* in the newspapers," Hilda says,
staring across the restaurant at the man. "And I heard he was
sick."

"You must have him confused with someone else," Laryea
reassures her.

Hilda stops fidgeting with her fork. She drapes an arm over the back of the chair, and takes a deep swig of her wine, which is no way to appreciate a good vintage. But it's as if the question mark knotting up the muscles in her neck and shoulders has dissolved away.

"You know, Laryea, I like your story very much. Now I want to tell you a story."

"Don't you want to wait for Mr. Shaik?"

"This is personal. Just for you."

"All right," he says, intrigued.

"I know you think I am stupid."

"Hilda! I've never thought that for a moment."

"Because my English is not so good, you believe I cannot think so well. But this is not true."

"Of course not. I'm hurt that you would even say—"

"Will you listen? You know why I have ask you here? To this restaurant?"

"Because of the ostrich. You said you wanted to try the ostrich."

"I had a phone call. From the police."

Laryea pushes his chair away from the table.

"Sit down. It is too late."

In the foyer, two men approach Mr. Shaik, who is really Mr. Dansua, politely but firmly remove his phone from his hand and wrest his hands behind his back.

> *You have won 450,000 GBP from Nokia Promotion. Please contact our agent Mr Mark Cole;*
> *Regards*

Nokia Staff
Nokia Online End of Year Lottery Promotion

There are three more men in plain clothes crossing the restaurant towards their table. Laryea had seen one of them in the gift shop on the way in, had even noted the slovenliness of his clothes, ill-fitting, creased, like the man had more important things to do than ironing.

"The police?"

"I thought you were trying to help us."

"I was. I am."

> LET US DO A GOOD WORK AND HELP THE LIVES OF THE SUFFERING, MY NAME IS Dr. Kenneth Dickson FROM NEW ZEALAND. RECENTLY MY DOCTOR GAVE ME VERY BAD NEWS WHICH IS VERY DISTURBING TO MY EARS, HE SAID THAT IN ABOUT THREE MONTHS TIME THAT I WILL SOON DIE OF MY ILLNESS. I HAVE SURRENDERED MY LIFE TO GOD AND I AM NOW A BORN AGAIN, I WANT TO DO A GOOD DEED BEFORE I DEPART. I WILL WANT TO SET UP ORPHANAGES IN MY NAME AND ALSO DONATE THE REST OF MY WEALTH TO THE MISSIONARY OR CHARITABLE ORGANIZATIONS.

"Come, *señora*. I don't know what kind of lies they have been telling you, but we can sort this out."

"You are the one with the lies, Laryea. But this is not the story I want to tell you."

"Then what?"

"I lied also."

"You?" He is trying to understand, but it is like struggling through thick and scratchy jungle to find the road he was walking only a minute ago.

"There is no Gael. No cripple son. No accident." Hilda grins, revealing the skewed incisor that Laryea has always found endearing, until now. It is the first time she's smiled since she stepped off the plane.

"Then you knew? From the beginning? This has been a set-up for . . ."—his head reels—". . . for eighteen months?"

"No. The police, they only contact me now, while we are still in Mexico. It is terrible shock. We are very angry with you. And that's why I fly out. To make sure you get what you deserve, *cabrón*."

> *I must use this opportunity to implore you to exercise the utmost indulgence to keep this matter extraordinarily confidential whatever your decision, as you stand as my only family today.*

"But I've seen photographs." Of a boy strapped to a plastic board, his little face swollen up like a red and purple flower with a stamen of plastic tubes sprouting from his nose.

"And *I* have seen papers that show you are going to pay us. Tax certificates. Letters from the bank. My husband has access to the children's wards. We have a camera." She shrugs.

*I want you to have it in mind that this transaction
is 100% hitch free.*

"You're saying you invented Gael? The surgery? But what
about Dr. Edwards? Dr. Friedman?'
    "I say you are not the only one, Laryea. We make up Gael
so you will feel sorry for us. So you will give us *el dinero*—the
money—instead of someone else. But I will not tell this to
your police or the judge. They will think Gael is real. That
you defraud us, the poor parents of a broken little boy. They
will not check. Mexico is so far away. And you will suffer for
this. You will suffer *mucho*."

*Write back as soon as possible any delay in your
reply will give me room in sourcing another person
for this same purpose. God bless you as you listing to
the voice of Reasoning.*

Laryea has never felt any doubt. Never felt any guilt. But
now, as the police cross the restaurant towards their table,
guns held low at their sides, an SAPS badge held before them,
opening a pathway between the tables like a magic key, he
can see that he has lost his golden glow. His honey is tainted,
has turned, in fact, to shit.
    And the forest is burning down around him.

ALGEBRA

a is for algebra

"It's all equations," she says. "It's all explainable." Like we could break down the whole universe into factors and exponents and multiples of x. Like there is no mystery to anything at all.

"Okay, what about love?" I shoot back, irritated at her practicality.

And she ripostes with: "Fine. xx + xy = xxx."

She has to explain the bit about chromosomes. This is her idea of a dirty joke. Later, I wonder if this was also her idea of a come-on.

b is for braggadocio

"Oh yeah?" she says, "Watch me." She sets down her beer, walks right up to the beautiful DJ boy who is coaxing blurry noise from the turntables, leans over the decks and, to his surprise, simply pulls into him. Tsepho snorts in laughter or shock. "That chic is mal," he says, saying it without the "k," pinning her as hipster rather than baby bird. And I smile and shake my head in bemusement. But really, I think she's out of hand. And I'm worried. Or angry. Or jealous.

c is for cellulite
She's immediately on the defensive, as if I've bust her doing something far worse. "Oh come on. It's precisely *because* it's so shite that I read it. I mean, who cares that celebrities have sweat stains or who's had liposuction or a boob job? It's ridiculous."

She turns the magazine around on the table to show me a picture of a big brand-name star naked on his balcony, a black bar tactfully positioned over his tackle, like the prudish stars in the *Scope* magazines of old, which were somehow more obscene than the Jelly Tot pink nipples they concealed.

"And yet, somehow," she says, grinning, "perversely fascinating."

d is for dilute
"We'll catch up on the weekend, I promise." But between work and DJ boy, I don't see her for three weeks, apart from a quick coffee during her lunch break at the pretentious little place on Kloof, where the boys are more coiffed than the cappuccinos, and a caffeine fix requires a whole new lexicon. And then she is vaguely distant. Not in a malicious way. Not intentionally.

e is for eject

"More like reject!" she snickers into her Oreo milkshake. I am not-so-secretly relieved that the DJ has gone the way of the architect and the film student and the would-be waiter-model before him. But then she bursts into tears so unexpectedly that the Rasta hawking beaded geckos to the tourists at the next table starts and stares.

"Hey," I say, helpless. I move to put my arm around her, but it is too awkward across the table. "It's okay." Racking my brain to complete my analogy, "You can just fast forward to the next one."

"You're such a freak," she says, punching my arm, but smiling anyway.

f is for friends

"Can't we just be . . ." she says, ever so gently pushing me away, smoothing her hands over her jeans. And I know it's a nervous gesture, but I can't help feeling like she is wiping me off.

We have kissed before, fumbling on the dance floor of Evol at 3 a.m. two Friday nights ago, clashing teeth, her open mouth warm and sour from tequila. But we left in separate cars.

"Yeah, sure," I say. "No worries."

"Don't be mad. It's just . . ."

But there is no "just" about it.

g is for glue

"Buy food, okay? I mean it!" The street kid with the yellow plastic water pistol takes the five-rand coin and says, "Ja, thanks my lady," twirls the gun around his finger, cowboy-style, and immediately goes on to the next car, like he hasn't already scored.

"You know he's not going to," I say.

"Yeah. Well," she shrugs.

h is for harlot

"That's not what I'm saying," she says. "Camille's cool. She's great. I really like her. I just . . . didn't think she was your type."

"So who would be my type then? You?" I am not desperate, bitter, resentful.

i is for intuition

"It's too hot to spoon," I beg off. Camille throws back the sheets, a little too aggro, and gets up to light a cigarette. I won't let her smoke in my bed. "It's cliché," I tell her. She sits in the open window, naked, and exhales out the side of her mouth.

"You should tell her," she says, flicking ash onto the windowsill on purpose, to piss me off, I'm suddenly, absolutely sure.

"The neighbors will see you," I say.

It's not a surprise that we break up within the week. I tell everyone it's because she was too corporate, too *Cosmo*.

j is for jetsetter

"You'll hate it. It sucks," I tell her, totally assured even though I've never been to London myself. "Why do you think everyone comes back? It's cold, it's wet, and you'll just end up in some shitty bar serving beer to a bunch of drunk Aussies and getting nostalgic for NikNaks."

"So come with me, then." But she knows I can't. Or won't.

k is for killjoy
She holds up her phone at the Radiohead concert so I can hear Thom Yorke singing for thirty seconds (I work out that that half a minute cost her six quid). And I get an SMS (which she calls smiss—like a slurred, missed kiss) from the Tate Modern, where she's been "attacked," she says, by an upside-down piano. "Sorry, can't talk now," I text back. "Working on a campaign to raise money for AIDS orphans." This is true, even if it is just another ad agency job. As if I could guilt her into coming home.

l is for Letraset
The postcards she sends me, old photographs of other people's lives that she buys in Camden Market or second-hand bookstores in Notting Hill, have my name in bold black fonts meticulously traced and shaded to transfer the letters onto the paper. I didn't know you could even still buy the stuff. I write her emails back. They are too cheerful, and full of details deliberately designed to make her homesick.

m is for matrimony
"It's just for the visa," she explains over the phone, sounding distracted. There is music pounding in the background like she is at a club, but it's band practice, she tells me.

"Since when are you in a band?"

"And he's gay. So stop worrying, okay. It's purely convenience."

Even the 7/7 bombs won't bring her back.

n is for neural
The way the brain works, there's no lapse between thought and action. You think about tapping your foot, twitching a finger, and you do. It's instantaneous. You can't catch the signals, exploding through your circuits, mid-thought. Like the moment you've sent an email, it's too late. And maybe this is why I am sitting here, cramped in economy class, flipping through the in-flight magazine without taking any of it in, because how could I? And in the blackness below, somewhere, is the Sahara. An arid wasteland. Or maybe the Mediterranean.

o is for occupational hazards
"Shit!" Feedback screeches from her bass, perfectly articulated by the acoustics of the little Soho dive where Here Kitty Kitty! have their rehearsals. "Sorry!" she yelps and the drummer, Roger (pronounced *Roh-zhay*—like the bloody thesaurus), steps up to help, finding it necessary to wrap his arms around her to adjust a knob. Roger is definitely not gay.

p is for poacher
"Look mate," Thesaurus boy says, standing above the ominously stained green velveteen couch, on which I have been crashing these last eleven days in the house in Islington she shares with him and three other people whose names I never can keep straight, all Brians and Ryans. "Of course, it's

cool and all, but I was wondering how long *exactly* were you planning on staying?"

"Oh yeah, sure," I say, sitting up, "Just until I get some stuff sorted out." Like selling your snide corpse to black-market organ dealers, I think, but don't say.

I know a lot of drummer jokes.

q is for quarantine

She catnaps on the tube on the way to meet her gay financier fiancé, Sean, to go over the paperwork of their little agreement. But I only wake her when we are already well past the Bond Street stop, almost out of the city, where the tunnels have opened up to trees and houses that are stacked like Legos. I have an idea that we will take boats out on a lake with the ducks, only to be caught, laughing, in the rain, or go hunting wombles on the common, or end up kissing illicitly in a vaulted marble alcove at the back of some dusty eight-hundred-year-old cathedral, while the tour continues without us. But she is grumpy from her nap and insists there is still time to head back. She leans her head against the window and doesn't talk to me, sinking back into the dark rattle of the tunnels.

r is for rewind

Every song on the radio speaks to me personally. I know this is a bad sign.

"I love you. Come home." I should have said. A thousand times.

I call her from the plane, swiping my credit card and by some miracle it goes through—the card and the call.

"Hello?" she says.

"Hi, it's me. I love you. Come home." But I am too aware of the people sitting next to me, the well-padded engineer who takes over the armrest, and the pale working-holiday visa holder going back to Durban to work on her tan, and how they are pretending not to listen to every word.

"Hel-*lo*?"

s is for shongololo

There is a psychological test police profilers use to determine if you are a psychopath, apparently. It's something like: you go to a funeral and meet a beautiful woman but she disappears before you can get her number. How do you arrange to see her again? The psycho's answer is kill someone else she knows—so you can see her at the next funeral.

The truth is people only come back from overseas for funerals or weddings. I am seriously thinking about faking my own death. I've already persuaded DJ boy to play at my wake. Sometimes I think I might have been faking my life.

t is for tongue-tied

"A break-up is a kind of death," she says, her arms hugged around her knees on the rocks above Llandudno where it's cold and windy and hardly a beach day, but she insisted. We have fallen back into cosy routine, like she has never been away, like our relationship is a theorem that will always be proved true.

"And you were right," she pulls a face, "about the rain."

"And the NikNaks," I add, distracted, rubbing the rock where some asshole has spray-painted a black skull onto the uneven surface. I'm wondering if turps would get it off, because you can't just paint over a rock like you would a wall, when she changes the equation completely by kissing me.

u is for unbeliever

She starts a new band, Remote Control Lover. I design her flyers—retro robots and rockets—and attend every gig and pretend I have to fight off her groupies. Sometimes I do. Her belongings start migrating into my flat, like buffalo across the plains, which makes me think about how they run off cliffs. Or is that lemmings? First her toothbrush and then her clothes and her books and a frayed poster of Barbarella, even though she's never seen the movie. I know it's serious when she starts putting up her photos next to my doodles on the refrigerator. All the pictures are flawed, with red eyes and bad cropping, although she insists, chasing me round the kitchen with a curry-flavored spoon, that she did it on purpose.

v is for vacant

"I just feel like you're not always there, you know?" She takes my fingers, shaking them once, affectionate, for emphasis. "Like you're not quite with me." Like there is something missing from our equation. Of course I'm defensive, but how do I explain that it's not going to last? That she'll come to her senses, that this is not the way it's supposed to be.

That I know this with absolute certainty.

w is for war crimes

"Well, maybe you should stop projecting your fucking insecurities!" It is shock and awe without the awe. We say ugly things and swear, which we always swore not to. She is too flighty, too irresponsible. She should just grow up. I am too repressed, too uptight. I should open my eyes and smell the roses. Mixing dumbed-down metaphors, inarticulate with fury. She moves out with her books and Barbarella. I take her photos off the refrigerator and burn the Letraset postcards. Someone else starts doing Remote Control Lover's flyers.

solve for ex
I write her letters and smisses and messages on the back of her new flyers (skulls and rainbows) to leave under her car wiper blades, but don't send them, don't leave them. I know she'd hang up, but I still bring up her number, speed dial 2 (1 is pre-assigned to voicemail), let my thumb hang suspended above the green call button. As if this is all it would take. As if this could be resolved with words.

y is for yoked
The grief is a fever dream, all sweat and damp, knotted sheets. I can't sleep. I can't breathe. There is a heaviness that drags down against my ribs, as if a cannonball has lodged in my chest, arrested mid-trajectory, and it is the lack of momentum that is killing me.

z is for zero
Which is nothing. An absence. What you have left when you take everything away. Or a starting point.

Unathi Battles the Black Hairballs

Unathi was singing karaoke when the creature attacked Tokyo. Or rather, she was *about* to sing karaoke. Was, in fact, about to be the very first person in Shibuya's Big Echo to break in the newly uploaded Britney's fourth comeback anthem—a hip-hop cover of "Wannabe."

It was, admittedly, early in the day to be breaking out the microphone, but Unathi was on shore leave, and she and the rest of Saiko Squadron weren't up early so much as still going from last night, lubricated on a slick of sake that ran from here to Tokohama.

Unathi stepped up onto the table in their private booth,

giving her madoda a flash of white briefs under her pleated miniskirt. When she was on duty as flight sergeant of the squadron, she kept strictly to her maroon and grey flight suit or the casual comfort of her military-issue tracksuit.

In her private life, however, Unathi tended to be outrageous. Back in Johannesburg, before she'd been recruited to the most elite mecha squadron on the planet, she hung out in Newtown, where she'd been amakipkip to the max. Named for the cheap multicolored popcorn, the neo-pantsula gangster-punk aesthetic had her pairing purple skintight jeans with eye-bleeding oranges and greens. A pair of leopard-print heels, together with her Mohawk, added five inches to her petite frame.

Here in Tokyo, her newly adopted home, she tended towards Punk Lolita. And not some Harajuku-wannabe Lolipunk either. In civvies, she wore a schoolgirl skirt cut from an antique kimono that had survived the bombing of Hiroshima (according to the garment dealer), and she'd grown her hair out into little twists that were more combat-friendly than her Mohawk. But the highlight of her look was a pair of knee-high white patent combat boots made from the penis leather of a whale she had slaughtered herself.

Now, standing on the karaoke booth table, the light of the disco ball glittered behind her head like a halo. As she raised the mic to her perfect, pierced lips, time shifted into glorious slow-mo.

Or maybe that was just the impression of First Lieutenant Ryu Nakamura—a street fighter in his spare time—and in love with Flight Sergeant Unathi Mathabane like a plant is in love with photosynthesis.

Around her, Ryu found that time went gooey at the edges, like unagi on a hot summer's day. Unfortunately, so did his tongue, hanging limp and useless in his mouth in her proximity, unless he was responding to a direct order. He'd been planning to spill what was in his heart via a romantic duet already queued in the karaoke machine.

But that was before a flailing phallic tentacle ripped through the wall of the Big Echo, sending glass and brick and people flying.

The tentacle was monstrous, a thick and glossy tendril of black hair the diameter of a compact Japanese car. It was equipped with eviscerating spikes, and the bulbous tip split open to reveal a mouth full of spiny black teeth.

The force of the initial attack flipped over the table Unathi was standing on. She hit the ground with a crack like a rupturing tectonic plate. A moment later the table smashed down onto her chest, driving the air out of her lungs. The bubbles of a mild concussion popped across her vision. In the background, Britney rapped the Spice Girls classic over a raunchy beat.

While Unathi struggled to get up, the tentacle made sushi of Saiko Squadron. It snapped Chief Engineer Sato's spine so violently that his vertebrae erupted through his stomach. He twitched and flopped obscenely, only inches away from Unathi writhing on the carpet. A spike gutted Ensign Tanaka and another tore Corporal Suzuki in half. And then it bit off Ryu's head in one neat snap of those spiny teeth.

The karaoke jukebox clicked over to the duet. *Looking in your eyes, there's reflected paradise.* And that might have been true if Ryu still had eyes, or, for that matter, a head. His body stood swaying for a moment, like an indecisive drunk. And then a bright, hot jet of blood fountained from the stump of his neck, spraying Unathi in the face like some vampire bukkake video. She managed to suck in enough air to scream. She'd had an inkling of his crush. It was in the way he showed all his teeth and scratched the back of his head whenever she gave him a direct order. The cheesy eighties duet cemented it. And now he was dead. Excepting herself, the whole of Saiko Squadron was dead. And, worse, there was blood and spilt sake on her white patent-whale-penis-leather boots.

"Someone is going to fucking pay!" Unathi growled.

She finally shoved the table off her chest and yanked herself to her feet, drawing her saber. But the tentacle was already withdrawing, slithering back through the carnage. She vaulted the upturned table (and the still-flopping Chief Engineer Sato) and leapt through the smashed remains of what had once been a wall. She landed in a crouch in her heeled boots and looked up to see the creature looming above the couture capital of Shibuya 109, a mall that made Johannesburg's glossy consumer temple, Sandton City, look like a fong kong flea market.

The creature resembled a toothsome Godzilla-sized hairball studded with gnashing sharky mouths beneath the tangle of matted hair, thick spiky tentacles with lamprey teeth of their own thrashing about and laying waste to historic pagodas and skyscrapers alike.

Unathi got to her feet and started running, not towards the creature, but towards her mecha, stashed eight blocks away on Takeshita Street—the only place she could find parking.

The giant robot—a Ghost VF-3—was painted in zebra stripes as a little homage to her home. It was sitting dormant, exactly as she'd left it, except for the parking ticket pasted onto the ergonomic claw of the mecha's left foot. Unathi yanked it off, folded it into an origami unicorn and left it on the pavement as a little "fuck you" for the meter maid—no doubt, like all of Tokyo's public servants, an android who could only dream of being human.

She scrambled up the front of the robot using the multiple revolving turrets of the massive chest cannon as footholds, only to spend the next five minutes sitting on the mecha's armored shoulder, searching through her oversized Louis Vuitton bag for her keys.

They were right at the bottom, sandwiched between her Hello Kitty vibrator and a bento box containing yesterday's uneaten lunch. She bleep-bleeped the immobilizer, and with a hydraulic hiss and an actuator hum, the robot's blank-faced head folded back on its shoulders, revealing the cockpit. Unathi bounced into the pilot's seat and started flipping switches.

Beneath her, the Ghost VF-3 started to thrum as the engines powered up. The decorative samurai armor spines on its back flipped down and fanned out to become interlocking fighter-jet wings. The whole street was vibrating now with the throbbing force of the engine. Windows in the neighboring skyscrapers were rattling. Unathi hummed the *Top Gun* theme to herself while she calculated the sudoku puzzle on the virtual display unit that would unlock the VF-3's weapons systems.

"Weapons activated," a serene female voice said as Unathi plugged in the last digit. A four. Like the four men of Saiko Squadron lying in pools of their own blood and spinal fluid back in the Big Echo. With a grimace, she hit the thrusters and the Ghost VF-3 burst into the sky, leaving a crater behind it in the tarmac. On the pavement, the origami unicorn caught fire.

The battle was a blur. Literally. Possibly because she was still drunk.

There were sweeping colors and motion lines as the Ghost VF-3 launched towards the evil hairball. There was a shuddering frame-by-frame slow-mo as one of the tentacles smashed into the mecha. Another as the VF-3 catapulted backwards—tearing through Shibuya 109 with a rumble of glass and concrete. In the streets below, ducking the falling rubble and the flaming, tattered ruins of high couture, fashionable teenagers screamed in an agony of loss.

Inside the cockpit, Unathi jabbed at the controls and broke out her nastiest tsotsi-taal. "Come on! Come on! *Msunu ka nyoko!*" until the Ghost VF-3 wrenched itself free from Shibuya 109, leaving a mecha-shaped imprint in the rubble. One of her wings had snapped right off. "For the love of kawaii!" Unathi cursed, pulling up the systems diagnostics check. They sure didn't make them like they used to. She had *told* her superiors at High Command they should buy Korean.

Apart from the broken wing, which would throw her flight patterns for a loop, the damage wasn't too serious. Some minor bruising to the VF-3's sidian heat diffusers, an annoying fritz on the rear-facing starboard camera visual systems, but at least the Reaver cannon hadn't taken a hit. Unathi yanked the joystick forward and the VF-3 bounded down the street towards the hairball, leaving a trail of cracked concrete under every armor-plated footfall (and at least one squished teen fashionista).

Unathi awoke feeling as if the oni of hangovers had squatted in her mouth. She sat up, her vision still bleary, and started hacking up blood. She wiped her hand across her mouth and looked around. The world oozed in and out of focus. A shadowy figure loomed and resolved itself into a mild-looking middle-aged man, his hand extended to offer her a handkerchief. "Here," he said, and she dabbed at the bloodstains round her mouth. From the carpet, a black cat with one white ear looked up at her curiously. There was jazz playing quietly in the background. Miles Davis, she guessed, but then her knowledge of jazz was pretty much limited to Miles Davis.

"Where am I? What happened?" she said, handing back the bloodied handkerchief. The man folded it up and tucked it into a pocket.

"Perhaps you should tell me?" the man said, tilting his head at the smoking VF-3 wreck lying sprawled in the ruins of what was once a tidy little kitchen. Actually, it was only part of the mecha; the head, one shoulder and the ripped chassis of half the chest cavity had partially melted to fuse with the shredded remnants of the Reaver cannon. Unathi felt a hitch in her throat at the sight. First her boots, now her VF-3. Was there no end to the horror?

She closed her eyes. The memory of what happened came in Polaroid flashes of the action.

The Ghost VF-3 crashing down into Shibuya Station.

The hairball swallowing up half a train, which disappeared into one of those gnashing mouths like it was a tunnel.

The VF-3 seizing the nearest thing to hand—which just happened to be a panty-vending machine—and hurling it at the beast.

Scorched panties drifting down through the sky.

Launching into the sky, locked together like fighting hawks, her damaged wing sending them spiraling in crazy loops.

And then, weirdest of all, in the moment just before two tentacles seized the legs and chest of the Ghost VF-3 and twisted, shearing through the metal with a screech, she had plunged the mecha's hands into the heart of the thing and yanked the hair apart like a curtain, revealing . . . a lurid smiley-faced flower.

"Would you like some spaghetti?" the man asked. He ducked under the sparking wiring of the VF-3's amputated arm to the stove, miraculously still intact, where a pot was bubbling.

"*Hai, baba.* I have to get back. I have to destroy that thing!" Unathi snapped, lurching to her feet.

"You shouldn't go into battle on an empty stomach," he said mildly, dishing out a bowl of spaghetti for himself. He added fresh basil.

Unathi narrowed her eyes. "You know, for someone who just had the flaming wreckage of a mecha crash into his kitchen, you're being suspiciously calm about all this. Who the hell are you?"

"Oh, I'm a writer. I used to work for an advertising agency, but I left. Not for any particular reason. I just didn't like it."

"What *do* you like?" Unathi said, still suspicious.

"I like music. I like to cook. I like to think about jogging. And you?"

"Who am I or what do I like?"

"Let's start with the first."

The question made Unathi philosophical. "Mecha-captaining and monster-battling aside, I guess I'm still just a girl from Soweto."

"That must be nice," the writer said.

The phone rang. It seemed to have an impatient tone. "Excuse me one moment." He ducked back under the mecha's arm and went down the hall to pick up the phone. It was a grey phone, slim and somehow nostalgic. "Hello?" he said into the receiver and then: "You again? I thought I told you I don't have time for these phone games." He listened for a moment, then held out the phone. "It's for you."

Unathi limped over, holding her side. She'd definitely broken a rib. Maybe several. She took the phone receiver and held it to her ear.

"Hello," a woman's voice said. It was a serene voice, like her mecha's vocal system.

"Hi," said Unathi, taken aback.

"Did you have some of Haruki's spaghetti?"

"No," Unathi said.

"You should have some. He's an excellent cook. You'll like it."

"Excuse me, do I know you?" Unathi was getting annoyed.

"Yes, we've met many times. Have I mentioned I'm naked? I just got out of the shower."

Oh great. Phone sex. Like that was what she needed right now. "Have I mentioned I have a giant hairball to track down and destroy before it consumes the whole city?"

"No. No, you hadn't. Perhaps you should go do that," the woman said.

"Is there some kind of point to this phone call?" Unathi thought about hanging up, but there was something about the woman's voice. The situation was eerily familiar. Not déjà vu exactly, but like she'd seen it in a movie or maybe read it in a book.

"Not really. I just wanted to say hello."

"Hello and goodbye."

"Oh and you should go to the suicide forest. It's beautiful this time of year."

"What?"

"Aokigahara. It's under Mount Fuji."

"I know where it is."

"I think it might be helpful for you. Well, that's all," the woman said pleasantly, and then, "Goodbye."

Unathi listened to the dial tone for a moment and then replaced the receiver. "What was that about?" she asked Haruki.

"I don't know. She phones sometimes. I don't mind so much."

"She said I should visit Aokigahara."

"Why would she say that?"

"I don't know, you tell me. She's your mystery lady phone caller."

"Well, maybe we should go check it out."

"Maybe we should. Maybe it'll lead us to the hairball."

"It could be a wild sheep chase," Haruki mused.

"You mean goose chase." Unathi hated it when people got their idioms muddled.

"You're right, I don't know why I got that confused," Haruki apologized. "But I know a short cut. It's this way, through the alley."

He led her out the back door into a small garden behind the house. There was a white and green deck chair with a book beside it. He helped her climb over the breeze-block wall and into an alley that ran parallel to the backs of the houses. The black and white cat jumped up onto the wall and watched them.

"I call it an alley, but it's not really an alley," Haruki said. "It's also not a way, because, technically, a way should have an entrance or an exit, but this doesn't. It's also not a cul-de-sac, because a cul-de-sac should have an entrance. This is more like a dead end."

"You're going to be a dead end if you don't stop talking. Get me to Aokigahara."

"All right, all right," the writer said. "Sorry." He was quiet for a while, leading her behind the houses. Both ends were fenced off with barbed wire. He was right: it wasn't a way or a cul-de-sac. Above them, in the trees, a bird sang like a wind-up toy or a spring unravelling. The cat jumped down and padded after them.

They came to a well. It had a cover made of wood, faintly damp with moss that had grown over the edges, with a metal handle set into it. She helped him push the cover off. Inside the well, it was very dark. A metal ladder descended into the black. It looked well maintained. There was a rich, cloying smell, like sarin gas or dead bodies. Maybe both.

"Ladies first," Haruki said. The cat jumped onto his shoulder. It looked like it was coming along for the ride.

Unathi sighed, looking down at her boots. At this rate, she was going to have to go on another whale hunt.

Unathi counted 439 rungs before she stepped down onto loamy earth.

"It's man-made," Haruki said, climbing off the ladder and brushing the dirt off his hands, "Possibly an old storm drain. Or maybe it connects to the subway. An abandoned line that used to lead to Aokigahara."

"Or straight to hell," Unathi said.

"That seems unlikely," Haruki said. The cat leapt off his shoulder and set off ahead. It looked back at them with an inquisitive meow, as if to say "Well, are you coming?"

They followed the cat and, after thirty minutes or so, the tunnel opened into a cement bunker with a rusted metal door that was wedged shut. There were signs that someone had been there recently. There were paintings stacked up against the walls. The top one featured a colorful theme park monstrosity, a sickly grinning mushroom with rolling eyes and melting edges. In the corner, there was a life-size sculpture of an anime boy with spiky hair and a death-grip on his erect penis jizzing spunk around his head.

"I recognize this," Unathi said. It was hard to forget a sculpture of a naked anime boy with a sperm lasso. "This is the work of that art factory. The one run by that famous guy who formed a collective of hungry young talent to mass-produce a range of work. What's his name again?" Before the aliens attacked and Unathi had been enlisted, she'd gone through a rigorous cultural immersion program, from the correct brewing of tea to pop-art politics.

"Ah, my namesake," the writer said, "Takashi."

"You said you were called Haruki."

"Yes, but we have the same last name. No relation."

"Yeah, okay. Whatever." Irritated, Unathi flicked through the paintings stacked up against the wall, until she hit one that was horribly familiar. She hauled it out to get a better look. It featured a lunatic grinning flower with rainbow petals. It was almost identical to the glowing face at the heart of the hairball.

"And I *definitely* recognize this," she said. "But why is this here?"

"Never mind that," the writer said, yanking at the rusted door. "This door is stuck."

"Not for long." Unathi grinned and broke it off its hinges with one well-placed karate kick (another advantage of the cultural immersion program).

They emerged into a forest. Sunlight streaked through the leaves in pale golden bars. Mount Fuji loomed through the foliage, tufts of cloud ringed around the peak like a hula hoop. The cat stopped to lick itself. The wind in the leaves sounded like ghosts laughing.

"It's lovely," Unathi said, surprised. That was before she saw the bodies hanging from the trees like gruesome Christmas decorations. Their faces were black, their eyes popping out. Asphyxiation does that.

They were hanging from belts or cables or the kind of mesh straps you might use to secure a mattress to the roof of your car, which Unathi had done only a few weeks ago when helping Corporal Suzuki move into his new apartment pod.

"The suicide forest," the cat mused. "Second only to the Golden Gate Bridge in the self-murder popularity stakes. Partly inspired by the tragic double suicide ending of the novel *Kuroi Jukai*, or *Black Sea of Trees*."

"I didn't know you could talk," Unathi said.

"I can't," said the cat. It gave her a huffy look from beneath its eyebrow whiskers.

"Why are they all bald?" mused the writer.

Unathi started. He was right. Whatever state of decay, whether their faces were still intact or the birds and squirrels had eaten their eyes and lips, whether their clothes marked them as disgraced salaryman or despondent housewife or lovesick teens playing out *Kuroi Jukai*, every corpse had one thing in common: their heads were entirely shaved.

"Something weird is going on," Unathi said, automatically reaching for her joystick and the diplomatic power of the Reaver auto-cannon's 20mm uranium-depleted tank-killer bullets the size of milk bottles.

"No shit, Sherlock," the cat said and then pretended it hadn't, earnestly rubbing a paw over one ear and then the other.

"Shhh. What's that sound?" Haruki said. Unathi listened. There was a buzzing whine, like a sick lawnmower or her Hello Kitty vibrator running on maximum speed.

"This way," she said, and ran off between the trees, quiet as a ninja in a library.

The buzzing sound was emanating from an electric hair clipper, wielded by a young man in a neon-green jumpsuit.

He was dangling from abseil gear, his feet wedged on either side of the unfortunate corpse he was shearing. It was a young mother, judging by the burp cloth still draped over her shoulder. No doubt the victim of social shame inflicted by one of the cruel mom cliques that ruled the city's playgrounds. As the dead woman's long black hair parted company from her scalp, it came to life. It writhed and twisted, so that green jumpsuit guy had to wrap it round his wrist to keep it from slithering away into the sky.

"Hey, you skabenga! What are you doing?" Unathi yelled, which was perhaps not the most prudent of plans. The young man startled so badly that he lost his grip on his anchor line. The rope screamed through the carabiner. He grabbed for it, but it burnt through his palm and came free, dropping him out of the air. He landed on his neck with a grisly crunch. The spasming hair wriggled free of his wrist and slithered away into the mossy hollows between the tree roots.

"Is he?" the writer asked.

"Dead," Unathi confirmed, kicking the corpse. The hair clipper was still buzzing in his hand. "Now what?"

"You could always follow the extension cable," the cat said.

"We could always follow the extension cable," Unathi said, ignoring the cat. She yanked at the electric cord attached to the vibrating hair clipper and started reeling it in.

The cable wound between trees, over glens and at some point, with little heed for electrical safety, right through a babbling brook.

"I wonder why they didn't use batteries," Haruki said,

jumping over the brook. The cat was back to riding his shoulder.

"We ran out," a voice replied from the shadowy glade up ahead. Unathi and the writer stepped into a ring of trees to find a slight man with glasses and a rumpled suit sitting atop an oozing mound with Mickey Mouse ears, pointy fangs and gargantuan cartoon eyes swiveling in opposite directions. Bright paint leaked down the sides of the mound and saturated the grass beneath it in camouflage whorls of color. It grinned at them and rolled its eyes.

Beside the mound an oversized generator hummed happily, a tangle of extension cords like Medusa dreadlocks running away from it to feed power to other hair clippers in other parts of the forest, shearing other suicides of their bewitched locks.

Gathered around the mound were young men and women in various shades of neon and states of industry. They'd formed an assembly line of sorts. On the far side, apprentice artists in grey jumpsuits sat at workbenches besides boxes and boxes of bowling balls. They stripped the paint off the balls, sanded down the surfaces and delivered them to the next work-bench where a girl with bright-pink hair and huge goggles airbrushed the iconic smiley flower designs onto them.

The flower balls piled up next to her, blinking happily, while they waited their turn at the next station, which aptly resembled a sumo ring. Several huge men and women wrestled with tangles of writhing suicide hair, wrapping it onto the flower-faced bowling balls. The hair resisted. As they watched, a tentacle of hair squirmed out of one man's grasp. "Look out!" he yelped. The hair slapped him aside. He flew out of the ring and landed with a fleshy thud at Unathi and Haruki's feet. "Urrrgh," he said.

Back in the ring, an artist in a red jumpsuit grabbed the end of the hair and cracked it like a whip. The hair collapsed to the ground, stunned. Two other artists leapt on it and wrapped it round the flower face before it could recover and stapled it down. It quivered and howled as the hair and the flower ball became one.

The final stage was a wooden platform raised like a dock. Cute artist boys and girls in school uniforms released the finished artworks into the sky. "Byeee! *Sayonara!* Get big and strong, you hear! Have a nice life!" They waved their hankies in salutation as the hairballs drifted off like balloons, already sprouting gnashing mouths and spined tentacles.

It was horrible.

It was brilliant.

The man atop the mound gave the mecha pilot and the writer (and the cat) a chance to take it all in. Then he stood up and threw his arms wide. "Welcome. I am Mr. Murakami. And this is my heap. I am king of it and all artistic endeavor."

"So you're the guy?" Unathi snarled.

"Ob-vious-ly." The cat rolled its eyes.

The slight, bespectacled man smirked. He stood up and skidded down the side of his mud creature, leaving behind a swathe of blues and greens. It groaned and swiveled its eyes to watch him. "It depends," the man said. "By 'the guy' do you mean one of the most challenging and thought-provoking artists of the twenty-first century? Who innovated the superflat style combining the best of otaku culture and Japanese pop aesthetics? Whose factory puts Andy Warhol's little art manufacturing industry to shame? Whose art has the capacity to shock, to titillate, to overturn the world as we know it?"

"I meant, are you the fucker responsible for ruining my boots?"

"Your boots?" Takashi shifted his gaze from Unathi's tits to her boots, which were no longer remotely white. They were splattered with blood and mud and spinal fluid and bits of writhing, haunted hair. "Is that whale penis leather?" the artist asked admiringly.

"Killed it myself," Unathi beamed.

"Divine."

Unathi turned grim. "And one of your hairball creatures has destroyed them. Along with half of Tokyo. And the whole of Saiko Squadron. Although, technically, they're replaceable. I mean, we have new academy graduates practically begging to be recruited."

"What can I say?" The artist shrugged. "Good art should exact a toll."

"*Hamba'ofa!* Exact this!" Unathi said, as she pulled her diamante-studded .357 Magnum from the holster on the side of her boot and pressed it to his temple.

"Wait!" yelled the cat and the writer at the same time.

"You got a better idea?" she said, her finger itchy on the trigger.

"Don't you know anything about art?" Haruki said. "Look at him."

Unathi looked at Takashi, beaming lunatically like one of his flower balls.

"He wants to die."

It sunk in. "Shit. And then his art will live forever." Unathi eased her finger off the trigger.

"And grow bigger and more infamous and ravage the whole world!" Takashi crowed.

"Shut up," Unathi said, lowering the gun and jamming it up against his crotch. "Unless you want to bleed to death slowly from a bullet hole in your hairy balls."

"Even more sensational! I'll take it!" Takashi grinned.

Unathi ignored him. "This writing you do, Haruki . . ."

"Yes?"

"Ever do art critiques?"

"I haven't . . . but I see where you're going."

"What?" Takashi said, panicky. "No, no, no, no. This is a time for action, not words."

"I'm thinking this suicide hair thing is interesting, but, you know, in my opinion . . ."—Unathi paused for effect and rolled her eyes—"sooooo derivative."

"No!" Takashi yelped.

"Shock for shock's sake," Unathi continued. "So tired. So very . . ."

"Don't say it. Don't you dare."

"So very Damien Hirst," she finished.

"Aaaaaagh!" Takashi tore at his hair. "I am nothing like that hack. You can't do this to me!"

"Already doing it," Haruki said, tapping away at his phone. "I'm uploading a scathing review to all the arts sites right now."

"Have mercy," Takashi moaned.

"Sorry, friend," Haruki shrugged, not looking up from his

screen. "I guess the text message is mightier than the mass-produced pop-art gimmick."

Takashi grabbed Unathi's hand, wrenched the gun up to his temple and, before she had time to react, pulled the trigger. A bright twist of blood arced away from his temple in slow motion. The artist's lips twitched in the faintest of smiles and then he keeled over sideways, revealing the bloody mash where the back of his head had once been. His blood started to mingle with the swirl of colors on the grass, muddying the bright hues.

Unathi looked down at the body. *"Eish,"* she said. "That's done it."

"Watch out," said the cat. Unathi and Haruki stepped back just in time to avoid being flattened by the scramble of neon jumpsuits fighting each other to get to the top of the globulous, seeping heap of color.

The battle was ugly. The hungry young artists climbed over each other, dragged each other down, punched each other in the face and the throat. And then they broke out the knives. After a while it got too messy to tell who was actually wounded and who was just slathered in paint.

"We should leave," the cat said. "The succession fight is only going to get nastier."

"But the whole world is screwed. Takashi's dead." Unathi gave the body a kick to emphasize her point, adding some of the artist's blood to the congealed stains on her boot. "His reputation is going to grow; the haunted hairballs will only become more powerful . . ."

"No," said the writer. "Ignominious suicide after a bad review? That's not a scandalous death that will lead to centuries-long infamy; that's a pathetic publicity stunt. His former students and factory colleagues will be the first to defame him. It's over. The hairballs will eventually shrivel up and die or get bought up by advertising agency execs to display in their foyers." He added, "But only ironically."

"Ouch." Unathi shuddered.

"Should we get back? I don't know about you, but I could murder some spaghetti."

"Early lunch?" Unathi checked her watch. It was only twelve. But then, hey, Tokyo was a fast place.

They started walking into the forest, back towards the bunker, the cat riding Haruki's shoulder. Behind them, the artists were still engaged in violent infighting. One of them had extricated herself from the melee and was filming the carnage. It would make a great video piece.

"So why did you leave Johannesburg, if I may ask?" Haruki said, heaving open the bunker door.

"*That* city? *Hayibo.* That city is too fucking crazy." She shook her head, ducking under the dangling foot of a suicide. "Hey, you have any idea when whaling season starts?"

Dear Mariana

Dear Mariana,

I have FAllen in love with your typwriter, typ½os and all. The tactility, the stacatto click of THe keys is so much mpore fuFILLing than the dulled ergonomics of my keyboard.

I always thought to be a writer yiu should have a magnificent old typewrter, polished black and roosting among the white sheaves of paper and crumpled mistakes like some prehistoric insect of curves and clivcks. I KNow this is cliche. But that it should be muse anddrug, hungry for you rather than the other way round. As all GOod drugs are.

So, while your typeweiter (ticking out these words, astonishing me with the immediacy of creation; ink on paper so much more tngible than pixels of 10-pt Times New Roman. It lends the wrods a sense of permanence that my computer lacks entirely. And look, I am getting better! My fingers are adjusting (finally!) to the rhythms of teh spaces. Anyway, I digress. It's this hopeless infatuaTion with this machine.)

So. Again. While your typwriter, being electric and that blond beige of deskbound electronics pre-candy-coated imacs, is not quite the slick black BEast of my imaginings, the novelty of the thing is delightful, and thus, inspiring.

I think, perhaps, it extends beyond the typewriter though, to your feng shui-ed house that bears my invasion a little uneasily I'm afraid. But ah, Mariana, what stories your things tell of you. Oh, don't worry, I haven't been prying. I'm not the type to snoOp, or at least only a litlte.

You've no idea how much you are embodied in this space. I can breathe you in these rooms. There is so much more I know from trning over the secret places of you, like the soft underbelly of some thorny beetle. For you can be thorny, honeybee. You can be a hellcat. Like Dante, who I am afraid still doesn't like me verfy much. He skulks around the house, tail puffed out like a toilet brush, quivering. It's that ridiculous name. I told you it would give any cat a complex.

Anyway. Sitting at your desk, my hands dancing over the typewriter like pale spiders, looking out at your view of the mountain, I feel at once diSplaced and at home. I have to confess to wanting to pull a MR. Ripley and neatly acquiring your life.

It's all spelled out so clearly in even just the surface of your possessions. No need to open drawers or read old letters when evrything I need to know of you lies out here, so naively exposed. A stranger could construct you from your things. Your books and CDs and photographs tell me more than billsor diary entries. It's all so naked.

You should be more careful

A list then to illustrate the pieces of the puzzle:

1) The pictures of your fucked-up slick-clique hipster friends and the total absence of photos of your fucked-up highbrow parents (or of me, I've noted, but it's been a while and I've already forgiven you this slight).

2) Your old fashioned rollerskates to take to Mouille Point, gliding along the promenade like rollergirl.

3) The sixties-style furniture of which you've collected quite a mismatched assortment.

4) Eccentric artwork done by those fu
000cked-up boho friends and glossy coffee-table books.

5) Obscure "cutting edge" electronica you know I have no tolerance for, beats and whines like the sonic nightmares of kitchen appliances.

6) Sartre and Tolstoy cosied next to Eve Ensler's twat and David Egger's monstrous ego – and all that other contemporary literary wanking you seem to go in for.

7) two-ply T.P., Clinique, Dove and a loot of Mac cosmetics in every shade.

8) A wardrobe full ofDiesel and EVisu, trading in your parent's high-priced fashion fetishes for your own.

9) And let's not forget the health-conscious single (!) girl's refrigerator, adorned with erotic fridge magnET poetry and more photos, stocked with coke light and heineken and single-serving portions of various easy-cook ingredients. One aubergine, 1 red pepper, one yellow, one onion, one plain greekstyle yoghurt, one pack of tofu, one butternut, one slab of butter, one litre of soy milk, omne thai-style green curry paste, one clasisc mnt sauce, one jar odf lemomn grass oeneoneoneone oeneoNEONEONE ONE ONE ONE

ONE ONE ONE EOINEJNEHEHE OEN df';hjlgkjlkjl ts
rghjrggjh eark,jfdz

Anyway.

While you are supposedly away, like Little Red Riding
Hood off into the dark woods to visit your sick grandma, I
will simply slide into your life as you would a pair of shoes.

I will change my star sign. You're Aries Tiger? I'll start
doing Pilates, drink green tea and eat at swish restaurants
where they serve sorbet between each course. I will go to
auditions and acting clases and feverishly type scenes for
countless unfinished plays that will never be performed on
this very typewriter, and chainsmoke Lucky Strikes in the
cxrisp office of your therapist and bitch about my mother.

The bitch has been calling, you know. Your mother, not
your therapist. And perhaps that's one thing I would not wish
to assimilate as your doting dopplegang, not even to have
something to talk about with my/your therapist. I can see
where you get your razor tongue from. Jesus. She leaves shrill
messages on your voicemail (for obvious reasons I don't pick

up) in that FUCKING posh tone of voice that sometimes creeps into your own like when we fgight, like a switCH. Snotty on-off-on-off, hotcold, hot-clolf. Like that fcuking cat.

Look, kust loojkj how upset I am just thinking about that fuCKIGN bitch makes me lapse into typois again. I HAve to go out

I'm back. I went to Spar. I got flour and potatoes and eggs to make gnocchi. For two. Although you won't be here. After all, you've been gone weeks now. Who knows when you might come back? I'll toast you though, all the same. I bought wine – Thelema red, candles, baby tomatoes, onions, peppers, garlic and home-made cannelloni from Carlucci's. More paraffin, too.

Sorry I lost it, your mother. . . No wonder you never told her. Her messages have become increasingly, I don't know, like there's a sense of nervousness to her soliloquys after the beep. I think she's worried. Suspicious. Maybe I'm imagining it.

I know I'm not imagining the other messages you've been getting. I know, I know. I promised I wouldn't snoop, but what if there was an urgent call? What if there was an emergency? You'd need to know wouldn't you?

Steve has been calling a LOT, M. And I mean a LOT. He seems terribly ------- familiar on the phone. On the answring machine, I mean. I'm not jealous. Really, I'm not. I mean, we're over, right? It's got nothing to do with me anymore. I'm just curious, that's all. I guess I ujst wish you'd told me. Thatsall. Were you seeing him before? You said you weren't that way inclined. You said you weren;t interested. I know, I'm sorry, I'm not jealous, I'm just sad. I still care aboiut you. I just don't like to thoijnk of anyone else toufching you

sorry. I;m sorry. I'm back again.

I'm afraid I'm going to have to do something about Dante. He's sort of a typo, too. Like we were. See, I'm not afraid to admit it now. You were right, we're not good for each other, we can't compromise. I know it was only a couple of months. I know I have issues with trust. And that was all part of it.

This whole thing has given me a lot of time to think and I've finally accepted it wasn't ever going to work. You're right. I can't own you, I don't want to. I'm sorry if all this Mr. Ripley stuff has been a little out there.

I think I've finally come to terms with it, Mariana. Wouldn't your therapist have been pleased? And after this I will be out of your life forever, I promise. Don't get me wrong, I'll always love you. You meant a lot to me and while I know things fucked up, that I fucked up, that doesn't change the way I feel. Part of me feels like you played me for a fool, all those lies, all those games. Oh it was fun for a while, the furtiveness of this delicious secret, like an affair, our own private reality that excluded the rest of the world.

It got too much though, you know? It all became really difficult, sore. And I still don't really understand. I mean I can understtqad your mother, but I don't get why you were so scared, why you pretneded in front of your friends. Were you ashamed of me, M? Or only of us? It's really sad that you denied yourself like that. It's not healthy M. You can'tg live a lie like that. I'm saving you.

But I still have to do something about that fucking cat. Oh, I put out those scientifically formulated maximum-nutrition vitamin-fortified pellets you feed the little fucker, but he's been steadfastly refusing to eat. I can't fuckging HSAndle it. I can't.

I was tempted to take some keepsake of you, to save it from the house, but there's nothing I really want. I did try to take one last photograph of us together but your flash is broken, so I don't know if it'll come out.

Anyway, sweetheart, it's getting late. You know part of me will always love you. I don't regret anything we had, anything that happened. But I think all this has showed me that I'm ready to move on. I think I'm going to be okay.

Love (always)

Claudia

RIDING WITH THE DREAM PATROL

July 29, 2017
Special Report by correspondent Lauren Beukes

[Cape Town] The view from the Mongooses' offices at an undisclosed location on the Cape Town Foreshore overlooks white-sailed yachts on a choppy grey sea and the distant industry of shipping containers being shuffled around by cranes and trucks in the harbor. On the other side, the bustle of the city bowl is reduced to the blank façades of buildings, the faint hum of traffic. It's an enviable view for a government department. It's a pity no one's taking it in.

That's because the Mongoose team, some forty-eight of them, are glued to their screens. A mix of programmers and "intelligence collectors," the elite surveillance unit is watching the greatest show on earth. You.

"It's actually very tedious," Lerato Makhetha says, looking

over my shoulder at the information scrolling across the screen. The Mongooses' thirty-six-year-old director of operations is barely five foot two with close-cropped natural hair, a petite Big Brother in heels and a Maya Prass dress. It would be easy to underestimate her. Also a mistake.

The info stream is harvested from cellular phone calls, social media, CCTV, cookies, browser histories and even embedded fashion catwalk cams, all feeding information straight into the Mongooses' servers.

"We've got algorithms in place to do the heavy lifting: detecting blatant abuse, unauthorized disclosures on flagged materials, problem phrases, links to and from blacklisted sites, criminal activities, scams, illegal pornography and so on. But at the end of the day, you still need a human being to sort through it all. Is this a real terrorist threat to national security or just someone blowing off steam on a blog?"

The work may be all about the subtleties, but Makhetha is not. Formed from the remains of the Hawks after they were disbanded, the Mongooses' mandate is, she explains, really simple: "To bite the heads off snakes in the grass and chew up the dirty little beetles trying to turn up shit and undermine our democracy."

"Relax," she says, brushing off my obvious discomfort with a laugh. "It's all in line with the Constitution. We're not the Gestapo here."

The truth is that they're more effective. In the age of social networking, sharing is caring and secret policing was never this easy. Whereas apartheid's Special Branch would have had to embed undercover agents to spy on union meetings, for the Mongooses, total transparency, at least for private citizens, is only one click away. A glance at Facebook events, your Flickr set, your Twitter feed or your Mxit friends list provides information on your known associates, recent whereabouts, political, social and sexual proclivities.

But the combination of RICA, which makes every SIM card traceable down to its GPS coordinates, the Protection of Information Act and the Corporate Responsibility Act of 2013 (CRA), which legally obliges corporations to cooperate with government demands such as shutting down cellphone coverage in a riot zone, for example, makes their job a whole lot easier. The Mongooses can not only monitor open networks but private ones too, including phone calls, emails and your Internet history. They can even track your current location using your cellphone's GPS—and they can shut down anything they don't like.

There are rumors that the unit also has a game design arm that creates silly apps for social networking, that rate your sex appeal on MeToo, for example, or create photoclouds out of your most popular Tumblr posts. But when I ask her about it, Makhetha says mildly, "That's classified."

Also classified is exactly what happens when a human operator confirms the algorithms. Makhetha won't comment on the rumors of secret detainments. "That's not strictly my department," she says, "If something like that was happening, it *would be* classified, but I can tell you, at least in theory, what the first steps in the procedure would be from our side.

"If it's just someone venting or making a stupid joke about blowing up the taxi rank because the drivers are on strike, we'll send them a friendly warning to cut it out. But if it's a genuine offense, say an info terrorist disseminating top secret documents about a government tender, we're within rights to act immediately, to disconnect them from the Internet and shut down their cellphone account until the matter is resolved in a court of law.

"We've got all this in place with the network providers as per the CRA. Of course the perpetrators still get a free and fair trial, but we have to shut down their communications immediately. It's about stopping the poison before it infects the whole system. I guess you could say we act as freedom's tourniquet."

The problem, according to critics, is that the tourniquet is not just cutting off the poison, but the circulation of a healthy democracy. One of the most outspoken detractors is Montle Hunter, head of Clear, a radicalized pro-transparency spin-off of Afrileaks, which the Mongooses shut down two years ago.

Clear calls the Mongooses "the dream patrol"—as in that's the only place they're not watching your every move (you hope). It's appropriate then that the only place Hunter agrees to meet with me is *in* a dream world of sorts—in the popular Filipino virtual gameworld, ShinyShiny.

Hunter appears as a bog-standard cyborg-orc, indiscernible from any of the other orcs wandering through the enchanted techno-forests of ShinyShiny. "This is me," he jokes. "Warts and all."

The truth is that no one knows what he looks like, or if Montle Hunter is his real name, or if he's a he at all, or only one person or the public face of a interchangeable like-minded collective of people. Hunter operates between the unregulated alternanets and darknets to avoid detection by Mongooses or the global info-terrorism unit, Int.pol.

When he goes out in public, he says, he has visual frequency distorters on hand to disrupt CCTV cameras. Meanwhile, Clear agents have fallen back on using old-school spy techniques: "We pass handwritten notes," he admits, a little sheepishly.

"The problem here is not that the South African government is spying on its people. Governments have always done that. It's that they're actively suppressing information using the Protection of Information Act of 2011, and I'm not just talking about critical state secrets or leaked diplomatic missives, the kind of real 'national security issues' it was designed to protect. We're talking about withholding basic information that affects people's lives on a day-to-day level."

He cites the Vaalwater cholera outbreak in November as a "classic example."

"Here we've got a municipal district manager who sees an outbreak of a fatal disease in his area, but he can't get the information on the water supply to find out if it's contaminated because it's linked to a hydropower station, which is classified because it falls under national security. As a result, 981 people died. We're talking about the basic capacity of government to do their job effectively. It's self-sabotage.

"There are some things that absolutely should be classified and top-secret, like, say, the blueprints of Pollsmoor Prison. But something like the housing lists should be public information. There are still people waiting for housing, and their impression is that their position on the list changes from month to month. And they might be right, or there might be serious dodginess going down, bribery and backhanders and corruption and illegal tenders, but we simply don't know. Because we don't have access to those lists, because they're classified. And why? Because people tend to get angry about housing screw-ups, which might lead to a riot, which might lead to them blockading the highway and overturning buses and burning tires, which then becomes a 'national security issue.'

"The problem is that you can justify almost anything as national security, and the guy who gets to decide what should be declassified is the same person who decided it was classified in the first place. So he's got the yes stamp in one hand and the no stamp in the other. It's mental. And all this is being sold to us as for our own good. 'Mama government and her Mongooses know best, now run along, dear, and write some more concerned letters to the newspapers.'"

When I try to raise some of these issues with Makhetha, she's very sympathetic. "I can understand that some people have concerns. But I'm afraid I can't discuss that, it's—"

"Classified?" I finish for her.

"Ah yes, your file says your communication style is antagonistic-sarcastic," she counters. "What I can tell you is that we know all about Clear. We've got keyword monitors set up on most of the major Chinese game servers, and we're already working on ways to embed nanoparticles in paper that will be able to relay the imprints of handwritten notes to our systems. What you have to understand is that this is a global issue. As fast as info terrorists can come up with new tactics, governments are working alongside to develop countermeasures."

As she shows me out, Makhetha adds mildly, "Of course you won't forget to submit the story for pre-approval as per the Media Patriot Act."

Of course not.

UNACCOUNTED

The ittaca is wedged into the uneven corner of cell 81C, as if it is trying to osmose right through the walls and out of here. It is starting to desiccate around the edges, the plump sulphur-colored frills of its membrane turning shriveled and grey. Maybe it's over, Staff Sergeant Chip Holloway thinks, looking in through the organic lattice of the viewing grate. The thought clenches in his gut.

He has been having problems with his gut lately. He blames it on the relentless crackle of the blister bombs topside. The impacts reverberate through the building, even here, three floors down. You'd think you would get used to it.

The Co-operative Intelligence Resource Manual does not cover this exact situation. The CIRM advises a recovery period for the delegate, a show of mutual respect to reestablish trust and, better yet, to instill gratitude. But the CIRM also advises that if a delegate is critical, it is critical to press on.

Terminal is not an ideal result. Terminal can be attributed to lack of due diligence.

The corridor stinks of urine. Not from the ittaca, which is anaerobic and recycles its waste through its body again and again, reabsorbing nutrients. Strip-mining food. It excretes sharp chlorine farts that puff from the arrangement of spongy tubes like organ pipes fanning down its dorsal side. Just one of the chemical weapons to watch out for in the ittaca's natural biological armament, according to *The Xenowarfare Handbook: Reaching Out to Viable Lifeforms*.

There is a splatter of piss on the door. He needs to have a word with K Squadron. He knows they're just frustrated. That camaraderie is sometimes expressed in casual acts of hooliganism. Still, the CIRM does not cover what to do when respect for your authority is fraying like the membrane frills of an ittaca's gastropod foot. When you keep hearing the word *maggots*, even though this is against protocol.

When they took occupation of the prison, there were ittaca med-scanners installed outside each cell, bacterial-powered screens monitoring vital signs: heart-rate, brain activity, adrenal spikes in the endocrine system that might indicate a prisoner about to erupt into violence. The first thing the military did was dismantle them.

They tore the screens off the walls, whooping and hollering, then piled up the ittacan tech in the open courtyard under the shadow of the guard tower—back when it was still standing—and set it alight.

Security risk, Command said. He never saw a formal directive. Good for morale, General Labuschagne said, when he queried it. C'mon, Holloway. Was he saying his people didn't deserve a little celebration? After everything they'd been through? It still made him feel uneasy, though. A waste of resources, he told himself.

He turned a mostly blind eye to the mulch moonshine being not-so-covertly distributed between the reserves because maybe the General had a point. But he circled the groups, making sure no one drank too much of the mildly psycho-tropic guano distillate, and made a note to find out who was brewing it. He'd have to have a word with them, too.

It all went wrong, of course. The light from the bonfire or maybe the music seemed to enrage the insurgents, drawing down a fresh assault by the blisters. Chip was the last one through the doors. Dragging Reserve Lieutenant Woyzeck with him, reeling drunk and swearing at him to let her go. Asshat. Shithead. Party pooper.

His eyebrows were seared off by the heat of a strike, the explosion scouring the reinforced coralcrete with venomous pus and shrapnel. Fucking Kazis, he heard, as someone slammed the door. He'd tried to discourage them from using the term as disrespectful to both the ittaca and those reserves of Japanese heritage. But the blisters are aerial suicide bombers, and what are you going to do?

You were fucking lucky, Chip, said Ensign Tate, leaving out the "sergeant," leaving out the "sir," because Holloway encouraged his people to call him by his first name. And was that grudging admiration in Tate's voice?

Chip found an unexploded blister in the courtyard once, deflated on one side and gagging on its own blood from the shrapnel tearing up its insides. Blisters swallow improvised weaponry whole, choking down nails and sharpened scrap metal and bits of coral through their gill slits, like an athlete carbo-loading before a game. Some of the reserves were using it as a football. He chased them off with a warning. But he couldn't bring himself to shoot it.

He can't blame the reserves. There isn't exactly much in the way of recreational facilities for them. Mainly they take pot-shots at the rats. Which are not rats, but something bald, skittering things the size of Rottweilers, with too many legs. They dig up body parts from shallow graves dug by the former regime and drag them around, scraping off the dried membrane with nubs like teeth, cracking the mantle spines to get to the marrow.

Let it not be said that the ittaca did not cast the first stone. Let it not be said that this was *ever* a good place to be.

Inside the cell, a spasm flutters through the ittaca's membrane, setting the spines along its mantle clattering. A xylophone made from insect's legs. Alive, then.

The ittacas don't bleed, exactly. They extrude a clear viscous liquid. Tacky, like sap. The first time, it took him forty-eight minutes and a full bottle of military issue stainEZ (guaranteed to take care of even the most stubborn bio-matter tarnish with just one drop!) to get the stickiness out of his uniform. He wasn't prepared for there to be a second time. But by the third, he wore an improvised poncho made out of a foil body bag.

He made a note of it in his weekly report. 1x body bag. He is careful to account for almost everything.

- 407 Military Reserve Soldiers (human) stationed at Strandford Military Base formerly known as Nyoka Prison Satellite Facility. (Temporary posting.) Broken down as follows: 241 Male. 113 Female. 53 NGS (non-gender-spec).

- 0 indigenous translators. (Complement of 7 were dismissed on charges of info leaks.)
- 123 ittaca delegates (alive) kept separate in 123 cells.
- 4 ittaca delegates (deceased) in morgue-lab.
- 18 blister delegates (deceased) in morgue-lab.
- 6037 blister delegates (deceased) processed through central crematorium.
- 550 TK-R surface-to-surface RPGs. Effective coralcrete penetration: 0.2%.
- 25 MGL-900s, HE grenades. Effective coralcrete penetration: 100%.
- 200 MXR-63 multifunction assault rifles plus parts + 80 000 x 45mm rounds.
- 50 000 x 30mm U-238 rounds, incendiary, armor-piercing + 5 x chainfed autocannons + mountings. Shelved. Useless. Who would have predicted that ittaca would be able to metabolize uranium?
- 263 268 carb-blasters (nutritional value as per military recommendations). Sufficient for 213 days of rations for full staff complement. They have been here for 189 days already. This does not fit the military definition of "temporary posting."
- 700 rebreathers, including ample issue for

visitors. And there are ample visitors. No rankings. No name tags. If it weren't for the rebreathers taken off their hooks, set back to recharge, they might be ghosts.

- 23 field decontamination tents
- 12 carbon atmosphere recyclers; includes 3 overflow tanks and 250 biohazard disposal bags.
- 24 x 12-tray silver sulfadiazine 1% topical cream packs for treatment of chemical burns. 1 tray missing.
- 1050 field-dressing packs plus standard meds.
- 800 standard saline packs plus first aid supply kits. All date-stamps have expired. (Bandages are bandages, aspirin is aspirin, General Labuschagne had said when he raised his concerns.)
- 499 body bags aka meat sacks aka take me home daddy.

Chip came here on the highest commendation. In the provinces, planet-side, he was a core cultural liaison with the ittaca in the villages. Strategically critical, they said. Hearts and minds. This was before everything went to shit. Sorry. Before relations devolved with the indigenous population and assertive action became necessary.

He learned the basics of the language, with its clicks and liquid gurgles, using a translator pod. But it turned out a lot of it was in the nuance of how you arranged your mantle spines. He was popular with the young potentials, which is how the ittaca describe their children. They would trail behind him on his rounds, popping and clicking, anthropological in their interest.

Command detonated the central guard tower in the courtyard. Too much of a target, the higher-ups said. It made no difference. The blisters kept launching themselves off the balconies of the apartment mounds surrounding the prison on a single propeller wing, spinning downwards like maple seeds, making that godawful crackling, screaming sound through their gills. Isn't static the sound of the Big Bang? Chip thinks, remembering the science shows he used to stream as a kid.

Before the siege intensified, before they'd been forced to retreat three floors underground, he used to walk the ramparts, taking in the view of the coralcrete apartments growing up in unsteady spirals, following chemical markers laid by ittaca architects. Even their slums are beautiful, he'd commented once to the sentry at the door. He'd been met with a blank stare.

The reserves found the ittacan architecture disorienting. The warren of grown tunnels intersecting at strange angles. They ended up sleeping in the cells. Six to a room. Not exactly army protocol. Not exactly good for discipline.

The results were inevitable. Soldiers cliqued up. They did things behind closed doors, regulation t-shirts stuffed into the viewing grates. Unauthorized sex. And other things.

What's the big deal. Chill. We're just blowing off steam. Tate and the others didn't say any of these things. They just stared at him and grinned those chimpanzee grins, all clenched jaws and contempt.

He included it in his report. He is careful to be accountable. He is careful to use neutral language. He is careful not to use the word "maggots."

Members of K Squadron (night duty) reprimanded for inappropriate behavior towards ittaca prisoners in Cell Block 3. Video evidence, taken by the relevant members involved, is attached.

He deletes that last part. Retypes it. Deletes it again. Leaves it at "videos were taken." Does not attach them. He is aware that it is a security risk to say even that much. He is aware that he isn't qualified to know what is inappropriate anymore.

Let's war.

He scrubs the videos. But he cannot shake the images. Or the sound of Tate's voice—the laughing that accompanied it—as he rounded the corner, on his way to dish out rations.

Maggots. Fucking maggots. Suck on this. Fuck you. Fuck.

There are items that he cannot account for. Things that were not on the facility inventory lists when he took over command of the prison, but that have mysteriously appeared. Bayonet tasers. Electrodes. High-density carbon-saws. A broken chunk of coralcrete in a pillowcase.

There are visitors. Irregular. Like ghosts. Did he already mention this? He's pretty sure they're MI. But they could just as easily be private contractors. Military development partners with an interest in developing new resources.

The reserves call them suits, but it's more the attitude than their attire. They wear sleek, expensive body-fitting hazmats. They don't carry identification or rank. They refuse to answer when he questions them. Should his people also be wearing protective gear? Has this been okayed by command? Why hasn't he received notification? Where is their clearance? Can he see some identification?

Don't ask, don't tell, one of the intelligence suits says to him, smiling behind her rebreather like it is all one big joke. Then she takes him into the ittaca's cell. This was two days after he made his report. Which received no official response.

You need to understand, the suit said. We're saving lives. Following orders.

And Chip has always been good at following orders, doing what needs to be done. But what he thinks is: *I am complicit.*

It was just a lark, *Chip*, Ensign Tate said, surly at being called into the cell that doubles as his office down here.

What Chip Holloway and the suit do to the ittaca in Cell 81C is not.

Not the first or the second or the third time.

He wishes the ittaca would fucking die already. He wishes the blisters would break through three floors and the whole damn moon and blow them all to smithereens. But mainly he wishes he could sleep and sleep and sleep. The exhaustion nags in his bones like arthritis.

You ready? asks the suit, appearing at his elbow. She flips open the viewing window. Looks like we don't have much time. Better stoke up the crematorium, baby. Oh yes, I brought you something. She reaches into the side of her toolkit and shoves a folded piece of plastic tarp at him. Surgical scrubs. Better than a rejigged body bag, she says.

She slides her chem-print keychain into the lock. The door grates open. In the corner the ittaca stirs, its spines clattering feebly. It resembles a clot of mustard. (Maggoty custard. A pile of pus-turd, he hears Ensign Tate's voice sing-songing in his head.)

Don't worry, says the suit, seeing his face—which has become something grey and sagging, something he doesn't recognize in the mirror. Like he is starting to desiccate, too.

She kneels down and snaps open her toolkit. Starts sorting through various unaccounted items, humming a tune he recognizes from the radio, sweet and catchy. Don't worry, she repeats, her back to him, laying out things with serrated edges and conducting pads and blunt wrenching teeth. You can't dehumanize something that isn't human.

TANKWA—KAROO

13h41.

The hottest part of the damn day and Rethabile is out in the thick of it, caught between the expanse of the reckless blue sky and the flat rocks, with sweat crawling down the back of his neck and sliding slick down his sides. He's off on a wild springkaan chase, because they need the eyes of the insectoid micro-drone in the sky if they are to protect themselves, protect their resources.

He tugs at the sodden Scorchd Afrika! t-shirt clinging to his skin. It's become a uniform, a way of telling Us versus Them, now that they've resolved Us versus Us. He doesn't even like EDM, he thinks.

The heat has its own gravity, smashing down in a way that stuns everything, even the fat desert flies. He squints against the light, trying to spot the giveaway gleam of the fisheye lens of the micro-drone. Maybe that's all they are out here,

Rethabile thinks, hollowed-out grasshoppers mindlessly responding to stimulus.

The gun holster chafes in Rethabile's armpit. He's not stupid enough to carry it tucked into the back of his cut-offs. Time was he wouldn't be seen dead in cut-offs. Time was he'd never held a gun.

Everything changes. Oh, you won't believe how fast it changes.

"Phase Three." Words he wishes he'd never heard, everyone bandying the phrase around the camp, breathless with importance and the footage coming down the x-fi.

Eleven days ago, they'd pulled up to Scorchd Afrika in Jamie's Audi A4, driving past the rusted sentinels of the gas drills strung with fairy lights, into the sprawling camp of converted shipping containers and wildly colored nomad tents and weird sculptures. A music festival in the middle of the remains of an old fracking operation in the nature reserve.

"Helluva place for a party," Rethabile sneered to Jamie, swatting at one of the buzzing drones that zoomed in to film them.

"Open mind, baby," Jamie sang back at him and went to hug some bouncy girls in Day-Glo catsuits. That'd teach him to date trendy white boys.

Helluva place for civilization's last stand.

Hippies, yuppies, techies, artists, aggressive young okes looking to get messed up, maybe score some chicks. All sorts. Like the sweeties. He could do with some of those now, Rethabile thinks, using his shirt to mop up the sweat on his face. Imagine: just walking into a café and buying a bag of licorice over the counter.

They're down to bugs now. He can get over the popcorn crunch, but the spiny legs that catch between his teeth still make him gag. Rethabile wasn't built for this. None of them were.

They got the news on the x-fi, before the Internet went down—turns out the Internet, like civilization, needs power. Accident in the Thokoza coal plant, too much power being drawn, the electrical grid overloaded. Eskom moved to Phase Three, which sounded innocuous enough—a little bit of load-shedding to keep things going. What they didn't say is that Phase Three means Eskom phoning the army and telling them to "get ready" because if the load-shedding doesn't work, the whole grid goes down. It takes two weeks to come back online. That's fourteen days of chaos in the dark. Get ready.

Scorchd had generators with petrol for a week, but gasoline couldn't keep the x-fi connections up for long. The news on the Internet was bleak. They all huddled round while DJ E-lise projected the live-feed from her retina input onto the white fabric wall of the medical tent. There were scenes of people being shot in the street. Riots, looting, a necklacing on the Sea Point promenade. They marveled at the images of soldiers with searchlights moving through Rosebank Mall, its shattered windows puking out luxury handbags and designer sneakers, ignored by the looters in favor of canned food and bottled water.

Half the camp bailed on day one of the news of Phase Three. They got in their four-wheel drives and their kombis and their bakkies and drove away until Crazy Eddie, the artist, got hold of a gun and threatened to shoot anyone else who tried to leave. With his shaved head, he looked like a poor man's Bruce Willis in bright orange Crocs and a camouflage kilt slung low under his pot belly. But a man with a gun is a man with authority, even wearing stupid shoes. He got them all breaking down the towering wooden sculptures they were supposed to burn and turning them into fortifications. "It's about preservation now, people," he pronounced, sitting on a leaning throne made out of car tires.

On day two, the music died. Crazy Eddie shot DJ E-lise in the head when she complained. "Power is life," he said and told them to bury her under a pile of rocks.

On day three, the x-fi finally went down, taking the news with it. They still had the springkaans, a hundred-strong swarm of tiny drones designed to broadcast the party to the outside world. Eddie had the techies turn their cameras outwards, patrolling the perimeter, but their range was limited and their batteries were dying—their grasshoppers fell one by one, but not before they'd captured human shapes moving out there. Eddie told them they had to "go dark." Rethabile had no idea where he got all the military jargon. Video games, maybe.

On day six, they took *all* the drugs and screwed for forty-eight hours straight—a bacchanalian up-yours to the apocalypse. They didn't count on waking up the next day, hungover, reeling, a little bit crazy. Crazier. Or maybe it was the heat climbing into their skulls and baking their brains.

On day eight, they started planning the insurrection. A Mfecane of their own, dividing along tribal lines, not

Moeshoeshoe versus the rednecks, but IT guys and hardcore chinas from Midrand against the artists and musos and the hey-shoo-wows.

Rethabile begged Jamie to stay out of it. They didn't have any skills, not like the others. What part did a media manager and a junior investment banker have in an uprising? But he wouldn't listen. Jamie had a strange light in his eyes, like a splinter of the bright broad sky had got caught in there. The desert does things to you.

There was fighting. Other people had brought weapons, in defiance of Scorchd party policy. They scrambled over the wood fortifications. They turned the sharp edges of mechanical sculptures into things that pierced and cut. Rethabile can't think about it too much—stabbing the girl with blonde dreadlocks in the throat and the fountain of blood that drenched him like sweat.

But no one was as mental as Crazy Eddie. No one was as ruthless. The insurrection was squashed. The pile of rocks got bigger. Jamie got a bullet in the gut trying to take control of the water tanks. It took him eight hours to die. Rethabile buried him with the rest of them. He cried till his eyes dried out.

Crazy Eddie was very forgiving. He said it wasn't Rethabile's fault Jamie was deluded. But now he would have to prove himself. There was one springkaan still transmitting, but it was down, somewhere to the east, among the rocks. They needed the drone. To find more water. To keep an eye out, because it was civil war out there, and the drones had spotted people moving around the perimeter. Strangers.

"Do you understand me, guy? I know you're bummed out about your friend, but it's Phase Three, man."

Eddie gave him the gun, placed it in his hands and patted it, like it was a baby needing burping. He had him pegged; figured that Rethabile wouldn't try to turn the gun on their leader.

Now, Rethabile scuffs at the dirt with his designer sneaker, which is splitting at the seams. He wanted to live. Is that so bad? When this is all that's left? He tries to imagine what the rest of the country looks like right now. Famine, death, cannibalism. He pictures the galleries and coffee shops in Braamfontein on fire, raging gun battles through the Constantia winelands, private security armies with machine guns taking control of the fenced-off suburbs. What's worse, he wonders, being ruled by private security like ADT or Crazy Eddie?

He swipes at his dry eyes with the back of his hand, too thirsty to be able to summon tears, and then he spots it: a glint in the grass. It's the chip embedded in the dying grasshopper's abdomen. The faceted glass of the lens is a cool, hard, all-seeing eye. He hopes Eddie is seeing this on their last monitor running on carefully hoarded gasoline. He hopes he gets extra water rations.

He scrambles up the hill and falls to his knees in the dust beside the springkaan. He scoops it up, and the metal wings of the micro-drone buzz in his hands. He could kiss it. His salvation. He looks towards the burning white orb in the sky and, sees, from this vantage point, a shimmer of road in the distance, and a shape that he'd mistaken for another rotting drill bit—a water tower.

"Thank you, sweet Jesus," he croaks.

"It's Frank, actually," a stranger says, stepping up over the rocks, blocking out the sun. He looks like a cowboy, but with a floppier hat. Rethabile shades his eyes, taking in the aviator sunglasses, dark-green uniform, the gun on his hip, the Parks Board insignia stitched on his epaulets.

"You one of those party people?" Frank says, his voice disapproving.

"Yes. No." Rethabile is not sure what the right answer is. He wants to run to the road, to climb the water tower and sink into the cool black depths and let the water cover his head and never come up.

"We've been trying to reach you people."

Rethabile jabs the drone at him. "Don't even try. The springkaan sees you. We got guns! You leave us alone! They'll shoot you if you come near!"

"Why would you shoot?"

"The war, you idiot." Rethabile is hysterical. "The civil war. Chaos! Cannibalism! We don't have enough to go around! It's safety first."

Frank takes off his sunglasses and folds them away in his pocket. "You have heatstroke, my friend. You need to get some shade and some water."

"Eskom! Phase Three!"

"Oh, that," Frank says mildly.

"Yes, that! All that!" And all this. The insurrection. Lord of the Springkaans.

"Ag, man." Frank takes out rolling papers and sprinkles tobacco into the fold. "There was some kak around that, but we came through."

"We came through?" Rethabile repeats dumbly.

"Sure. Come on, man. Are you kidding me?" He sticks the roll-up between Rethabile's lips and lights it for him. "This country doesn't fall apart *that* easy."

EXHIBITIONIST

I'm feeling fractal by the time I reach Propellor. There is already spillage out the doors, which can only be a good sign, seeing as it's just gone six thirty, but it makes me feel edgier.

"You're late." Jonathan latches on to my arm at the door, and swishes me inside through the crowd. I can't believe how many people there are, crowded into the gallery, but of course it's not just for me, or for my retro print photographs.

Most people are here to see Khanyi Nkosi's sound installation, fresh returned from her São Paolo show and all the resulting controversy. It's the first time I've seen it in the flesh. The thing is gore-deluxe, red and meaty, like something dead turned inside out and mangled, half-collapsed in on itself with spines and ridges and fleshy strings and some kind of built-in speakers, which makes the name even more disturbing—*Woof & Tweet.*

I don't understand how it works, but it's to do with reverb and built-in resonator-speakers. It's culling sounds from around us, remixing ambient audio, conversation, footsteps, glasses clinking, rustling clothing, through the systems of its body, disjointed parts of it inflating, like it's breathing.

It's hard to hear it over the hubbub, but sometimes it's like words, almost recognizable. But mostly it's just noise, a fractured music undercut with jarring sounds that seem to come at random. Sometimes it sounds like pain.

It's an animal, right? Or alive at any rate. Some lab-manufactured plastech bio-breed with just enough brainstem to respond to input in different ways, so it's unpredictable—but not enough to feel pain, apparently.

"It's gratuitous. She could have done it any other way. It could have looked like anything. It could have been beautiful."

"Like something you'd put in your lounge? Please, Kendra. It's supposed to be revolting. It's that whole Tokyo tech-grotesque thing. Actually, it's so fucking derivative, I can't stand it. Can we move along?"

I run my hand along one of the ridges and the thing quivers, but I can't determine any difference noticeable in the sounds. "Do you think it gets traumatized?"

"It's just noise, okay? You're as bad as that nut job who threw blood at her at the Jozi exhibition. It doesn't have nerve endings, okay? Or no, wait, sorry, it does have nerve endings, but it doesn't have pain receptors."

"I meant, do you think it gets upset? By all the attention? I mean, isn't it supposed to be able to pick up moods, reflect the vibe?"

"Christ knows. I think that's all bullshit, but you could ask the artist. She's over there schmoozing with the money, like you should be."

Woof & Tweet suddenly kicks out a looped fragment of a woman's laugh, which startles me, before sliding down the scale into a fuzzy electronica.

"See, it likes you."

"Don't be a jerk, Jonathan."

"There's a journalist who wants to interview you, by the way. And he's pretty cute."

My stomach spasms. This is another thing Jonathan does to keep me in my place, to make it razor that we're not together. My shrinkable tells me I'm still in love with him. Well, actually, he didn't: he let me figure that out for myself, which cost a little more, more wasted time, when apparently he had the answer all along.

What my psych does tell me, of his own accord, after this revelation, is that I should cut Jonathan off, get some distance, recover a sense of self. He uses a lot of shrink-speak that doesn't translate—it only applies to someone else's ordered life, where the rules work. But it's complicated. Jonathan was the one who orchestrated this exhibition—or should that be exhibitionism, because isn't it my soul being laid bare here?

I know Jonathan is intending to sleep with me again. It's been real casual since we broke up, only a couple of times, but it's still happening, even though he's seen at least two other women that I know about in between. Just fuckbuddies, he says.

I met the one, Marinda, at a party. One of those awful media types, hanging off him like she was his handbag. Old bag. Thirty-eight at least. An editor at one of the pushmags he works for occasionally. One of the perks of the job—fraternizing with the help.

Of course, Jonathan is thirty-two, so he's right up there with her. Closer to her than me. And was it just imagination, or did she scope me with just a shade of pity? First time we met, I asked to take her picture. Jonathan kissed me on the head, whispering, "You cunning little fox, sweetheart. You just guaranteed yourself a publicity splash. We'll have to make the event worthy of the write-up."

But I was more interested in reducing her to planes of color, the hard sculptural form of her bones. The print I went with was an accidental, a misfire, while I was adjusting the light settings. She is sitting on the edge of the twist of spiral stair on the fire escape outside a party. The focus is on the shapely knot of her knee, one hand resting in the dark fall of her skirt, the other touching her mouth, although you can only see the angle of her jaw tilted out of frame. It makes her look vulnerable.

I glance over at my pictures, partially obscured by the swilling crowd. Only one of my prints has turned out perfect. An image that appears abstract, but on closer inspection resolves itself an anonymous blur against the edge of a doorway, wrecked wood and the liquid swirl of graffiti, the paint still wet and dripping in runnels, so that it is all sharp-focus texture.

The others have not come out so distinctively, and Sanjay is still a tad uncertain about the whole shebang, about how the critics will take them all. The overexposed and under-, the bleached, washed-out, over-saturated with color, the ones with blotches and speckles and stains like coffee-cup rings, or the buttresses of white that frame the horizontal top and bottom, where the canister has cracked and let the light slip inside. My favorite is called *Self-Portrait*. A print from a decayed piece of film. 1m x 3.5m. It came out entirely black.

Jonathan propels me in the direction of Sanjay, who is standing in deep conversation with two other people. The one is clearly money, some corporati culture patron or art buyer, the other, I realize with a shock, is Khanyi Nkosi. I recognize her from an interview I saw, but she is so warmly energetic, waving her hands in the air to make a point and grinning, that I can't match her with her work.

I realize I can't deal, and checking that Jonathan is intent on pushing through the queue at the bar, I detour back towards the entrance and the open air—only to skewer someone's foot with the blue velvet heels I bought for the occasion.

"Hey! Easy!"

"Oh god, I'm sorry." Shit, I really, really, really need a cigarette. I wonder if I can make it to the spaza down the road and back before Jonathan notices.

"No worries. You're the artist, right?"

"Um, yeah. Yeah, or the photographer, anyway. I'm not, I mean, the thing—*Woof*—that's not mine."

"Yeah, I'm Osiame. I'm from *Sonar*?"

"Oh, right. The journalist, right? Hi." Vaguely, I note that he *is* cute, but I'm distracted by nerves.

Osiame touches my shoulder, which only irritates me more. "Do you have a drink?"

"No. Someone's getting me one."

"Oh, okay. Listen, if you want, we can talk later. I know it's your opening and you've got things to do, people to schmooze."

"Actually, do you want to get out of here?"

"What?"

"Just for a sec. I need some fresh air. And a smoke."

"Isn't that a contradiction?"

"You want to come?"

"Oh. Okay, sure."

We're not the only people hanging outside. I cadge a cigarette from a blonde, familiar from other events, with fucked-up hair, cut ugly on purpose.

"She makes me feel conservative," I confide to Osiame as he lights up for me. "But that doesn't make it into the copy, okay?"

He holds up his hands. "Do you see me making notes?"

I inhale deeply. "So, can we go ahead, get it out of the way? The interview."

"Am I allowed to take notes now?"

"Yeah-yeah." I wave my hand.

He hooks a mic into his phone and points it at my mouth. "So. What's with the old school?"

"Didn't you read the press release?"

"Let's say I didn't."

I quote it from memory. "Adams's use of non-digital format is inspired by her fascination with the capacity for error . . ."

"Okay. Let's skip the press release."

"Ah, it's just—film is more interesting than digital. There's a possibility of flaw inherent in the material. It's not readily available, so I have to get it over the Net, and some of it has rotted or it's been exposed even before I load it in the camera, but I don't know that until I develop it."

"Like *Self-Portrait*?"

"And it's not just the film. It's working without the automatic. The operator can fuck up too."

"Did you fuck up?"

"Ha! That's the great thing about working with damaged materials. You'll never know. Actually, it's the same in audio. Digital was too clean when it first came out, almost antiseptic. The fidelity was too clear, you lost the background noises, the ones you don't even pick up, but it's dead without the context."

"Like a sound aura."

"So they had to adapt the digital to synth analogue. You can do the same thing in photography. Apply effects, lock out the autofocus, click up for exposure, all to recreate the manual. It's contentious though, now the audio techs are saying it's been nonsense all along, just nostalgics missing the hiss of the recording equipment. So it's reverted now again. Who knows."

"So you're looking for the background noise."

"Yeah. Or something like." I drop the stompie, twist it under my heel. "Got enough?"

"Yeah. I'm good. You give good soundbite," he says admiringly, flirtatious even.

The gallery seems less oppressive. I'm less freaked, even when I overhear some over-groomed loft dwellers giggling into their wine. "And this. I'm so tired of Statement! Like she's the only angst child ever to embrace the distorted body image."

"Oh, I quite like the undeveloped. Because she is. You know, still young, coming into herself. The artist in flux, emergent."

"Well precisely. It's so *young*. You can't even tell if it's technically good or not, it's all so . . . damaged."

Amused, I'm about to lean in, to point out that *Self-Portrait* is not actually that at all. That under the black is a photograph of a photograph, clutched in my fingers, captured in the mirror with a reflected flash of light. That it's all meant to be damaged. But then I realize I don't have to make my motives transparent.

I'm distracted by a flurry of activity at the door. There are people shoving, wine spilling from glasses, yelps of dismay.

"This is a private function!" Jonathan yells, spouting clichés at the rush of people in black who are pushing in through the crowd, their faces blurred like they're anonymous informants in documentary footage. It is so disturbing, it takes me a second to catch on that they're wearing smear masks. Another to realize that they're carrying pangas.

A few people scream, sending out a reverb chorus from *Woof & Tweet*. The crowd pressing backwards. But then the big guy in front yells, "Death to corporate art!" and Emily, the woman who dissed my work, laughs scornfully. "Oh god! Performance art. How dreadful gauche." And there are murmurs of relief and snickers, and the living organism that is the crowd now pushes forward again to see.

Osiame grabs my arm and pulls me back out of the front line, because I haven't moved this whole while, just as one of the men (women?) grabs Emily by her hair and forces her to her knees, spitting with rage, "Don't you dare make me complicit in your garbage!"

The black-clad one raises the panga, pulling back Emily's head by the roots of her hair, exposing her throat. Emily raises a hand to her mouth, pretends to stifle a yawn.

"Are you going to chop me into little itty-bitty pieces now? Oh please. This is so melodramatic." And it is. The crowd is riveted. But I didn't think this kind of promo stunt would be Sanjay's thing.

The man jerks her head back further and, bowing his legs, moves his arm as if to slice across her throat, only at the last instant—so late that she winces back involuntarily—deflecting to a side-swipe—not at her, but at *Woof & Tweet*, just in front of them.

The thing emits a lean crackle of white noise. The audience is rapt, camera phones clicking, as the others move in, five of them, with one guarding the door, to start laying into it. It's only when the artist starts wailing that it becomes apparent that this was not part of the program.

The pangas tear into the thin flesh and ribs of Khanyi Nkosi's thing with a noise like someone attacking a bicycle with an axe. The machine responds with a high-hat backbeat for the melody it assembles from the screams and skitters of nervous laughter. It doesn't die quietly, transmuting the ruckus, the frantic calls to the police, and Khanyi wailing, clawing, held back by a throng of people.

The bright sprays of blood make it real, spattering the walls, people's faces, my photographs, as the blades thwack down again and again. The police sirens in the distance are echoed and distorted as *Woof* finally collapses in on itself, rattling with wet, smacking sounds.

They disappear out into the streets as quickly as they

came, shaking the machetes at us, threatening, don't follow, whooping like kids. With the sirens closing in, one spits on the mangled corpse. Then, before he ducks out the door and into the night, glances up once, at the ceiling. No one else seems to notice, but I follow his gaze up, to the security cams, getting every angle.

I'm sick with adrenaline. The woman who was taken hostage is screaming in brittle hyperventilating gasps. Her friend is trying to wipe the blood off her face, using the hem of her dress, unaware that she has lifted it so high that she is flashing her lacy briefs. Khanyi is kneeling next to the gobs of her animal construct, trying to reassemble it, smearing herself with the bloody lumps of flesh. There is a man trying to comfort the girl with the jagged blonde hair, but he is the one weeping, laid waste by the shock, while she lights cigarette after cigarette, her hands shaking.

There is still a prevailing undercurrent of thrill, a rush from the violence, because no one was hurt, except the thing. Everyone is on their phones, taking pictures, talking. Osiame is shouting above the ruckus, to his editor no doubt, and there are even more people trying to wedge into the space, so that the cops, who have finally arrived, have to shove their way inside.

Self-Portrait is covered in a mist of blood. I move to wipe it clean, although I'm scared the blood will smear, will stain the paper, but just then Jonathan takes my wrist, wraps his arms around me and kisses my neck.

"Don't ruin the effect, sweetheart," he whispers, his breath hot against my throat. "Do you know how much this is going to be worth?"

I glance up at the cameras again. The beady red lights, the unblinking lenses recording everything. Already the cops are asking for the footage. Jonathan kisses my neck again and grins. "You were magnificent."

DIAL TONE

A t first, she chose them at random. Opening the phone book, she'd drift over names with her fingertips.

"Hello?"

In time, she would refine her methods. She'd choose names she liked the sound of. Gamboni or Ndudlu. It was less fickle than chance. It allowed her to feel more attached.

"Frenkel residence?"

Sometimes she didn't look at the names at all. The symmetry of the numbers was enough. She'd find patterns, repetitions. Some combinations had a cadence that she found pleasing. She made little mantras out of them. 93-0-12-12. 426-526-4. 88-9-12-59. Skipping rhymes.

"Sandy?"

Sometimes, but only sometimes, she would just dial. Haphazard configurations. Although this worked least well of all.

"Is that you?"

She found an old-fashioned rotary phone in a junk shop. She liked the click of the dial spinning back when she released it. She liked the solid weight of the handset. It was carbon-colored, a muted grey, a plastic pigeon color. It was scratched. The woman sold it to her for peanuts.

"Hi? Can you hear me?"

Her name wasn't listed in the phone book. On the form from the phone company, she'd left that particular box unchecked.

"Helloooo? You're going to have to phone back. I can't hear a thing."

She liked it best when there were ghosts on the line. It had only happened once, though. When she heard the woman's voice, so confident, mid-stride, she'd been taken aback. Talking about avocados. Of all the banal things in the world. And then the man had said:

"Who's there?"

She kept hoping it would happen again.

"Is anyone there?"

She pretended she was part of their conversation. She pretended she had strong opinions about avocados. They couldn't hear anything she said. Perhaps she was the ghost.

"I think you have the wrong number."

She had rules. She learned to avoid women. When she could, when it was possible. Sometimes the phonebook didn't say. There was only so much she could tell from the crisp initial.

"Who the fuck is this?"

She was careful. She crossed names off. She never phoned

the same number more than twice. Not after the man whispering fiercely into the phone. Pervert. Freak.

"Time to follow. When you hear the signal, it will be twenty-two hours forty-two minutes and thirty seconds. "

She tried the Internet once. At a café with neon lights and coffee and a skinny kid playing computer games with fast-moving square-faced men and guns. The waitress had a tiny stud in her nose. She had asked her if everything was okay.

"Four. Three. Eight. One. Five. Two. Four. is not available right now. Please leave a detailed message after the tone."

She had left a message. For Goldenbaum. B. 788-166-0.

"Hi! We're not in at the moment . . ."

Only she didn't say anything. She thought she might have. Until the machine cut her off.

"Hello? Hello, hello, hello?"

She listened for the question mark. For the anticipation.

"I'm sorry. The number you have dialed does not exist."

Sometimes she would just pick up the handset and listen to the dial tone. Sometimes that was enough.

GHOST GIRL

You might think of a city as a map, all knotted up in the bondage of grid lines by town planners. But really, it's a language—alive, untidy, ungrammatical. The meaning of things rearranges, so the scramble of the docks turns hipster cool while the faded glamor of the inner city gives way to tenement blocks rotting from the inside. It develops its own accent, its own slang. And sometimes it drops a sentence. Sometimes the sentence finds you. And won't shut up.

I'm walking through the gardens on my way to an exhibition on Pancho Guedes, the crazy post-modern Surrealist Mozambican-Portuguese architect, because that's my major (only three and a half years to go) when a voice drifts down out of a tree: "Hey, cute student guy, wait up."

A girl drops down from the branches where she's been perching like some tree frog in black amongst the squirrels and starts strolling along behind me, imitating my walk like a bad mime.

I turn, irritated. "What are you doing?"

"Attaching," she says. "It's what the dead do when they get lonely."

It's obviously an art-school prank or, worse, a project. Like that tosser, Ed Young, who stages pointless events with buckets of fried chicken and beer and strippers with scarily over-inflated boobs and pouted lips, like they'd been blowing up balloons and the balloons blew back. Campus is only a block away.

"I'm really not interested," I tell the girl still riding at my heels, like she's a surfer who has caught a wave. She busts me looking around furtively for the rest of her posse, for someone with a video camera.

"Oh don't worry," she says, "I'm all yours. Rule 285a, subclause iii. *Only the embodied attachee, also known as the 'living', will be able to physically observe his or her attacher, also known as the 'apparition'.*"

"Oh." There isn't a whole lot more to add.

She giggles. "I just made that up." And then, wistfully, "They're not much for rules on this side."

"Look, could you leave me alone?" I say. And by the time I look back, she is already gone. Which is why it's all the more annoying to find her waiting for me in the lecture theater the next day.

She's sitting in my usual place, last chair, second row from the back, so I can sneak out for a smoke break if the lecture drags. She's swinging her legs like a kid, which I guess she is. She can't be older than fourteen, the eyeliner crayon-scrawled around her eyes as if by a toddler with more enthusiasm than hand-eye coordination.

I slide into the row, intent on ignoring her, when Noluthando rolls up—the last person I wanted to see after the drama last weekend.

"Sekwa, 'sup sweetcakes?" my sometime girlfriend says. "You've been keeping a low profile." She throws herself into the seat beside me.

"Hey," I say, annoyed. "Can't you see—?"

But apparently she can't. Because she sits down right on top of the girl.

"Crap," the girl says and pops like a bubble, leaving a smoky shimmer in the air behind her.

"Don't look at me like that," Noluthando says, tucking her arms across her chest like a police barricade. "I mean, I know things went a little south on Friday . . ."

"A little south" is her euphemism for getting wasted, having a screaming argument with the bartender over whether he gave her two full shots of Jack or not, projectiling a liquid dinner all over the windscreen when I was driving her home (which means my car will probably reek of cheap bourbon forever) and then grabbing the steering wheel on the highway, pretending it was Grand Theft Auto. Luckily we didn't hit any pedestrians for extra points. But that's not the reason I'm looking at Nolly like that. I'm not even looking at her. I'm looking at the space where the girl was.

The girl is waiting for me on the stairs, sitting hunched, staring at the scuffed silver toes of her spray-painted Doc Martens as if they could reveal the meaning of life, or maybe a scrolling news bar, à la CNN.

"Finally," she says, scrambling to her feet. "I thought you'd come look for me at least."

"Clearly I didn't need to," I say. I'm not even freaked. Much. It's weird how people can adjust to anything. One moment you're going about your normal life. The next you're talking to dead girls.

"Who was that woman?" she says, bouncing alongside me. "Your energy was all tangled up. Like you'd been having se-ee-eex," she sing-songs.

"You jealous?"

"Mmmf," the girl says, noncommittal. "If I was, I could just, you know, eat her heart or something."

She sees my face.

"Kidding!" she says. "Unless, you know, you really wanted me to."

I give her a look.

"So, don't you want to know how I died?" the girl asks.

"Not particularly."

"Come on. Ask me. You know you want to."

"All right. Fine. How did you die?"

She gets a little crease between her eyebrows, which are over-plucked. It makes her look even more little girl under the makeup.

"I committed suicide. Over a boy." She points to a high window in the Tugwell Hall res. "I jumped out of that window. I would have lived, probably, only the oleander tree that used to be there broke my fall and a branch snapped right through me and my blood ran down the branches and clotted in the leaves and mingled with the poison sap, ruby dark against the white bark."

"Really?"

"No. But wouldn't that have been romantic?"

"I don't have to listen to this."

"Okay, I'm sorry," the ghost girl says. "It was consumption." She coughs, delicately tragic, like Nicole Kidman in *Moulin Rouge*.

"You know that's TB, right? Millions of people have it. Coughing up, what do they call it, sputum? It's this bloody phlegmy stuff that clogs up your lungs like custard."

"Gross."

"Yeah. That's what I thought. Busted." She has the grace to look guilty for all of 2.3 seconds.

"Don't you have somewhere to go?" I say, dropping the hint like a dump truck of sand.

She shrugs. "No."

"Wow, your room is really messy," she says with admiration, excavating a book from the landfill of papers and sketches and a take-away pizza box. It's the one on Frank Gehry. Now thirty-seven days overdue. I know because the university library sends regular curt reminders to my inbox.

"Can you—just put that down. Don't touch anything."

"Is this real?" She turns the book to show me a picture of the Frederick R. Weisman Art Museum with its swells of hard angles, more structured than the abstract swirls of the new Guggenheim, but still damn cool. "Like a real building? It looks like he just crumpled up a bunch of tinfoil and built that."

"Even the strangest concoctions of our imaginations have

to do with humanist values," I say, quoting his interview from the *New York Times*. I only know this because it was an essay topic. Discuss.

"What does that even mean?" the girl says.

"It means he feels like his creativity is enough social responsibility. He doesn't have to prove anything by building homeless shelters."

"So, I was wondering. That John Edward guy?" My mouth is half-full of sandwich—peanut butter and white bread with the mold cut off, because it's the end of the month and my wallet is bare, never mind the cupboard.

"Oh, he's got it all right," she says. "Serious talent." She is sitting on a cleared section of desk next to the skeleton of my model-in-the-making for the new university sports center. I've restarted it and abandoned it six times already.

"Because I read this thing about how it's cold reading, you know, picking up cues from the audience and just throwing out random stuff, seeing if anyone bites. Apparently he's not very good at it. Has these hardcore non-disclosure agreements because the filming takes five hours of guesswork."

"Nope. He's the real deal."

"Oh."

"You seem bummed."

"Well, it's just that nobody ever has anything really juicy to say about the afterlife. It's just hi to Aunt Mathilda and look after DeShawn and your gran misses you."

"Maybe John Edward just attracts really dull ghosts."

"Really?"

"How would I know?" she snaps. "Have I ever been to America?"

———————

"It's too serious. It's boring," the girl says, lying hanging upside down from the couch, her hair on the floor, her legs stretched up like exclamation marks. She's watching me cut and glue the balsa wood onto the frame of the model, sitting on a carpet of newspaper because I can't be bothered to clear the desk.

"That's the brief, numbskull. Have you seen the old sports center? It's hideous. You have to start with the purpose of a thing and build on from there."

Actually, I'm proud of it—the clean modern lines, the glass, the eco-friendly features. It's practical.

"I still think it's boring," the girl says.

"Good thing no one's asking you."

"Good thing no one's ever going to build that boring thing!"

"Good thing ghost girls can't be architects!"

"Good thing ghost girls never wanted to be!"

We're both grinning.

"You know, for a pesky emo dead girl, you're okay."

"At least I'm never boring."

"But I promised!" Nolly yelps, turning from the freezer door and the bottle of vodka she's stashing to chill for half an hour. "It's Sarah's going-away party. People don't just go to London every day."

"Actually—" It's like a rite of passage for young South Africans. Working holiday visa. Earn pounds. Blow them on cheap beer and backpacking around Spain.

"You know what I mean! Don't be a dick, Sekwa."

"Come on, Nolly, you know I have to work on this project. I'm way behind. It's part of my year mark."

"That's just pathetic. It's Saturday night, you fucking loser."

"Don't swear at me."

"Then don't be such a spoilsport! It's one night. How much difference is one night gonna make?"

"She's not even my friend, Nolly. I barely know her. I don't think we've ever even had a conversation."

"I can't believe you're doing this to me!"

"Can you close the freezer please? You're letting the cold air out."

"Fuck!" She screams the word, reaches into the compartment, plucks out the frozen chicken and hurls it across the room at me. "Fuck you, you fucking fuck! You asshole!"

The chicken misses my head. Not by much. It leaves a dent in the paint on the wall. Nolly has the presence of mind to take the vodka with her when she storms out.

"That girl is crazy," the ghost girl says, dabbing up shards of rapidly melting ice from the floor with a dish towel.

"Look who's talking," I snap.

Sunday night Nolly and I break up. Four and a half hours of arguing later, we're back together. I don't know how this works. Another fight like this and we'll be engaged.

The make-up sex is almost worth it, until I catch the ghost girl out of the corner of my eye, sitting on the desk, watching with her head cocked like a scruffy dark bird.

"Baaaaaby, where are you going?" Nolly says, as I disentangle myself and lurch towards the bathroom, grabbing my t-shirt from the end of the bed.

The girl takes the hint and follows me in. I shut the door behind her, clutching the shirt over my groin.

"Sex is pretty silly," the girl says, like she's been giving this a lot of thought.

"What are you doing? Seriously. What the hell?"

"I was curious."

"This is inappropriate on so many levels."

"It's not my fault. There's so much stuff I've missed out on."

"So you're just gonna watch me have sex? No ways. Forget it. You're just a kid."

She hunches her shoulders, like she really is a scrawny bird about to take flight, when Nolly's voice calls from next door. "Sekwa? What are you doing in there? Giving yourself a pep talk? I can go easy on you, baby. Just come back to bed."

I lower my voice. "You're being creepy and I want you to cut it out. Now."

Ghost girl glares at me. "Whatever. I'll catch you later. When she's gone."

The next day, I am hungover from an overdose of sex and emotion and lack of sleep and an unhealthy amount of vodka, which Nolly brought back with her, because after all that, she ditched the lame going-away party and went out with her friends. In other words, I'm not in the mood for communing with spirits, unless it's more vodka.

But the girl is waiting for me, playing with the neighbor's ginger cat in the apartment's scrubby communal garden. I walk right past her.

"So, don't you want to know how I really died?" she says, dropping in step beside me.

"No."

"Come on."

"Nope."

"Please?"

"Not a chance. Not even vaguely interested."

"I could tell you how you're going to die."

"Don't even think about it."

"You're going to—"

"Shut up. I mean it."

"You're so un-fun."

"Well at least I'm not obvious."

"What do you mean?"

"I mean, couldn't you just—"

"What? Leave you alone? Stop bugging you? Eat someone's heart? I could you know. Just give me the word." She bares her teeth like a little animal.

"No! I was saying couldn't you be a little less predictable? You know. The black make-up, the Docs, the whole gothic romance? It's so hackneyed. It's embarrassing."

She looks like I imagine someone does when you rip out their heart and take a giant bite of it in front of them. Her eyes turn bright and liquid and then she pops like a bubble.

And I'm alone.

———

Pancho Guedes authored over five hundred buildings in Mozambique and more on paper, fantastic architectural whimsies, partly inspired by the Surrealists and partly by African art, all of it fermented in his brain. The bastard offspring of his imagination are sci-fi rondavel curves woven into the stark angles of wood carvings and Cubism.

He was intent on maintaining purity of vision for his students. He didn't want them corrupted by European influences. When Malangatana asked to see his art books, he reportedly snapped, "These are not for you," and squirreled them away.

When the revolution came, he lost everything. He moved to Portugal. Went back to the drawing board.

Most of his major works are designs only: storeys that were never built, stories that were never completed.

Nolly has a car accident. I should have seen this coming. I'm her speed dial 2, so I'm the one Jaco, the witness, calls when he finally finds her phone lodged between the passenger seat and the gearshift among a confetti of broken glass.

I'm the first on the scene after Jaco, who was on his way to the casino for a bit of a razzle, he says, after the tow-truck drivers and the paramedics, but before the cops, who have been dealing with an armed robbery in Observatory.

"Has she been drinking?" is the first thing they ask. The tow-truck driver warned me about this, that her insurance might not cover her if she has.

"No," I lie. "I gave her a nip, to get her to calm down. Better than Rescue Remedy, right?" I hold up a bottle of Teacher's that has been rolling around in my trunk since the last party we went to. It is almost empty.

"Have you been drinking?" they demand to know.

The hospital is schizo. This is not a good thing for a hospital to be. The historic thirties façade with its palm trees and turrets looks like a genteel resort asylum, maybe the kind of place Gatsby would have come to dry out.

But the modern section screams of functional bureaucracy, a thoughtless graft by a careless surgeon who didn't give a damn about the messy stitching or adding another arm to a patient who already had two.

The incinerator smokestack vents black smoke into the sky above the prim turrets, the morass of medical waste miraculously transmogrified. Ashes to ashes.

It takes me twenty minutes to find parking.

Casualty is a mess of humanity. There is a line of people in various states of trauma, like they're posing for illustrations for a medical dictionary.

There is a woman ODing on the floor, her limbs stuttering reenactments of eighties dance moves while the nurses try half-heartedly to restrain her. There are two cops wedged on either side of a man with a fake leather jacket and a knife wound to his head. There is a pool of blood on the floor, bright red and frothy. I manage to stand in the edge of it. I don't notice this until a nurse, too tired to be pissed off, points out the bloody crescent moon of sneaker prints I have tracked across the sickly mint of the linoleum. The nurse has hollows under her eyes so sunken they seem to be trying to swallow them whole.

Nolly has already been whisked right in. Store this for

future reference, kids, just like rocking up outside a club in a limo, making your entrance en ambulance will get you bumped straight to the front of the queue.

"Well, look who it is," the ghost girl says. I almost don't recognize her. She is wearing a purple and chocolate pleated dress, all seventies retro, and a pinstripe fedora like she's trying to bring sexy back.

"This isn't a good time," I say.

"Is there anything I can do?" the girl says.

"I don't know. Is there?"

Maybe it comes out sharper than I intended.

The X-rays come back. Nolly's ribs are cracked, not broken, which is lucky, because they could have punctured her lungs. It's hard to breathe blood. Her sternum has a hairline fracture, her heart is possibly bruised, but only a cardiologist can say, and they're in short supply at three in the morning.

Her left ankle is bust, her right arm broken in two places. Her face has split like a seam where the steering wheel leapt up to meet her mouth, like an over-eager lover moving in for the kiss and clashing teeth. Full frontal into a tree will do that.

They won't be able to determine if there is any damage to her brain until she regains consciousness.

"But she was just talking to me," I explain.

The nurse shrugs. "Head injuries."

"Did you know?" I ask the girl, when we're finally admitted through the double doors and into ICU, standing hushed beside Nolly's bed like it's Snow White's glass coffin, or maybe Lenin's, if we're going by the puffiness of her poor swollen face.

The girl doesn't answer. Something occurs to me. "Did you do this?"

I eventually find her huddled in a maintenance closet. Her tears spill down her cheeks and the end of her nose and then disengage with physics completely and float up towards the ceiling like condensation on a windscreen when you're speeding in the rain.

"Leave me alone."

"I'm sorry."

"You should be."

"At least I came looking."

"I guess," she sniffs.

"Neat trick," I say, indicating the glassy beads of her tears drifting up over us and away into the air.

"Thanks." She wipes her nose with the back of her sleeve.

"Can I join you?" I don't wait for an answer, just plonk myself down beside her, ducking my head under a shelf laden with cardboard boxes of rubber gloves and swabs. I pull the door closed with the toe of my sneaker.

"If someone finds you in here, they'll think you're a total freak," she says.

"Won't be far off, then. But not nearly as much of a freak as you."

She smiles despite herself and punches my arm. "You're the freak."

"No, you."

"You!"

We sit quietly in the dark for a while.

"So how did you die? Really?" I ask her.

"I can't tell you."

"Because it was really horrible? You can't remember?"

"You'll think I'm lame."

"What, you mean you weren't consumed in the terrible fire in the orphanage, refusing to leave little Becca's side? You didn't drown in a tragic yachting accident? Get run over trying to save a kitty in the middle of the road?"

"You're not funny."

"Just tell me."

"I fell off a bench."

"How high was this bench?"

"Normal bench height. Two feet off the ground or whatever. I sort of missed when I sat down."

"You sort of missed?"

"Oh, like you've never miscalculated! Look, do you want to hear this or not?"

"I'm sorry."

"So I thought the bench was closer than it was and I kinda fell back and I was laughing and I hit my neck on the strut on the back. Right here?"

She touches the tender little hollow among the wisps of hair where the vertebrae of the spine connect with the skull, the keystone holding the human body together.

"And that was it."

"Jesus."

"Yeah, he didn't show up. I was expecting him to, you know? But no one did."

It takes time.

Nolly cries a lot and demands more painkillers. We play cards. She cheats. I let her. The brace they've locked her in looks like scaffolding, but like scaffolding it's temporary. It'll come off, eventually.

Her family upgrades her to a private hospital, a private room. It's always full of flowers, so I bring her other things to take her mind off the pain: books and homemade chocolates from the German deli in town. At the ghost girl's insistence, I pick up quirky stuff that might amuse her at the flea market, like a menagerie of porcelain circus animals.

Her family and friends buzz around her bedside. Her brother gives me looks like it's all my fault. Maybe it is.

"I thought he was dead," I say, still shocked. It seems impossible that he would be here, in person at the National Gallery.

"You think a lot of crazy things," the ghost girl says, dancing ahead of me, hyped up like a puppy on the beach barking at the waves. "He's only eighty-four. C'mon."

A woman at the entrance presses a badge into my hand as the crowd seeps into the gallery. It reads "Pancho Guedes— Retrospective" in seventies-orange. It's a belated official opening because Pancho was away, getting an award at a Biennale or something.

I guess I would have known about all this, his being alive, the opening, if I'd been paying attention, going to class, all the normal stuff. But I've been visiting Nolly every day.

It's the word "retrospective" that threw me, made me think he was deceased.

The gallery is packed, the crowd expanding outwards to fill all available space, so the latecomers, including us, have to be corralled into the nineteenth-century portrait room. We can't see anything past the bodies standing straight and tall, stirring gently like a field of mealies as the speakers go on about Pancho's Habitable Woman and hysterical buildings and the architect as witch doctor.

Afterwards, the crowd flushes through the main gallery and out into the courtyard, aiming single-mindedly for the cocktail snacks.

"You have to eat sushi for me," the girl says, mournful. "I never got to. It always looked too disgusting."

"It still does," I object.

Maneuvering past the buffet table scrum, looking for an opening, I realize that HE's standing right behind me, talking to the museum curator and a journalist taking notes.

The girl figures it out at the same time. "Isn't that the guy?"

And then the little cow trips me, deliberately, so I practically fling myself into the bony arms of the museum curator.

"Watch the steps," Pancho says, mildly, turning to me, a glass of water in his hand. "They're badly designed."

"Mr. Guedes." I pronounce it with the Portuguese slur on the "des," but that's the only thing I get right.

Later I will spend half the night lying awake thinking of all the things I could have said. Engaged him on his idea of an imaginary Dadaist Africa, for example. But I mangle it totally.

"I'm a big fan, a huge fan. Such a big fan."

They stare at me, the journalist, the stick-insect curator

and the famous architect with his sticky-up white hair and over-bright eyes.

After a pause, Pancho says, "Well, thank you," waiting to see if I have anything to add, but equally ready to turn away politely. I lurch for the opening.

"I just wanted to ask . . . I'm studying architecture, and I was wondering if you had any advice? For me. That could be useful . . ." I trail off lamely.

He taps my collarbone once and says, "Young man. You have to find your own sense."

I will spend the other half of the night trying to figure out what that means.

Nolly called it off yesterday.

She said I've been great and she appreciates everything, but it's like that movie *Saw*? She's got this new perspective, and she's realized it's never going to work between us.

"And seriously, baby," she said, taking my hand, "you need to get your shit together."

As I'm leaving, the nurse calls me back to hand over a black bag full of junk: origami sculptures made from recycled blueprint paper and books and a porcelain flea-market menagerie.

"At least she ate the chocolates," the girl says, trying to cheer me up.

The university has been very understanding. Within reason. My tutor has given me an extension, but deadlines are like lintels; they can only be moved out so far before the whole thing comes crashing down around your head.

I stare at the model sports center and seriously consider smashing it to death with a frozen chicken. The girl stands next to me, her head tilted to the side, fingers pressed to her mouth, assessing it.

"I mean, I know it's supposed to be a sports center and everything. But it's not the kind of place you could live," is her considered conclusion.

I snort. "This coming from the person who doesn't."

"Live, you mean? I live. Kinda. With you. Except when you want to be alone. For sex and stuff."

"Yeah, about that. Maybe you should get your own place."

"Yeah, about that. Maybe you should make me one."

So I do.

It's tough for a ghost girl to get a lease agreement these days.

It's a monstrosity. It's the best thing I've ever made.

It's part Pancho, part Frank, part Escher, part Sekwa.

"And part Ruby," the girl chimes in.

"Well, finally. Is that your name?"

"No," she says. "But wouldn't it be romantic if it was?"

We stay up thirty-one hours straight constructing it out of balsa and yeah, bunched-up tinfoil. When the balsa won't bend and buckle the way I need it to, we shear cool drink cans and beat them flat. Unhinged parabolas soaring up to pseudo turrets, plunging back into crenellated organic fissures and a spaghetti snarl of cables, like the energy lines that connect people, like "se-eee-x." We populate the grounds with broken porcelain animals standing in for the traditional human figurines.

"It's a strange concoction of the imagination all right," the girl says, admiring.

"And a homeless shelter," I add. "My social responsibility here is done. The question is, when are you going to move in?"

"Are you nuts?" The ghost girl squinches up her face with perfect teen incredulity. "What, I'm just going to shrink down to size? I can't do that. The actual question here is, when are you going to build me the real thing?"

The examiner's notes are snippy. "The work shows vigorous creativity, passable technical skill and a total inability to meet the purpose of the brief."

I fail.

It's worth it.

NON-FICTION

Non-Fiction

Adventures in Journalism

I never wanted to be a journalist. The newspapers seemed all bore and gore—column space crammed with crime scene mop-ups, politicking and mawkish personality profiles. I also never planned to stay in Cape Town. When I came to the city in 1996, after a year of semi-feral gypsying around the world, it was supposed to be only for one indolent summer. I fully intended to return to Johannesburg, my hometown, to pavements slick with jacaranda blossoms and malls slick with money and skies bristling with violence at the tail end of sultry afternoons.

Naturally, I wound up doing both. And almost a decade later, I find myself standing behind Khayelitsha's taxi rank with Mr. Klaas, in his black and gold shirt and oversized Ray-Bans that come in somewhere between pantsula and *The Sopranos*. We are musing over a liquid smear of blood and scuffed gravel that seem to indicate that someone wounded or dead had been dragged away during the night, behind the stalls that sell sweeties and fruit and entjie cigarettes to commuters.

Whatever act had been committed here wasn't the point of the story I'd been commissioned to do by an Italian magazine, which activated its international correspondents in random scatter-shots with only a broad theme to guide us. Like we were enthusiastic entomologists set loose, bringing back intriguing specimens in our butterfly nets from which the editors could pick and choose.

In this case, our brief was as simple as "slums." The photographer and I had crashed a wedding party in Langa, intervened between feuding hair salons in Chinatown and eavesdropped on the phone calls sold roadside by entrepreneurs with mobile Telkom units. And all the while, we trailed a scraggle of children, an informal escort who tirelessly (and tiresomely) chanted "umlungu, umlungu," in case the community hadn't already noted the whiteys in their midst.

In our wanderings, we'd met an amateur boxer and muscleman shebeen owner who also ran a games arcade in a dank shack across the way from his drinking hole, learned how to prepare smileys, the delicacy made from sheeps' heads, and meticulously recorded the process for brewing traditional mqombothi beer with a nqali owner who quickly learned to ignore our pestering while she stirred the thick, fermenting sorghum mix in a metal drum.

It was inevitable then, that we'd eventually come to Mr. Klaas and his vigilante group, the Peninsula Anti-Crime Association or PEACA. At the crime scene behind the taxi rank, Mr. Klaas grunts and turns away, striding back to PEACA's office in a converted shipping container, pointedly ignoring the cluster of hopeful petitioners awaiting his attention. Inside, he explains, by way of our translator Themba, that PEACA was set up to prevent ex-struggle soldiers being let loose in the community without jobs— "like lions among the sheep," says Mr. Klaas ominously.

This way, he says, the lions are set to protect the kraal: they intervene in domestic violence or recover stolen goods, where the police cannot or will not assist. Like the case of the woman waiting outside, who does not trust that the restraining order she got from the courts will protect her from the boyfriend who has sworn to kill her and dump her body in a nearby dam.

"You see," Mr. Klaas says, not bothering to remove his shades, "there are some cases the police cannot actually at all solve. According to a number of certain rules the police should follow, like the Constitution, the Bill of Rights, they can't enter all these areas. But PEACA is everywhere. PEACA does not have any boundaries."

It's not entirely unlike my position, now that I've come to terms with it. I have an all-access pass to the city built into my job description. It's landed me in precarious positions, like meeting with vigilantes (Themba will berate me later, saying he had to soften my questions, that I must be careful), but it's also provided opportunities for more entertaining and even frivolous encounters.

I've come at the city from every angle. Sent by tourist magazines to go scuba diving, spelunking and skydiving, I've seen the land stretched taut as a canvas painted in Mondrian blocks, rushing towards me through howling sky, inched down a rope into a darkness squeaky with bats under the Silvermine mountains and faced down a quintet of ragged-tooth sharks in an old-fashioned copper diving suit in the Cape Town aquarium.

But mostly, it's the cold-blooded interrogation I get off on. Journalism gives me license to intrude, to ask queasily personal questions of people like Riaan* (not his real name), a tattooed twenty-eight-year-old who knowingly passed HIV to his wife, Lizl*. Sitting in the downstairs coffee shop of the multinational corporate the couple work for as AIDS educators, I asked them if they were still in love, after all they'd been through. "We've been married for six years now," Riaan said, rubbing the back of his hand, marred by white scars from punching in his car window, because, ironically, he's the bitter one. "But if you watch Oprah Winfrey, you'll know that love thing is just a phase."

"Like an infection," Lizl added, straight-faced.

Or of Roxy*, at the up-market brothel the Cape Ranch, who used to work the bedrooms but now does the front desk, who was very quick to answer when I ask if she'd want her fourteen-year-old daughter to get into the business. "No. I've got—she's got big plans for herself. And I want her to stick to them. Ja. Even if she got retrenched, like me, I wouldn't want her to. Rather get a waitressing job or something." Or of Julie*, a hockey player with a bandaged toe (a mishap in the outside world rather than a fetishist turned violent), who said that working at the Ranch got her off drugs, helped her learn to enjoy sex and was paying for her kids to go to private school.

It's not always easy. In a stale room in Retreat, Michel*, a Rwandan refugee, is reluctant to talk and, even more so, to be photographed. "The people we live with, we don't talk about this. There were people who killed who left Rwanda to come here as refugees as well. Hutus and Tsutsis. We don't know who they are or what they have done." He lends me a documentary video instead, that he keeps behind the battered fifties kitchen cabinet that would fetch good money, something I know from doing a story on antique shops.

And in a bed at the Brooklyn Chest Hospital, where Joseph* is dying, my eighteen-year-old half-brother Thabo, who is translating and acting as photographer's assistant, has to intervene. "He's really tired."

"Five more minutes," the photographer says, because we have to get this shot, the sharp sculptural geometries of Joseph's bones, his body limp and brittle as the thin white voile curtains framing the windows.

Of course, it didn't mean anything to Joseph that his image was the perfect embodiment of the twin pandemics of AIDS and tuberculosis, that the photographs were ideal for the World Health Organization report we were contributing to, that they might inform and educate and maybe even incite people to action. "What is it going to do *for me?*" Joseph hissed through his teeth, flipping the question.

When I first moved to Cape Town, I would get lost. The geography defied me, despite having the landmark of Table Mountain to navigate by, and it didn't help that my job sent me careening around the city from rough-hewn Bellville (cellular chip technology, kiteboarding) to an exclusive boys' school in leafy Rondebosch (teen sexuality) to the low-income apartheid estate Bonteheuwel (graffiti artists, taxi drivers). I would usually be able to get myself home by steering a random course in approximately the right direction, but it was always a surprise when I'd round a corner and reconnect with an area I knew and a missing piece would slot neatly into place.

While the unexpected shortcuts I find while driving reconfigure the physical construct of the city I carry in my head, the encounters I have recalibrate my understanding of it.

My lazy conclusions about a proposed nuclear pebble-bed reactor are thrown off course, for example, after lunch with an energy expert from the University of Cape Town, who says if we could capture the poisonous substances expelled by coal plants the same way we separate nuclear waste, it would be hailed as an environmental breakthrough. "The irrational phobias against nuclear power are usually the domain of rich people in rich countries," he says, "In South Africa, thousands of people don't have any power at all, and thousands more die every year from paraffin fires." But nuclear power is "unfashionable." He declines to be quoted by name for fear of losing out on grants.

This comes into perspective, traipsing around Barcelona, in Khayelitsha, with a pair of cable thieves named Godfrey and Andile who explain everything in the third person, as if they are not actually the ones who "climb up the poles, *mos*, like this one, like Tarzan," to break the power cables and steal the copper intestines for resale.

This time we have collected a following of adults, chanting "iz'nyoka," inspired by the Eskom TV ads that vilify people like Godfrey and Andile as "snakes." Godfrey shrugs it off: "No, they are not talking about us. It is iz'nyoka because the electricity is very quick to kill you. It bites you like a snake. On TV, they tell you, it can kill you first time."

The context expands again, in a labyrinth of shacks in Nyanga, where there is no electricity at all, not even the illegal connections that sag in snares across the dirt roads elsewhere. Our guide Pele tells us that here people live in fear of tsotsis who come in under cover of the absolute blackness to rob and rape. "Hooo. You won't find me here at night," he says.

He takes us to visit his friend David who lives in a miserable shack that smells of damp and bare earth. There is a battered fridge in one corner, used as a cupboard, and in another a metal drum in which a fire can be built, because the paraffin stove (the kind that sets neighborhoods ablaze) doesn't provide enough warmth.

And David's home forces me to shift and intertwine the categories again. On the walls, made of ragged pieces of cardboard and chipboard, there is a clothing-store poster advertising a competition to win twenty grand for your child's education—all those zeroes insistent above the grinning faces of white children. But there are also patches of faded blue wallpaper, adorned with cats and monkeys in frilly Edwardian outfits, all floppy hats and capes. It reminds me with a wrench of a Tamboerskloof home where the filmmaker couple (allegedly with a cocaine habit, but that didn't make it into the décor magazine story) had covered their little blonde daughter's bedroom in a similar wallpaper.

Likewise, the image of Joseph dying of AIDS and TB, which the WHO never used, becomes inextricably tangled with a story I did on an upmarket swingers club and my meetings with Karl*, the middle-class teenage vampire who swaps swigs of blood from open wrists with his Goth friends.

But all of these are only snapshots. The encounters are glancing, a single serving before I move on to the next story. As much as I am driven by curiosity and the desire to distill the world in words, I don't follow up unless I'm paid to. I have no idea how much longer Joseph lived or if Lizl and Riaan are still married, if he is still angry, whether Julie still turns tricks in an over-plush room with lace curtains, or if PEACA's warning to the violent boyfriend turned physical, as it so often has in the past. And I still I have no idea who was injured or killed behind the taxi rank.

While the complexities of the city I've internalized are expanded by my experiences, they are also limited by what fits on a page, but always there are new connections, new circuits rewired and re-contextualized. And I've learned to use this in my fiction, to find the telling details that speak to a subtext, to develop an ear for how people speak and speak differently, the revealing dialogue that will be bolded for emphasis on the magazine page. I've stolen the journalism techniques for novel research, talking to cops and artists in Detroit, refugees, music producers in Johannesburg, location scouting in Chicago. Every person I speak to gives me a new perspective, a different lens. It's made my writing more than it would have ever been. And it's still an excuse to go adventuring.

ALL THE PRETTY CORPSES

Pop culture has a nasty habit of producing them. You know the type: the girl in the trunk with her long bare legs dangling over the bumper, the torture victim in the basement in a dirty camisole and panties, matted hair masking her face, the broken ingénue with her dress fetchingly rucked up, one high heel kicked off and blood pooling under her.

The murder victim becomes a puzzle that has to be solved. She is the sum of her injuries, of the violation done to her, rather than her life.

We focus on the gory details—the exit wound of the bullet, the angle of the knife, the pattern of the blood spatter, the DNA under her nails, the defensive cuts on her hands. We learn this from TV. *This* is what is important: what was done to her. Passive voice. Because there's no subject anymore. Only object: the dead girl; the body. And a body doesn't mean anything. It's an empty snail shell. It's okay to look. There's no one in there now.

But there was once.

Which is why I wanted *The Shining Girls* to be a book that is as much about the victims' stories as the killer's.

Serial killer folklore maintains that they often have a type. Ted Bundy was into young women with middle partings and brown hair, for example. But what if my killer was not into physical characteristics but some inner quality that shone out of young women? Bright, full of spark and curiosity, engaged with the world, kicking against convention, pushing past their doubts and fears. What if the story was more about their lives than their deaths? What if the pretty corpses had voices, and that's part of why they were cut down?

I was interested in writing women who were exceptional in ordinary ways, who didn't quite fit in, who took a stand and would have made some kind of contribution in their fields if they hadn't been robbed of their potential: from a microbiologist to an artist, an architect, an activist, a single-mom welder, a transsexual dancer, an economist.

If the violence in the book is shocking, it's because it is supposed to be. Because real violence is. All those pretty corpses and the raging gun battles and torture porn on-screen have made us virtually immune to violence and the ripples it sends out. But it should be gut-wrenching. It should be traumatic. It *should* be about the victim.

Of course, in the real world, real violence is rarely perpetrated by a serial killer. Usually it's someone the woman knows. A partner or husband or friend or neighbor. But the truth about violence is that it is *all* domestic. As in every day—playing out with tedious regularity in any number of configurations. Ask any cop, any social worker, any paramedic or crime reporter. Bodies lose their flavor. Often they don't even make the news. Especially if they're not a pretty corpse or a celebrity, if there's no whiff of scandal. Especially if they're poor.

Writing this book was very personal.

In 2009, Thomokazi, a friend of my family, was attacked by her abusive boyfriend. He stabbed her, poured boiling water over her, locked her in his shack in one of Cape Town's desperately poor shantytowns and walked away, like she was nothing.

She lay there for five days until neighbors were alerted by the moaning and the terrible smell, and called the police. They broke down the door and summoned an ambulance. There were flies thick on Thomokazi's skin, but she was alive, if half-mad with pain. We didn't know it was already too late. With burns, the infection sets in deep, the same way violence does in society. After repeated trips to hospitals and clinics, she died four months later, waiting for treatment in an emergency room. She was twenty-three. The public hospital put it down as "natural causes," because maybe that kind of thing is.

I tried to help the family. We tried to get justice. Three months after Thomokazi was buried in her traditional home upcountry, I accompanied her sister to court. But before the case was called, the prosecutor summoned us into his rooms and told us—furious—that he couldn't try the case. He wrote an angry report to the police pointing out all the holes in their investigation. "Holes" was the wrong word, though, because there had been no investigation.

The police docket was one pathetic page—the dead woman's statement. The cops hadn't bothered to interview anyone, to check the medical evidence, even to warn the family that the attacker was forbidden to stalk or harass them. We watched him swagger out of court, his new girlfriend, maybe nineteen, trailing two steps behind him like an obedient dog.

The only witness to the crime was Thomokazi. It was her word against that of her attacker, and she was dead. And the dead cannot speak for themselves. But I thought I could. I got the case into the papers, because I'm middle-class and I have a voice and I know how to use it—and I believed in justice. With the support of the prosecutor, I got the investigation reopened. I gathered hospital records, the names of witnesses who could testify that her boyfriend had punched her before, pulled out her hair. I found out which neighbors had called the cops, tracked down the paramedics.

Then her family phoned me. They couldn't bear to go through it all again. They couldn't face having to exhume her body for a police autopsy. They couldn't talk about it anymore. All the words had been used up. They asked me to let it go.

I still haven't been able to. I'm still angry. About the violence that happens every day, about all the girls and women like Thomokazi whose deaths go unmentioned, who will never have a voice, whose obituaries come down to their autopsies. As Kirby, the survivor in *The Shining Girls*, says: How am I supposed to let this shit go?"

How are any of us?

At least in fiction, unlike real life, you can get justice.

JUDGING UNITY

J ustice Unity Dow does not take crap from anyone. Not from the Botswana government: she took the state to court as a young attorney in 1990 over her right to pass citizenship on to her children, and consequently had the law overturned. Not from the senior South African Judge Hlophe, whom she called out publicly when he introduced her salaciously at a legal conference as "the woman I'm going to be spending a lot of time with." Nor from Botswana's state counsel (and special presidential advisor), Sidney Pilane, who found himself spending an unexpected week in jail for contempt of court during the contentious Basarwa land case. And certainly not from a journalist who crosses the line between her private life and her public persona.

"None of your fucking business," she says in reply to a relatively innocuous biographical question, not even bothering to raise the register of her voice, which makes the effect all the more shocking. Her face has stiffened into cold severity, as if someone has plunged a needle of Botox into her. There is no question that she is in control. Nor will I dare to try to pursue this line of questioning. I suddenly, acutely, empathize with Sidney Pilane.

The weird thing is that we have already crossed the line. Until this moment, she has been the most generous of hosts, throwing open her home and her life to us for the weekend to reveal the woman behind the formidable reputation. As a High Court judge and one of Botswana's leading novelists, she is taking a risk, giving us the all-access backstage pass, but that doesn't mean she has to like the vulnerability.

The first time photographer Pieter Hugo and I meet her is in her chambers at the High Court in Lobatse, and I am immediately struck by the sharp curiosity that radiates from her features. She comes across as driven by uncompromising ideals, but unlike some of her redoubtable colleagues, she is also warm and wickedly droll. She connects with people readily, but at the same time, you are aware that she is measuring you up—and keeping something of herself in reserve.

I quickly learn to keep my notepad stowed. She is an impatient interviewee, especially if the questions are ones she has been asked a thousand times before (like how she became a lawyer: by chance, a teacher's recommendation) and she becomes cagey whenever she catches me jotting down her words.

In conversation, however, Unity is genial, opening up about the twenty-one-year-old AIDS orphan she has taken under her wing, or sweeping us off on a driving tour of

Mochudi, the tiny village where she grew up, and where, she says, "if you went even four houses from your home, you were out on a major adventure." Now, she flies around the world as a matter of course, attending conferences on human rights and doing book tours.

She is at her most open at home, with her family, and especially around seventeen-year-old Natasha, the youngest of her three children, cool in her purple Converse sneakers. Natasha is protective, admonishing me to "write good things" about her mother, but also candid: pointing out, with a teen's affectionate exasperation of a parent's foibles, the notes Unity writes to herself in the front of books she's reading—brief diary entries caught in airports and train stations.

At a dinner party at Unity's non-traditional timber house (the unconventionality upset the neighbors no end), her sister, Tiny Diswai, claims "That sister of mine has balls!" Her friends agree, laughing and teasing her about the time she threw the prosecutor in prison. Unity waves it off, dismissive rather than humble.

Her notoriously convivial gatherings of friends include Gaborone's intelligentsia: artists, writers, activists, educators and an AIDS immunologist, among others, tonight embroiled in sparring banter about the education system and international crime tribunals over red wine and slightly singed steak on the braai. Normally, these affairs evolve into dancing until dawn, but perhaps subdued by the presence of journo and photographer, the party tapers off at one in the morning, which is perhaps lucky, considering what is to come . . .

The coincidence is absurd. It is an event peeled from the pages of one of her books, akin to a Nazi prison camp guard rocking up on Berhard Schlink's doorstep or a gang general in the 28s asking Jonny Steinberg for a light on a street corner.

In the morning-after wake of the party, a young woman arrives at the gate, pleading that she has been attacked. Natasha pounds on the shower door: "Mma? I *really* need you." While the High Court judge hurriedly gets dressed, Pieter and I go with a discomfited Natasha to unlock the gate, where a cowed girl with disheveled hair and soaked-through sneakers is waiting, clutching her dirty t-shirt. When Natasha slides opens the gate, she moves in complement to open her hands briefly, to show us the rip down the front of her shirt, exposing her breasts. She is shaking.

Inside, at the kitchen table, she fondles a mug of tea overloaded with sugar, while Unity quizzes her in Setswana, cool and calm, already having procured her a clean shirt, a sweater. I can't follow, but in the gaps, Unity explains. The girl was hitching a ride home from the golf course where she works, when three men stopped to pick her up in a van. They pulled off the road in the dark and told her, "We've been looking for someone like you." Unity says, "What she's saying is that they wanted her for a ritual murder. For dipheko or muti."

And this is where the absurdity comes in. It is one thing to chance upon the one house in this semi-rural neighborhood that just so happens to belong to a High Court judge known for her work on women's rights; it is another entirely when that judge also happens to have written a novel on this exact issue—*Screaming of the Innocent*.

Her book is based on real events. In 2001, there was a riot in Mochudi over the unsolved ritual murder and mutilation of schoolgirl Segametsi Mogomotsi, reduced to bloody parts for superstitious and powerful men—an atrocity, Unity says, that happens at least two or three times a year in this otherwise urbane country of 1.7 million people, where education and medical care and even land are dispensed for free.

"Nobody was ever brought to trial," Unity says, which makes it all the more difficult for me to understand why she is not now insisting that the trembling young woman with the bruises on her arms go to the police. But I don't intervene. I have not been privy to all the details, and she is a judge, after all, with a long and lauded history.

We drive most of the way to the young woman's village in silence, stopping only once, briefly, to survey the place where she says she was attacked. When we drop her off and watch her walk into her modest house, I realize I never asked her name. She raises one palm as we pull away, the rescue affected.

It is only on the way back that Natasha asks the question: "What happened to her?"

And it's now that Unity throws me, flipping my suppositions with a canny dissection that reveals a judge's experience, but also a novelist's raptor eye. She has been weighing this all along.

"I hear a lot of witnesses," Unity tells her daughter. "She wasn't telling the truth." There were holes in her story, Unity explains, which shifted like the dust does here, during the drought.

For starters, she was too old, at twenty-one, well beyond the age of the budding virginal pubescents required for such gruesome medicine. She claimed she escaped from the van into the darkness and thorn bushes, and found refuge by breaking into a yellow house just across the way, failing to see the lights or hear the noise of the braai at Unity's house or the local bar around the corner. And she only came for help at ten in the morning. "I've worked with women who have been attacked," Unity says. "In these kinds of situations, you can't sleep. You go for help at first light."

She was hesitant about the details of the assault. There's no doubt that there was one. But not the way she described it. Unity guesses it was probably a boyfriend, maybe one her parents disapprove of, which would explain her reluctance to go to the police or tell her mother. But then she adds, "Poor kid. Nobody deserves to be attacked."

When Pieter and I first arrived in Gaborone two days ago, it was to find the papers infested with stories about women: a brouhaha about Miss Botswana refusing to be photographed in a bikini, a school principal under investigation for taking one of his teen pupils off into the bushes at night, the "passion killings" that have become an epidemic here, committed by jealous boyfriends or husbands who often turn the gun on themselves afterwards.

The subject of women's rights is one that will always itch under Unity's skin. After she overturned the law with her landmark case in 1990, she set up the Metlhaetsile Women's Center (which provides legal aid to the women of Mochudi); in 2002, she became the first woman High Court judge in the country.

But she found her new role constrained her. "As a judge, you have a different voice, a powerful voice that has to be used very carefully," Unity says. "You're making powerful decisions that can affect other people's lives. I can't just pick up the phone and give a comment to the newspaper because there's confusion as to whether I'm speaking as an individual or whether this is an official position from the court. It's the retreat and self-censorship that made me write novels. I'm still talking, but from a safe harbor through fiction."

In her novels, her passion seeps through the page like a watermark, overwhelming her protagonists, but not her sense of story or characterization. "What moves you at any point is what I write about," she says. And what moves her is AIDS and violence against women in *Far And Beyon'*, cultural identity in *Juggling* and muti murders in *Screaming of the Innocent*. I ask her if this event will make it in to her next book. She shrugs, noncommittal. It not quite everyday, but neither, in her experience, is it remarkable.

Her new book, *The Heavens May Fall*, is due out later this year. The title is inspired by a Latin saying, "Let justice be done or the heavens fall," but it also seems a good précis of her life. I get the idea that with her stubborn and uncompromising will, Unity Dow would be capable of bringing them down herself.

INNER CITY

"Hey, watch out," João says, yanking me back under the safety of the overhang as a black garbage bag drops onto the rubbish piling up on the landing, like the silt of the mine dumps that used to rise up around the city. He's nineteen years old, with a sharp face, a blunt nose and pit bull puppy eagerness. He pokes his head out from the safety of High Point's undercover parking lot—an action hero checking for snipers—and then beckons me over to safety.

It's 2008. I'm researching my book Zoo City. *Historically, the idea of the great South African novel has been all about the journey into the interior, the wide expanses of Karoo scrublands that expose the interior of the soul. I wanted the journey of my story to be vested in more corporeal things. Forget the soul, I wanted the sparking nerves, the guts, the pounding heart of the cityscape.*

João explains that the building's elevator is not working.

The water goes off periodically; people try their taps, cursing and cranking them wide open. Forget to close them and when the water comes on again, it floods the sinks and bathtubs, spilling down the walls. The last time this happened, it drowned the elevator's electrics. It will cost a million rand to fix. And in the meantime, building management has told residents it's okay, as a temporary measure, to drop their garbage onto the landing rather than lug it down twenty-four flights of stairs.

We carefully skirt the garbage drop zone to the edge of the landing, which looks down onto the street: me, João and his young burly partner, Mike, and my fixer, Johnson, a Zimbabwean recommended by a photographer friend, whose job is to escort me through the wilds of inner city Johannesburg. Tour guide, translator, bodyguard. We have agreed he should leave his gun at home. "It just makes more trouble," Johnson says, and we are not here looking for that.

Hillbrow is the place of breathless TV specials: documentaries following paramedics on New Year's Eve, dodging refrigerators thrown from tenement-block windows in some kind of high bacchanalian consumer backlash; Louis Theroux cringing coquettishly behind private security guards in bulletproof vests storming up the stairs of abandoned buildings that have been hijacked by squatter slumlords.

As a teenager, my friends and I used to drive through here on our way to the alternative club, the Doors, where you had to check your goth-wannabe weapons at the door. We never told our parents where we were going. Singing along to Tori Amos or Sisters of Mercy, jumping red lights on the lonely streets, always with that jagged catch of danger in our throats that made us feel restless, electric, alive. Because if there's one thing everyone knows about Johannesburg, it's that it's capital-D Dangerous.

I read everything I could on Hillbrow: Bongani Madondo and Charl Blignaut's essays on the nineties scene, Ivan Vladislavic's restless meditations, Kgebetli Moele's spiky provocation of a novel, Room 207, but it was a blog about the death of Johannesburg that got under my skin. I won't name it, but it's one with those smug, hand-wringing then-and-nows contrasting photographs of how vibrant the inner city used to be and the wrack and ruin and decay it has fallen into.

The thin subtext of the captions and comments is that it's because of "the blacks." Always the blacks. As if apartheid's (white) secret police, the ironically named Civil Cooperation Bureau, didn't meet at the Quirinale Hotel on Kotze Street in Hillbrow to orchestrate atrocities, assassinations and political unrest in their efforts to derail democracy. As if a hundred years before that, Cecil John Rhodes and the (white) mining magnate Rand Lords didn't scheme in the library of the gentlemen's club downtown to bring the colonial empire snaking into the interior on railway tracks and the corpses of countless dead.

But for all its shrill hysteria, the photographs on the blog don't lie about the decay. Businesses have fled the city center to soulless business parks surrounded by soulless townhouse complexes in Midrand, a purpose-built suburb halfway between Johannesburg and Pretoria.

The premises they left behind *have* become dilapidated, boarded over and, in extreme cases, bricked up, to prevent them being gutted for copper piping or taken over by squatters. A few kilometers away, Forest Town, the suburb where I grew up, where President Jacob Zuma now lives, has jacaranda trees that bloom in purple archways over the streets. Whereas the Hillbrow "blossom" is the plastic bag, tangled and shredded in the branches of spindly trees.

There are a thousand pocket worlds in the central city, rubbing up against each other. The students and arts scene in Brixton and Braamfontein, the black hipster hang-out of Newtown around the Market Theatre and Café Sophiatown, the suits and shiny cars in Bank City by the Diamond Building. Hillbrow has always been a separate animal.

The twin towers of High Point used to be the most desirable blocks in the most cosmopolitan neighborhood, packed with restaurants and bars and clubs. When my dad was considering divorce in the seventies, he planned to buy an apartment here as the perfect swinging bachelor pad.

That was before Hillbrow turned bohemian: sex and drugs and rocking disco soul thanks to the likes of Brenda Fassie, the "Madonna of the townships," who hung out here, got high here, made love here, in the middle of the hip multiracial scene of artists and musicians and gays and lesbians in the eighties and nineties.

Now it's the place people bring their hopes, packed up in amashangaan, the ubiquitous cheap plastic rattan suitcases used by refugees and immigrants from small towns in the rural areas, looking for work, looking to break in. Low income, high aspirations.

Mike, swaggering for my benefit, goes to the edge of the ledge and calls down to a man on the street who is tossing away his cigarette: "Hey pick that up, you can't throw your *stompie* here!" Each building is a private fiefdom and the security guards are the protectors of the realm with batons and mace. What happens across the road is none of their concern. They manage the building, keep crime out, deal with troublesome tenants.

"We caught a rapist in the building. It took three days, but we knew he lived here, so I stood outside the gate with the woman who was, you know . . ." João takes a swig from his Coke to hide his discomfort. It is exactly the same red as his canister of pepper spray. "Until the guy finally came out and she pointed at him and we grabbed him and took him down to the cops.

"But there was this other time, I felt kak, hey, because I had to evict this old black guy who hadn't paid his rent. And I had to hit him with the baton to get him to move because he wouldn't go. And it made me feel swak, like he must think of old times, like apartheid, this young white oke beating him, but it's my job, what am I supposed to do?"

Johnson nods in understanding. When he's not playing fixer for journalists, he runs his own security firm for other buildings in Hillbrow. He has the same problems with tenants, but even more so, he says, with their guests. "As a security guard, you learn to understand the characteristics of people. You can get to know people in the building and their behavior. But visitors are a problem. You cannot understand the visitors."

There are old attitudes that endure. The ghosts of the city. But people find ways to live with ghosts, and that's why we're here, because despite the horror stories, the flying refrigerators and the drug dealers on the corner with their sharp shoes and cellphones, and the low-rise across the way that João says they raided last week with the cops to bust a sex-trafficking operation, Hillbrow is somewhere people live.

The city *has* changed. Cities do. It's in their nature. Like language. Tsotsi-taal (gangster-speak) is the word on the street here, a patois of English, Afrikaans and Zulu that has stolen the best slang from other tongues and remixed them.

And maybe that's the best way to think of Hillbrow and the inner city. As a remix.

Unlike the manicured pavements of the leafy suburbs or the glossy consumertopias of Sandton and Rivonia, the city streets are flush with people. Hawkers sell cheap plastic flip-flops alongside sandals handmade from Nguni leather, in front of cellphone shops and Internet cafés and fashion boutiques and a church occupying a reclaimed mall. Flyers pasted to a brick wall advertise the services of the Prophet Nkhomo, the St. Paul's Preschool, safe abortions, youth worship services. The big brands are moving back in—KFC and Jet fashion—to compete with the cheap clothing stores and the place on the corner that does Lagos-style chicken. It's seventies Harlem: hectic, alive, on the rise.

As Moele describes it in *Room 207*, the city of gold is actually the city of dreams. Because dreams, like ghosts, are unpredictable. They can be good or bad. You have to live with them.

It's driven home when we venture downtown to the Central Methodist Church. I have been intending to set a major scene in *Zoo City* here, and have arranged with Bishop Paul Verryn to attend the Sunday night service.

We're here a few months after a nationwide outbreak of horrifying xenophobic violence, where black South Africans turned on black Africans. A group of Somalians were thrown off the roof of a building, like refrigerators. A Zimbabwean man was burned alive in the streets.

There is a forty per cent unemployment rate. Someone has to carry the blame, and the middle classes are safe in their suburbs with their high walls and their private security and their jacaranda trees. So it's the "blacks" again. Blacker than black. Us versus them. The colonials knew this, exploited this, indoctrinated this. They taught that there is always someone blacker than you.

People have fled to the church to take shelter from the violence, the same way activists hid out here during the struggle against apartheid. But now there are new struggles. There will always be a struggle. It's the legacy we're left with, from all those whites with all their schemes.

The friends who drop me and Johnson off outside the church are reluctant to let us go. There is a mob clustered around the fence and the Portaloos around the church. The anger in the air is a living thing.

It is the first time I feel a spike of fear. Nothing like in Hillbrow (which was daytime, admittedly), not even when a boy brushed past me and hissed, "Put your cellphone away, they'll rob you." And not like driving to the Doors a decade ago, the acupuncture prick of dread. This is a pitchfork twisting my guts like spaghetti. "Don't worry," Johnson says. "They're my people. Zimbabweans." And although there are also Malawians, Zambians, Congolese, he's right. Far and away, the greatest numbers are those who have fled Mugabe.

We make our way inside the church, to the upper pews. There is a constant murmur, people talking through the preamble of announcements and hymn-singing. Kids tumble over the stairs. There are chains of coughing, babies crying, a choir of cellphone ringtones. A man is coughing bloody sputum into a tissue, his whole body wracked with the effort. He has no shoes. His bare feet are like knots of wood, his toenails cracked and yellow.

We find a place to sit next to a nurse, Melanie, dressed immaculately in a white linen suit, just as Bishop Verryn is about to deliver the sermon. He seems exasperated. "It is not satisfactory for you to live like this. I am not saying I don't want you here, but I worry about the humanity of people in this place." He seems worn down.

It has taken this to make me realize that dehumanizing is not only something that other people do to you. It can be self-inflicted, too. Switch off the light behind your eyes. Focus on the lowest rungs of Maslow. Get through the day, however you can.

From the pulpit, Verryn rails against the city council that keeps trying to move them: "Treat us like human beings. Don't move us like furniture, because we are not furniture." Outside, a young man tells me, "They use us like a ball. They kick us everywhere." He also says they go looking for trouble, seeking out Zulu guys and beating them up. Reprisals for the way they have been treated. He is thinking of going home. Even with no jobs, the messed-up politics, Zimbabwe is better than here. But he can't afford the trip. He is stuck.

Melanie, the nurse, explains that she came here via Harare, via London, via Cape Town. She offers to show me where she sleeps and confides, "I don't have friends. Only to share my jokes with, but not to share my secrets." She doesn't tell me how she manages to keep her white linen suit so spotless.

It is surreal or maybe hyperreal, following her down the stairwell to the basement, pushing and shoving through a crush of warm bodies in the dark, stepping over people who are bedding down for the night, on a scrap of cardboard for a mattress if they are lucky. On bare concrete if they are not.

We break free into the basement where the women and children sleep, the sum of their belongings arranged around them in amashangaan and battered suitcases. We are standing shoulder to shoulder, packed like tin cans. I cannot see how there will be room to lie down. Several women are bathing babies in buckets. "From Musina. The border," Melanie says. "The guards demand sex sometimes for getting you across."

I reel away from the horrors of a refugee camp condensed into a church building, out into the crisp Joburg night air, where young men cluster restlessly on the pavement, and into a warm car that will whisk us back to the suburbs. I feel shaken and raw.

"How was it?" my friends ask, and Johnson, who has been tjoep-stil, dead-quiet this whole time, bursts out in furious contempt, "It was pathetic." He shakes his head in disgust. *"Pathetic."*

I'm speechless. He told me earlier about how he came to South Africa as a refugee fourteen years ago. How his wife is a refugee. How these are his people. And now he is denouncing them.

It's a coping mechanism, I realize. He is distancing himself from the possibility that he could ever find himself living through a similar experience. He is saying that somehow he would be different in the same circumstances. We all want to be the exception. We all want to believe it couldn't be us.

But then we were only visitors there. Who can't be understood. Or understand. We can only imagine.

On Beauty

A Letter to My Five-Year-Old Daughter

Dear K—,

I tell you that you're beautiful all the time. But never just that word—"beautiful"—with all its connotations and reductions.

I say: "Baby, do you know you're beautiful and smart and funny and kind?" Because it's the combination of all those things that make it true.

And you say, "I know, Mama," with tolerant impatience. Not because you are vain, although you like to wear colorful clothes and a mermaid tail and a fairy princess dress and a tiger hat, and you have already decided that you like your hair to be brushed in a particular way. But because this is not especially interesting to you. It's a self-evident truth, like saying that mountains are high or tadpoles are wriggly.

You are much more interested in figuring out the world.

It intrigues you that black is the hottest color. You pick up snails in the palm of your hand and bring them home. You observe that "every car is going to a place" with melancholy philosophy. You wonder whether there is a Cat Jesus and if he hangs out with Father Christmas. You wish you could climb into books and you stop me reading mid-story so that you can talk to the characters, berate the bad guys or warn the goodies about what's about to happen.

You are full of spark and empathy. You are driven by endless curiosity and ferocious righteousness. You are opinionated. You speak up and you speak out. But you are also sweet and caring. You used to burst into tears when you stood on someone else's toe. You are still sensitive, but you're learning to put it in perspective.

Like beauty.

When you were two years old and we were watching Erykah Badu sing the alphabet on *Sesame Street*, you said "She looks like you, Mama"; and what you meant is beautiful.

I try to show you the range of physical beauty. I point out the posters of Paralympians who are beautiful and strong in their wheelchairs or with their prosthetics, and the punk black girl with green dreadlocks we pass in the mall, the old lady with her button necklace, the boy princesses in the documentary I made on a female impersonation beauty pageant.

I change the words in stories as I read them. Whenever a girl is described as "beautiful" I add "and brave" or "and clever." I ignore the words "fat" and "thin." But soon you will learn to read by yourself and I won't be able to apply the filters.

And that's what is so wonderful and terrible: that the world rushes in, and you are hungry for it, and I cannot control it.

You come home with other notions of what beautiful is and how important it is in relation to other things. That beautiful is not who you are, but how long your hair is.

And soon, too soon, you will realize that there are other definitive parameters that are so narrow barely anyone fits into them. That "beauty" is white and young and skinny and blonde. And soon, too soon, you will grow up and worry about all the stupid, poisonous slang we feed ourselves—words like "muffin top" and "thigh gap." You will worry about being sexy instead of sexual. Of looking good instead of reveling in your body.

We battle about watching *Barbie and the Dreamhouse* or *Monster High* because they're all about clothes and boyfriends and popularity, like the Kardashians for kids, and I try to nudge you to *My Little Pony* and *She-Ra* and *The Powerpuff Girls* and even *Winx Club*, where they have cool outfits *and* go on adventures. Where it's about more than being beautiful.

And I cannot believe that this all starts so young. That our culture wants to box you in and limit you to being merely physically beautiful. As if that is enough.

As if that is anything at all.

It makes me so angry. How the world treats women makes me afraid for you. Not just stupid advertising or bad kids' TV shows or salary disparities and lack of maternity leave, but the ugliness of men who hate women with casual ferocity, only one mouse click away.

Or the violence and horror and repression of women that happens a stone's throw from here, to people we know, and across the world to people we don't, people who are attacked for all the things I love in you: curiosity and a sense of adventure, for daring to go to school, or having an opinion or wanting a choice in their lives.

I can't control that. I can't control or stop the things people will say, what magazines will tell you that you can or can't wear, the way men will call after you in the street and think they're doing you a favor, how your physical self will be turned into a weapon against you, in the outside world and, worse, inside your head.

I can't filter it, I can't protect you from it. That's the worst way to live your life—sheltered from the world. But I can arm you as best I can. I can try to nurture your self-confidence. I can try to tell you what real beauty is.

It's everything you are already. Right now.

Hold on to that. Hold on to it as tight as you can—your delight, your burning curiosity, your sense of humor, your mad imagination, your clear sense of justice, your joy in your body, in running and climbing and swimming and playing and dancing.

Real beauty is engaging with the world. It's the courage to face up to it, every day. It's figuring out who you are and what you believe in and standing by that. It's giving a damn. You are interesting because you are interested, you are amazing because you are so wide open to everything life has to give you.

Your first teacher told you that one day you would grow up to be a great woman. And you will. But you will also be a beautiful woman—in all the ways that count.

GLOSSARY

ADT: leading provider of residential and commercial security solutions in South Africa, as well as an American security company

Ag: similar to *oh*

Amakipkip: multicolored popcorn, a popular packaged snack in Johannesburg, and another name for the sartorially colorful fashionistas known as the Soweto Smarties

Amashangaan: inexpensive, large red and blue checkered carry bag

Anti-retroviral medicine: a combination of drugs that suppresses the HIV virus and slows the progression of HIV to fullblown AIDS

Bakkie: pickup truck

Black Label: a mainstream South African beer often associated with the working class

Bra: similar to *bro* or *dude*

Braai: outdoor barbecue

Bukkake: genre of pornography originating in Japan in which several men ejaculate onto a woman or another man

Chinas: friend, pal, buddy. Considered outdated in some circles where *bru* or *bra* is more common

Dipheko: the Setswana word for *muti*, meaning traditional medicine or magic

Eish: interjection expressing resignation

Entjie: half a cigarette; see also *stompie*

Eskom: originally the Electricity Supply Commission (Kommissie, in Afrikaans) of South Africa, and the official name of the company since 1987

Fong kong: slang for a cheap knock-off

Hai, baba: similar expression to "*no, sir*," *hai* means *no*, while *baba* is a deferential term of address

Hamba'ofa: comparable to *fuck off*

Hawks: special investigations unit of the South African Police Service

Hayibo: expression of disbelief, sometimes expression of irritation

Hectic: slang expression indicating amazement or shock

Heita: hello

Iz'nyoka: snake, also slang for electricity thieves

Ja: yes

Jelly tot: soft fruit-flavored sweets

Jozi: short for Johannesburg

Kachi abadi: shanty town

Kak: feces, used as an expletive comparable to *shit*

Karoo: a semi-desert region of South Africa

Kawaii: the quality of being cute, Japanese usage

Kif: slang expression similar to *cool*

Kloof: a ravine or valley

Kombi: minibus used to transport passengers

Koppie: a small hill rising from the African veld

Kraal: a traditional African village or extended settlement, also an enclosure or contained area for domesticated animals

Kwaito: a popular genre of music, a mixture of South African disco, hip hop, R&B and raga, with a heavy dose of house-music beats.

Laaitie: younger person, esp. a younger male such as a younger brother or son

Llandudno: a popular surf beach and surrounding wealthy suburb in Cape Town

Los: to leave something or someone alone, to drop a matter

Lucas Radebe: a famous South African soccer player, retired in 2005

Madoda: term for a friends/guys

Mal: expression similar to *crazy, mad, nuts*

Mashambas: the countryside, rural plots, homesteads

Matric: short for matriculation, refers to final year of high school or Standard 10

Mealies: maize or corn

Mfecane: a period of chaos and warfare among indigenous communities in southern Africa between 1815 and 1840.

Midrand: an area between the expanding city limits of Johannesburg and Pretoria

Miggies: midges, fruit flys

MK: uMkhonto we Sizwe, the former armed wing of the ANC

Moeshoeshoe: a Sotho chief and contemporary of the Zulu king Shaka, famous for military victories against white settlers

Moffied up: from *moffie*, a derogatory term for a gay man

Mos: used as an interpolation, similar to *after all, of course, you know*

Msunu ka nyoko: comparable to *fuck your mother's cunt*

Mqombothi: a home-brewed low-alcohol beer made from maize and sorghum

Mugu/s: fool/s, idiot/s, sometimes spelled *moegoe/s*

Musina: border-crossing town between South Africa and Zimbabwe

Muso: a musician or extreme music fan

Muti: traditional or herbal medicine, or of medicinal or magical charm

Mxit: South African mobile social network

Ndincede nkosi undiphe amandla: Please, God, give me strength

Necklacing: the mob-justice act of killing by placing a tire around the neck and lighting it on fire, used on political informants in townships during apartheid

Nguni: a breed of cattle indigenous to South Africa; also refers to a group of peoples and languages

NikNaks: common brand of packaged snack made from corn

Nkosi: thanks

Nqali: a traditional speakeasy that serves sorghum beer

Oke: Similar to *china*, *bra*, *bru* and *boet*

Oni: from Japanese folklore, often translated as demon, ogre or troll

Ordentlik: well-behaved, proper

Otaku: a Japanese term for people with obsessive interests, commonly anime and manga fandom

Pantsula: a young urban black person (usually male) whose attitudes and behavior, especially regarding speech and dress, are trendy and current. Also a style of dance.

Panga: a machete

Rof: rough, especially do with character

Rondeval: a circular building with a conical roof, often thatched

SAPS: South African Police Service

SASKO: a ubiquitous South African bread and flour company

Scope: a weekly men's porno magazine in South Africa, published from 1966 to 1996. The nipples on the centerfolds were concealed with stars.

Scorpions: the special investigations unit of the National Prosecuting Authority, with special powers above and beyond the police, preceding the Hawks. Controversially dismantled and merged with SAPS in 2008.

Shebeen: an informal drinking establishment in a township

Shongololo: millipede

Simunye: "We are one," a saccharine slogan for TV channel SABC1 used just after the end of apartheid playing into the notion of South Africa as a "rainbow nation"

Skaam: embarrassed, remorseful, shamed

Skabenga: a gangster, bandit, or robber; a scoundrel or rascal

Skeef: sideways, askance

Skollies: hooligans, criminals, unsavory characters

Spaza: a small unofficial store, often operating out of a private house

Springkaan: grasshopper

Stompie: a cigarette butt; also a bit of gossip, as in "picking up stompies"

Swak: literally, weak; bad

Tata ma chance: I'll take my chances, a slogan for the National Lottery

Telkom: a wireline and wireless telecommunications provider in South Africa

Tjank: whine, whimper

Tjoep-stil: completely silent

Tsotsi: a criminal, gangster, thug or robber

Tsotsi-taal: a mixture of several languages mainly spoken in South African townships

Unagi: Japanese for freshwater eel

Vaya: go

Yiba nam kolu gqatso: Be with me in this race

7/7 bombs: series of coordinated terrorist bombings utilizing the public transit system during London's morning rush hour on the 7th of July, 2005

About the Author

L auren Beukes (*The Shining Girls*) is an internationally award-winning and best-selling South African author. Her critically acclaimed writing ranges within crime, noir, mystery, thriller, horror, science fiction, nonfiction, graphic novels, screenplays and literary fiction.

Beukes's novels include *Broken Monsters*, *Zoo City* and *Moxyland*, and she was the editor of the anthology *Maverick: Extraordinary Women from South Africa's Past*. Her graphic novel work includes Vertigo's *Survivor's Club*, an original horror comic with Dale Halvorsen and Ryan Kelly; the *Fables* spin-off *Fairest: The Hidden Kingdom* with Inaki Miranda; and a *Wonder Woman* issue, "The Trouble with Cats," in *Sensation Comics 9*, written for kids and set in Mozambique and Soweto.

Beukes's nonfiction has been published in international magazines including the *Hollywood Reporter*, *Nature Medi-*

cine and *Colors*, as well as the *Sunday Times Lifestyle*, *Marie Claire*, *Elle* and *Cosmopolitan*. Her film and television work includes directing the documentary *Glitterboys & Ganglands*, which features Cape Town's biggest female-impersonation beauty pageant.

Among her many honors, Beukes has received the Arthur C. Clarke Award, the University of Johannesburg Prize, the August Derleth Award for Best Horror, and the Strand Critics Choice Award for Best Mystery Novel, and her books have been regularly featured in best-of-the-year roundups by outlets such as NPR, Amazon, and the *Los Angeles Times*. Her fiction has won praise from the likes of Stephen King, George R. R. Martin, James Ellroy and Gillian Flynn, and her writing has been translated into twenty-six languages.

Lauren Beukes lives in Cape Town, South Africa.